SWIFT WATER

SWIFT WATER

BY
EMILIE LORING

GROSSET & DUNLAP
PUBLISHERS   NEW YORK

To

CHARLES C. SHOEMAKER

TO WHOSE SYMPATHY AND ENCOURAGEMENT
I OWE MUCH OF MY PROGRESS ALONG THE
ROCKY ROAD OF AUTHORSHIP

Chapter I

A RESPLENDENT roadster, yellow with black trimmings, shot down the main street of Garston violating laws both human and divine. As it approached the crossroads in the crowded business section a man in uniform held up an authoritative, white-gloved hand. With a wicked, little smile of defiance the girl at the wheel kept on her impetuous course. The officer stepped into the path of the car. As it passed him with hair-raising nearness he jumped to the running-board. Commanded in a voice which did curious things to the girl's pounding heart:

" Pull up to the curb."

From thickly fringed, brilliantly dark eyes in a startlingly white face she appraised him. Admitted:

" You win, Tyrant."

He was still on the running-board as she stopped the roadster in front of a building. He saluted in response to a hail from a gay party passing in a luxurious touring car before he demanded:

"Where's your license."

With tormenting deliberation she produced a slip of paper from her envelope purse.

"Here it is. Please don't beat me," she mocked penitently.

Triumphantly she watched the slow color rise under his bronze skin as he examined it. He wasn't quite so hard-boiled as he wanted her to think him. Neither was his uniform of the regulation traffic brand. It was of A. E. F. vintage, one silver bar on the shoulder, a caduceus on the collar, a discharge stripe on the sleeve. His implacable voice belied his color as note-book in hand he tapped the license:

"This really is your name?"

"Of course. I'm Jean Randolph."

Did it mean anything to him or was she imagining a slight tightening of his jaw?

"Your car has a New York registration. What are you doing here?"

Jean resented his tone, resented his direct gaze which stripped off her self-complacency, resented having wasted her most charming smile on a mere traffic officer, resented the surge of terror which had swept her as he had stepped in front of her car, even now there was an all-goneness in the place where her knees should be. She answered flippantly:

"Doing here? Nothing much. I've come to spend the winter with my father and — and — you may take it from me " — her voice waxed indignant — "I'm not **any** more pleased to be in your one-horse little city than you are to have me here." She waved a contemptuous hand; "Is it dead or just sleeping?"

"Father's name?"

She had the sensation of having inadvertently stepped under an icy shower.

"Hugh Randolph. I suppose you know who he is?"

He ignored the question as he made another entry in his book. She was conscious of eyes, millions of them, regarding her from the windows of the building. She felt the color rising to the brim of her soft white hat. Protested indignantly:

"Nice way you have of saying 'Welcome to our city!' — Lieutenant."

For the first time the man's gray eyes met hers, steadily, disconcertingly.

"Quite as nice a welcome as this visitor deserves." He returned the license, handed her a slip of paper. "Present this at court tomorrow morning at ten." He stepped from the running-board. "Drive on!"

Jean regarded him levelly and settled back behind the wheel.

"And if I don't care to drive on?"

"Parking limit at this curb five minutes. One of those summons is about all a visiting motorist can get away with in this town," he suggested imperturbably, touched his cap and walked away.

The girl watched him, noted his springy step, the determined set of his shoulders. He was slim without suggesting thinness. Must be about thirty-five, she decided. Back at his post he saluted almost continuously in response to waves and smiling nods from passers-by. She sniffed indignantly. Started her car. Said to herself:

" Big Chief stuff. If he's a regular policeman why that uniform? Perhaps the city's out of traffic cops today and he's filling in. No, he made out that paper as though it were all in the day's work. He belongs in the movies with his lean face and poker calm. My heart turned turtle when he stepped in front of the car. For the first time in my life I was really frightened. The Terrible Twin suggested ' Make it snappy,' when he held up his hand. Father'll be furious when he sees this summons. Why let him see it? "

A slight frown contracted her brow as she regarded her reflection in the small mirror above the windshield. Skin even yet curiously white under the rich sun tan which is popularly supposed to complement the satin blackness of hair which showed beneath the brim of her hat. Critically she regarded her white tweed suit, with its suggestion of soft yellow cardigan. Made a little face at the girl in the mirror.

" I don't believe that officious traffic cop could tell this minute whether you were sixteen or sixty."

The business section of the city behind her she drove slowly along a boulevard lined with tall trees blazing with color. Browns, yellows, crimsons, scarlets, the leaves ran the gamut of fall shades. Above swaying tops loomed a rosy cloud looking for all the world like a fluffy strawberry mousse. Low down behind the spacious houses glittered a river, rimmed with gorgeous foliage, sapphire as the heavens it reflected. Scarfs of mist, diaphanous as malines, pale as a mermaid's hair in moonlight, floated above it. Dusk lingered in the distance awaiting the sunset signal before resuming its stealthy approach. The beauty caught at Jean's breath. She had forgotten the frost-tinged splendor of a New England autumn.

The clear air rhymed and chimed. Bells? The music drifted down from the sky, like silvery rain from countless rockets. It fell softly, liquidly, swelled, swung into deepening sonorous chords.

A carillon! She remembered now. When the religious sects of Garston had united in one congregation, under one roof, her father had presented the church with bells in memory of his mother, who far ahead of her time had believed that different creeds should, to the advantage of their souls, spiritual influence — and incidentally finances, enroll under one banner. Also he had loaned for a parsonage Hollyhock House, the home to which his great-grandmother had come as a bride. She remembered her own mother's caustic comments when she heard of his generosity. Quite unconsciously she sighed. Life in the Randolph family had its complications. She hated this chill sense of self-condemnation — as foreign to her experience as snow in the tropics — which had persisted since her encounter with the traffic man.

" Darn him! " she muttered under her breath. The road rose gradually, bordered by lovely, old houses staring down through sunset bright panes upon the city at their feet. As she passed the brick parsonage tucked into a pocket of the high ground like a red and white handerchief, she wondereed if the occupants appreciated the choice old finish of the rooms. She shot the roadster up the drive to Hill Top, her father's home. The house spread as might a just alighted airplane. The ells were like wings resting on velvet lawns. The body seemed all glittering, fiery eyes as the windows reflected the slanting sun. Behind and below the hill glinted the river. As the car stopped a man lazily approached. His china teeth, like miniature tombstones fashioned to withstand the wear and tear of time, gleamed whitely in welcome. Ezry Barker! Doubtless he had been christened Ezra, but " Ezry " he had been since to all his world. A glow banished the still lingering chill in Jean's conciousness. She was sure of one person in Garston who would approve of her. He had been head gardener on the place since long before she was born, and her devoted slave and ally against discipline ever since.

" Sure Jean, it's mighty fine to get you back. Come to stay? "

He vigorously pumped her slender hand.

" For the winter. It's wonderful to see you, Ezry. How come that you are doing this though? " she waved to the car.

" Heerd you was comin'. 'Pointed myself a com-mittee of one to welcome you. Guess these flyin' women ain't the only ones to git a glad hand when they come home. How's yer Ma? She comin' ? "

His green eyes were alight with affection, his voice gruff with tenderness. Jean's throat tightened. She had hoped that her father would meet her. Silly! Nearly running down an idiotic traffic-cop had done things to her nerve. She smiled radiantly at the awkward man.

"Ezry, you're a dear." The smile left her lips. "No, Mother isn't coming. She's — she's hard at work on a new story."

"Been terrible successful, hasn't she? Didn't suppose when she left us ten years ago we'd be seein' her pictures in all the papers. You goin' to be one of them authoresses, Jean?"

"No, Ezry. Nature used up all the genius she intended for our family when she made Grandmother a great singer and Mother a writer. I have no talent, no parlor tricks. I play the organ creditably, that's all. I want you to show me the garden tomorrow. I've heard of its beauty."

"Sure thing. I've got another job, too. I'm sexton of the Community Church."

His voice dripped with pride. Jean teased:

"You! A churchman. I can't believe it, Ezry. Perhaps you'll take me sometime." As she ran up the steps, he answered good-naturedly:

"'Twouldn't hurt you none. Say, Jean, been gittin' into trouble so soon? Seems though I see th' old symptoms. Didn't fetch the Turrible Twin along with ye, did ye?"

"I'm afraid I did, Ezry."

"She sure was a glutton fer trouble that c[...] chuckled and started the car.

Jean stood quite still on the threshold of th[...] which had been hers ten years before. She migh[...] left it yesterday. Nothing had been changed. [...] cretonnes mauve and green and rose — softly glea[...] mahogany — red coals behind the iron grills of [...] grate — books, juvenile books on the shelves — [...] closet! A surge of anger, rebellion, swept her. H[...] many times had her naughty double, "The Terrib[...] Twin" been incarcerated there, in "the Dungeon" t[...] "good little Jean" should come out? She would ha[...] to count up. As though to exorcise the unpleasan[...] memory she pulled open the doors. Gazed in daze[...] unbelief. Transformation. Magic. "The dungeon" was a powder-room. As out of character in the old house as a Follies girl in the play of Hamlet, but oh, how charming.

The inside of the doors were mauve lacquer and silve[...] Above the dressing table hung in the same color, th[...] walls were mirrored. A light glowed in pale pink shades as the door opened. A mauve bench with silver top was before the table laden with crystal appointments.

Her father had planned this. He did care — her mother had brought her up to think him a hang-over from the glacial age — she remembered now how troubled he had been as one governess after another had refused longer to combat the Terrible Twin — her mother had been annoyed merely because the constant

terfered with her work — she had determined
a name for herself which would warrant break-
se from the small city of Garston. He had
Jean that her defiance of control would bring
piness to her and anyone who loved her, he had
seriously:

Opposition sends you plunging ahead. You think
ance spells courage. It doesn't. Nine times out
ten it spells lack of intelligence. Some day when
u're caught in swift water whirled and tossed and
bmerged you will remember this." Today when that
cious traffic cop —
There he was again, prying into her mind with his
ool, steady eyes. She crossed hurriedly to a window.
Not too dark to see the hillside which sloped from the
house to the pink tinsel river. Half way down a
chimney poked its head above the land behind it.
That meant her log-cabin playhouse tucked into a
shoulder of the hill still stood. A star pricked through
the sky. The Left Wing of the old house where resided
her maternal grandmother, Contessa Vittoria di Fanfani, " the glorious Fanfani," was spangled with lighted
windows.

Curious arrangement that his mother-in-law should
have come to make her home in Hugh Randolph's
house. To be sure the Left Wing was an independent
establishment, a little bit of Italy, from servants to
furnishings, set down in a New England homestead.

What was her father's reaction to the Contessa's
presence? What had been his reaction to the de-

parture of his wife and only child ten years ago? Jean remembered her unbearable longing to run back as over her shoulder she had gazed unhappily at the home she was leaving, but, she had too much of her father in her to show emotion. Darn the Randolph reserve! Detestable thing! It was everlastingly edging in between her and the gay acquaintances with whom she played round. No one of them would have felt apologetic because of a divided household. Try as she would she couldn't help the feeling that it was a disgrace. She and her mother had lived smoothly, merrily — in all the years no one had looked at her as impersonally, as distastefully, as had that traffic —

"Forget it," she stormed aloud before she again picked up the trail of memory. She and her mother had kept eternally on the move for atmosphere. Education had been snatched here and there — culture had been supplied by travel, her eager interest in life and people. Suppose she had disregarded her mother's protest and gone to college? What would her life have been? Sometimes the slightest contact swung one into another path, she had lived long enough to learn that. Not her mother's argument, but the certainty that Madelaine Randolph needed her as a sort of anchor to windward had held her.

Her mother was popular, unbelievably successful in her work, always there had been devoted admirers in her train. For three years Hugh Randolph had spent the week-ends with them. Then intervals between lengthened until finally his visits ceased. Once Jean had heard him protest furiously:

" I refuse to stand about holding your mink coat —
which you bought for yourself — while you allow men
to implant a lingering kiss upon your hand, Madelaine."
After that he had insisted that his daughter's expenses
were his affair. She had seen him seldom. A month
ago, suddenly, startlingly, he had announced that he
wanted her with him in Garston."

Why? the girl demanded of herself again as she had
asked him in a letter. She had told him of gay plans
for the winter. He had answered:

" Never mind, ' Why? ' Do as you like, of course,
but I want you here."

She had hated the thought of months in the small
city, but good sportsmanship pricked through selfish-
ness. She owed so much of the beauty of her life to
her father. She would go. When she had told her
mother of her decision, Madelaine Randolph threatened angrily:

" If you go to Garston, Jean, I shall start for Reno.
It's just like a domineering Randolph to crash into our
winter plans. I need you as a — a chaperon," she
had added with a self-conscious glint in her dark eyes.
The great emerald on her finger seemed to gleam sar-
donically.

In spite of her protest Jean had come and a nice
mess she had made of it at the start, she reproached
herself, as her eyes rested on the crumpled summons
she had flung to the desk. What was the white package
beside it? She answered a timid knock:

" Come in! "

A pink-cheeked maid in black satin frock with snowy collar and cuffs entered. Her dark eyes snapped with excitement, her rich voice was uneven as she explained:

" Madama la Contessa send me to do all things for you, all time you here. Signor Randolph have only Filipino men for servants. I try to please Signorina, ver' much."

" You mean that my grandmother loaned you to be my maid? "

" *Si! Si!* Signorina."

" What is your name? "

" Rosa."

" Very well, Rosa, unpack my bags in the other room. I will give you the keys to the trunks when they come."

The girl curtsied.

" I make a vera hard try to please. Madama la Contessa send this."

She held out a note. The pale pink envelope, the sickish fragrance which drifted out with the sheet of paper transported Jean back fifteen years. She remembered the advent of those rosy scented notes, remembered her mother's face as she had opened them, remembered the scorn in her voice as she had tossed them across the table to her husband with the remark:

" La Contessa, the glorious Fanfani, is still the center of a group of celebrities — to hear her tell it."

As invariably Hugh Randolph would answer:

" She has a marvellous voice and extraordinary beauty, Madelaine."

"Am I not as beautiful? Am I not as talented in my way? Aren't editors beginning to realize that I am in the world? She is out on the highways and I'm plodding along in a narrow, little country road because you insist upon carrying on the manufacturing plant you inherited."

"Cheer up! You may be the world's best seller and then you can chuck home and husband," Hugh Randolph would console caustically.

She had heard that unfriendly duelling till she had sworn that if that was what a narrow country road did to a woman's disposition life would never catch her and chain her to a circumscribed outlook. Jean shook off the past. What unpleasant memories parents could pile up for their children. Honesty compelled her to acknowledge from what she had observed of her companions that the children could do their bit at piling. She opened the note. Read:

Dear Child —

It is arranged that you and your father are to dine with me tonight. A small party. One of the rocks of the Community Church here — New England granite, — and his daughter, hard as nails — my old impressario Zambaldi — and a man with a divine voice. I am doing my best to pry him out of his present dull job. He belongs in opera. Make Rosa your own while you are here. She knows her business. Carlotta trained her.

VITTORIA.

Three hours later Jean appraised herself in the gilt-framed pier glass in the long drawing room at Hill Top. The bodice of her billowy, orchid tulle frock fairly conservative in the front, was cut to show her smooth-skinned back to a jeweled slide at the waist. Her petunia satin slippers with their exaggerated spiked heels were brilliantly buckled; two diamond bracelets sparkled on her left arm. She had accepted the frock quite as a matter of course when the modiste sent it home, but, viewed against the Victorian setting of this old drawing room, she was uncannily aware of wraiths of nineteenth century ancestors raising transparent ghostly hands in shocked consternation and disapproval.

" Jean! "

She wheeled from puckered-brow contemplation of the looking-glass girl with her rouged lips. Hugh Randolph was in the doorway looking absurdly young for a father — he had been absurdly young when she was born, she remembered, only twenty-two. Straight. Tall. Almost as lean as that officious traffic cop — curious how the officer's face flashed on the screen of her mind — his hair had whitened since last she had seen him. There were deep lines between his nose and chin. She ran to him with both hands extended. He caught them hard in his. His usually inscrutable eyes glowed as though small lamps had been flashed on. She gave his hands a little squeeze as she announced unnecessarily:

" I'm here, Hughie."

The name she had called him when as a little girl they were the best of comrades. His face which had been curiously pale under its bronze flushed with slow color. He returned the squeeze before he laughed:

" So I perceive. Sorry not to have met you on your arrival with a band and fireworks — the return-of-the-heir, stuff — but as I was about to start, I was waited on, I think that's the technical term, by a delegation from the plant."

" Ezry Barker was on hand. Dear old thing. Moderate as ever. He never will be a ball of fire."

" No, he's in the slow-match class. He gets there though. I left my proxy on your desk. Like 'em? " he looked down at the glittering gems on her arm.

" Like them! Hughie, they're gorgeous. And the powder-room is beyond words! How did you know that I was mad about bracelets? "

" I have a friend who doesn't care for jewels, who has a sympathetic understanding of other women's love for them. She suggested bracelets as my welcome-home gift. As to the powder-room, I thought we would exorcise the ghost of the Terrible Twin." He released her hands and picked up the frail velvet wrap which matched her slippers in tint. " We'd better get a move on. Madama la Contessa keeps her dinner waiting for no one. We will go through the garden-court."

Who was the woman who didn't care for jewels who could bring that tone into her father's voice, Jean wondered as she walked beside him through the fragrant dusk. Shrubs were but a faint blur. From a shell in the hand of a spectral nymph water dripped into a pool. The sleepy croon of the river stirred the scented air. In the east a copper disc peeked cautiously above the horizon as though to make sure that the world was safe for moonlight. She slipped an arm within her father's.

" It is good to be here, Hughie."

He pressed it tight against him.

" I felt like a brute tearing you away from the white lights and — the celebrities who flock about your — mother."

" I'm glad now that you persisted. I haven't seen La Contessa — I called her ' Grandmother ' once the last time she was with us and she almost snapped my head off — how is she? "

" Lately for the first time I have thought her vitality waning. In years she is what most of the world would call old, especially the youngsters. In spirit she is the most youthful person I know, she has no age-conscious-ness — which fact has kept her brilliant, interesting, even fascinating. Several months ago the doctor warned her to go slow. Since then she has changed. Were she anyone else I would suspect that she is fright-ened. Not a word of this to her. She is all excited now over the conviction that she has discovered a marvel-lous voice. Zambaldi, her one-time impresario, is dining with her tonight to confirm or challenge her opinion. Here we are, and not more than a moment to spare," he added as a servant in blue and cream livery swung open an elaborate iron grille and a major-domo bowed low in the tapestry hung foyer.

Hughie was right. Age had tapped her grandmother on the shoulder, Jean agreed, as she crossed the wide music room to where Contessa di Fanfani stood under an intricately carved balcony. A few choice paintings by old Italian masters, antique plaques, were set in walls paneled and pillared in mahogany. Embroideries, a rare tapestry were flung over the balcony rail. Photographs of celebrities, elaborately framed, costumes and sprawling autographs in the manner of a passing generation, crowded one another on small tables. A harp, a piano of gold inlay, put pulse and heart into the decorative rhythm of the room.

Never a large woman, Contessa Vittoria di Fanfani, in her sleeveless frock of emerald green velvet had a shrunken look, like a gorgeous flower whose petals have been lightly touched by frost. She was beautiful in spite of — perhaps because of — the perfection of her make-up. Her hair was ruddy with henna, and charmingly waved, her cheeks were delicately flushed, her skin was velvety, her mouth fashionably rouged, her dark eyes brilliant. Her throat, the spot where Time lays its most cruel touch on a woman, was collared in diamonds and pearls. With operatic abandon she caught Jean in her arms, pressed her lips to her hair:

"*Dio mio!* It seems ages since I have seen you. Mr. Calvin, I want you to meet our little girl. Mr. Luther Calvin and Miss Calvin, Jean."

Jean, somewhat embarrassed by so evident a play to the audience, acknowledged the introduction with a

smile which faded as she regarded the man and girl beside her grandmother. He was small with a narrow,
high face, eyes curiously still, agate eyes, cold as glass
marbles, a thin, cruel mouth, a Napoleonic nose, hair
so black and glossy that it made her think of patent-
leather pumps she owned which hurt her they were so
unyielding. He would hurt too, she decided, if he had
a chance. A fanatical old tyrant, if she was a judge of
human nature. Salvation stuck out all over him.
Having acquired it himself — his brand — he'd bend
his energies to converting the world. Electric currents
seemed to cross and spark as his eyes met hers. He
bared his gold inlays in the travesty of a smile. He
was faultlessly dressed in evening clothes. His daughter's hair was as dark, as lacquered as his, her eyes as
chillingly still. Her rose chiffon gown glittered with
tiny crystals. Brittle. Jean had the feeling that if
she touched either of them they might chip.

She turned to the white-haired, thick-set man beside
the Contessa. She didn't like him either, she decided
in a flash. He was the antithesis of Luther Calvin.
He looked as though his too abundant flesh were in
imminent danger of boiling up over his collar. The
Contessa presented him:

" Jean, this is Signor Zambaldi, the great impresario.
Our child has not a voice, Luigi, but she has a way with
the organ."

The Contessa's stilted use of English always amused
Jean. She spoke as a foreigner might who was laboriously acquiring the language. She, who until she was
sixteen, had lived in the State of Maine.

The girl's inner self retreated and banged a door against Zambaldi. She hated his pasty touch, hated the feel of his thick lips on the back of her hand. His voice was as smooth as cream, his English perfect as he complimented:

"Signorina needs no attraction but her beautiful face. If she is not the marvel I have come long miles to hear, where is your *rara avis*, Vittoria *mia?*"

"It is a man, not a woman. It has amused me to keep you guessing. Here he is! You'll thank me on your bended knees when you hear him sing, Luigi." The Contessa's voice shook with eagerness. Her long jeweled earrings glittered, swung, quivered, as might a seismographic needle recording a subterranean disturbance. Her excitement was contagious. A little shiver wriggled down Jean's spine as her glance followed her grandmother's. Her eyes widened in unbelief. Crossing the room beside a slender woman smartly gowned in a flowered frock — his wife, evidently, they seemed of an age — was the traffic officer who had held her up. For a fleet second his eyes met hers. Could he be the man with the voice who was to be pried from a dull job. She would call directing traffic anything but dull. Into her astonishment rasped the Contessa's whisper:

"*Dio mio*, Jean, close your lips. Have you never seen a good-looking man before?"

Jean choked back an hysterical gurgle. Had she been staring open-mouthed? Small wonder. A police-man — a policeman in the last word in evening

clothes — the dinner guest of the glorious Fanfani!
Incredible. As the Contessa swept forward with the
little impresario in tow, Jean caught her father's arm.
Mimicked her grandmother's intonation:

"*Dio mio,* Hughie, what is that traffic cop doing
here?"

Hugh Randolph looked about the room, frowned at
her as though he suspected a sudden attack of
aberration:

"Traffic cop! Where?"

"The man who just came in."

"He! A traffic cop! Where did you get that crazy
idea? That is Christopher Wynne. The minister of
the Community Church of Garston."

Chapter II

A MINISTER! The word echoed and re-echoed through the corridors — otherwise empty, she'd swear — of Jean's mind as the dinner prepared by the Contessa's Italian chef progressed. *Antipasto* gave way to *brodo e parmagioni* without registering the change in flavor or consistency. Each time she glanced under a fringe of lashes in Christopher Wynne's direction — steel to magnet — she was provincially conscious of the bareness of her back. If only she had a scarf.

Tapers, a profusion of them — thin blades of light as many — heavy laces — color and scent of flowers — massive silver — crystal frail as a breath — sheen of velvet — flash of jewels — liveried servants impersonal as the tribe Televox — the glorious Fanfani theatrically effective in a high back palace chair. Jean was subconsciously aware of it all as a background for her confused thought.

A minister! How could he be and look like that? He was so — so human. To be sure her acquaintance with members of his profession was as slight as her acquaintance with higher mathematics. Church at-

tendance had been limited to Christmas and Easter.
Always Easter. Sometimes Christmas. Fortunate
that none of the guests were relying upon her for conversation. She had been placed at the opposite end of
the table from the Contessa. Christopher Wynne and
Zambaldi were discussing music with their hostess.
Miss Calvin, Susie, her father called her, between the
clergyman and Hugh Randolph at Jean's left, was
listening to them, still eyes narrowed as though in
calculation. Luther Calvin — as controlled as an ice-
machine and about as glowing — at Jean's right was
talking with the woman who had entered the room with
Christopher Wynne. His wife? Curious the resem-
blance between them. They couldn't have been married long. A minister's wife! Frightful destiny! How
dare she look so smart? She was as lovely as she
was modish. One could imagine a man being quite mad
about her. Her hair was silky blue-black, her eyes
luminously gray, like water with the sun on it — when
she laughed her large mouth dimpled adorably at the
corners. As though she felt Jean's intent scrutiny she
looked at her and smiled. A lovely smile which sank
into the girl's heart as might a glowing star into the
depths of a rather lonely pool. Her voice was low with
a vivid note:

" I was telling Mr. Calvin, Miss Randolph, of Chris's
experience this afternoon as traffic officer."

As though he had waited for an excuse to cut in
Hugh Randolph asked:

" Why was he called upon, Miss Wynne? "

Miss Wynne! Impulsively Jean inquired:

" Aren't you *Mrs*. Wynne? "

" No, I'm Constance, Christopher's twin." As she looked at Hugh Randolph to answer his question Jean sensed Luther Calvin's annoyance at the interruption of his monopoly.

" It was Luke Carter's shift at the Crossroads this afternoon. His wife is ill. Chris was at the house this morning and realized that Carter was needed at home. He went to City Hall to explain to the Chief. Not a man available to take Carter's place. Chris directed traffic during the police strike, he is in the Reserve, so he volunteered to serve for Luke. The Chief was only too glad to get him. Made him swear, first, though, that he would let no ministerial soft-heartedness interfere with discipline. He needn't have worried. Chris has a firm conviction that motorists who jeopardize the lives of others are unsafe persons to be at large."

" Did he reap a good-sized crop of law-breakers? " inquired Luther Calvin with a tightening of his thin lips.

" He'd like to turn the thumb-screws on the poor offenders, old inquisitor," Jean thought, as she eyed him with poorly repressed contempt.

" I haven't heard, Mr. Calvin. Chris reached home only in time to change. We managed to slide in just before the doors were closed." She took advantage of a lull in the conversation at the other end of the table to inquire:

" Did you have any thrilling experiences this afternoon, Christopher? "

Her brother laughed reminiscently.

" Near-thrilling. A flivver laid down and died in the middle of traffic at the Crossroads. Coroner's verdict, old age. Two cars piled up on it. Then — "

Jean caught her breath. Was it her turn?

" A saturnine gentleman in a frock coat with velvet collar and a posy in his buttonhole engaged me in earnest conversation while a car with a curious sag to its back axle passed. He was not so engaging, however, that I failed to note the driver and the number of the weighted car. I phoned the Chief and they caught it with the goods before it crossed the city line." He smiled at his hostess. " And you insist that my job is dull."

Jean dared with a hint of defiance in voice and eyes:

" Is that all? You had me all excited. Didn't you arrest a motorist or two? "

His eyes met hers.

" Sorry to disappoint you, but, that is really all that happened — out of the ordinary. Of course there are always petty law-scoffers. You were saying, Contessa — "

Jean's cheeks burned. All that had happened " out of the ordinary." He had classed her with the herd. She had been smartly slapped and set in a corner.

Later in the drawing-room her indignation waned under the magic of Christopher Wynne's voice. The face of Zambaldi who was accompanying him on the piano was pasty from emotion, his red-rimmed eyes liquid pools. She glanced surreptitiously at Calvin.

He sat with finger-tips together, lips clamped, his face like stone, his eyes still. New England granite, her grandmother had said, as hard and as cold. The Contessa in another palace chair, glistening nailed finger-tips soundlessly keeping time on its arm, red spots of excitement out-rouging the rouge in her cheeks, kept her eyes on the face of the impresario. From the scores of music on the piano Christopher Wynne sang song after song. He protested as Zambaldi produced another.

" No more. Remember that there are others who are not so music-mad as we are."

Zambaldi mopped his moist brow with an elaborately monogrammed handkerchief, fine as a spider's web, as he seated himself beside the Contessa.

" Will you tell me why with that voice you became a preacher? " — disdain ineffable in the last word — " when you could have become a world famous singer? "

Luther Calvin unclamped his lips. Protested caustically:

" I object to your scornful use of the word, preacher, Mr. Zambaldi. Have you forgotten that the good book says: ' How then shall they call on Him in whom they have not believed? And how shall they believe in Him of whom they have not heard? And how shall they hear without a preacher? ' "

Zambaldi's grunt was skeptical.

" All preaching isn't done in the pulpit. I've seen a singing voice accomplish what talking never could have done in years."

Still standing beside the piano Christopher Wynne agreed:

"So have I, Signor Zambaldi. Because I deeply appreciate the interest you and the Contessa have shown in my voice and because I want you both to understand that I shall be neither lured, prodded nor frightened into opera, I'll tell you how music influenced me. I was serving my second term as interne at an hospital when I went overseas. All my forbears had been physicians, I had no thought of any other profession for myself." His eyes and voice deepened as he went on:

"For a year I served on what the French called the Front of the Front, mending broken bones and torn flesh, relieving pain, helping the agonized to slip peacefully away. Ministering to the men's bodies, I felt helpless to bring light into the dark places of their hearts and souls, that they might approach their rendezvous with death in peace with themselves, in the assurance that they were but passing on to renewed life."

"*Dio mio!* Who but a dreamer like you expects anything but shadows after death? We begin life with a cell, we will end when life goes out of it," interrupted the Contessa bitterly.

Christopher Wynne shook his head.

"I can't believe that. You wouldn't had you seen life go out as many times as I have. You would be convinced that unused vitality and strength and experience won by valiant living was of use somewhere. There is no waste in nature. Over there I realized that had I been in closer touch with spiritual realities I might have helped more.

" One night far, far back of the lines I heard men singing. A New England company starting for the Front. I can't tell you what that music did to me. It crashed barriers of doubt and indifference, it roused a new purpose. Picture to yourself inky black heavens shot through and through with search-lights, the accompaniment of distant guns, of airplanes droning overhead, men singing with lusty fervor:

" ' O God, our help in ages past,
      Our hope for years to come;
   Our shelter from the stormy blast,
      And our eternal home.

   A thousand ages in thy sight,
      Are like an evening gone;
   Short as the watch that ends the night,
      Before the rising sun.' "

The rich voice ceased. For a few seconds the air billowed with melodic waves. Someone camouflaged emotion by a cough. The spell was broken. Through misty eyes Jean regarded one listener after another. The song had made as much of a dent in the composure of the Calvins as it would on the face of a granite ledge; Zambaldi was having trouble with his nose; Constance Wynne's eyes were starry as she gazed at her brother; the tragic lines in Hugh Randolph's face had deepened

as he frowned into space. Jean, who many a time un-
emotionally had struck the sonorous opening chords of
the hymn on the organ, felt as though a ten-ton tractor
had ploughed up her emotions. Cheerfully she could
have pinched the Contessa when she observed triumphantly:

" Did I not tell you, Luigi? Not since Battistini in
his prime have I heard such beauty and freedom in
upper notes. Mr. Wynne not only has a voice but
dramatic ability. He had even you in tears with the
story of his — shall we call it conversion? Do not
despair. We will have him where we want him yet.
There is more than one way to get what one is after."

Christopher Wynne flushed darkly. He opened his
lips to speak. Closed them. Zambaldi implored tear-
fully:

" But think — think what you could do for men's
souls with song, Mr. Wynne! " He gesticulated with
his soft white hands as he went on:

"With that exquisite pianissimo of the same vital
quality as your full voice. You don't bleat, you don't
yell, you don't gasp. Somewhere you've learned that
there can be more of passion, more of sorrow in a
beautifully turned musical phrase than in all manner of
sobbing. *Dio mio!* Your voice would waft men
straight to heaven."

"Heaven! " Calvin's downeast twang was intensified as he protested fanatically:

" The opera and all that goes with it leads straight to
hell."

Zambaldi bristled like a bantam cock.

" Narrow men like you, Calvin — "

Christopher Wynne's laugh had a boyish quality.

" Have I precipitated a battle by my simple state-ment of cause and effect? It is always a mistake to turn one's heart inside out for inspection, sometime I'll learn that. Con, I have work to do at home."

His sister rose.

" Good-night, Contessa di Fanfani. I'm not entirely grateful to you for having emphasized the beauty of Christopher's voice. I'm not any too resigned to hav-ing him work as he is working in this small city. I know that I shouldn't have said it, Chris, but just this once I had to."

Her brother protested:

" Small city! Not for long. Garston is expanding industrially, it's due any minute now to burst from the chrysalis of custom and tradition, a great, brilliant, indestructible moth of progress and achievement." Jean felt his eyes on her as he attested: " It's growing. It is neither dead — nor sleeping."

Later as he said good-night, he reminded:

" I'll see you tomorrow at ten, Miss Randolph. Sorry. But it had to be done."

Not until the brother and sister and the Calvins had departed did Jean realize what he had meant. The summons. Court. Of course he would be there to testify against her. Darn! And he a minister!

As she and her father bade their hostess good-night the Contessa boasted:

" *Dio mio!* You think Zambaldi and I are beaten, Hugh? We are not. When we go after a voice we get it, especially a voice in accord with old Italian traditions, not to be found among the singers today." She tossed her head, her black eyes, set in dark rings of fatigue, sparkled like those of an ancient and ill tempered bird as she threatened:

" Christopher Wynne has impracticable ideas as to the mission of a clergyman, thinks he should give his time to the spiritual needs of his people, not to the business side of the church. I will start something which will sweep him out of the pulpit into opera." Her body shook, her long earrings quivered with excitement. Zambaldi laid a fat, pudgy hand on her bare arm. Chided:

" Now, now, Vittoria. No tantrums. It is bad for your voice." Madama la Contessa sank back in the palace chair and began to cry.

The impressario waved a protesting, I-can-manage-her hand as Jean started toward her. Hugh Randolph drew his daughter from the room. As they crossed the foyer they could hear the excited voice of the Contessa and the conciliatory rumble of Zambaldi's. In the garden Jean asked curiously:

" Why, *why* did a man so alive, so — so — to use an absurdly overworked word — but it is the only one which expresses him — so vital, a young man like Christopher Wynne go into the ministry? It is incredible in this age and generation."

" He told you why."

" But he could have done as much, more good it
seems to me, in medicine. Surely physicians minister."

Hugh Randolph stopped to look thoughtfully up at
the stars before he asked irrelevantly:

" Why out of all musical instruments did you select
the organ to play? "

" Why — why — I don't know, unless because its
tones seem to satisfy something in here," she laid her
hand on her breast. Her voice was tinged with embarrassment as she added, " Sounds like sheer sentimentality, doesn't it? "

" No, I understand. Christopher Wynne went into
the ministry for the same reason doubtless, in response
to an urge within him. Remember what Napoleon
said when he saw Goethe? ' There's a man! ' I
always have that feeling when I meet Christopher
Wynne. I'm not religious, but always I feel his spiritual vitality."

" Will the Contessa succeed in prying him from his
dull job? "

Hugh Randolph stopped to light a cigarette. In
the flare of the match his face looked white and drawn.
The light from the laughing moon, riding high in a
chariot of fleecy clouds drawn by a tandem of shaggy
white ponies, silvered the nymph of the fountain.

" It depends upon what she does. The desire is becoming an obsession. She has a devilish ingenuity in
ferreting out the weak spots in character, of piercing
to the quick. I like her. Have always liked her. I
admire people who do things, but I wouldn't trust

her. She would scrap courtesy, principles, honesty any time to get what she wants."

"How she dramatizes life. She was the glorious Fanfani in Madame Butterfly when she caught me in her arms. I was embarrassed to tears. Curious that she should interfere in a man's life. She is always egging Mother on to be independent, to work out her destiny, as she expresses it."

"That is because your mother's career doesn't affect her. She would do anything to get her own way. You never would be mean or dishonest but you have a strain of that I'll-have-what-I-want-and-let-the-world-go-hang quality yourself, Jean. Watch your step."

The girl opened her lips to protest indignantly. Thought better of it. Asked:

"But why should the Contessa set her heart upon juggling the Reverend Christopher into opera? What will she get out of it?"

"Glory. She is a deposed celebrity clamoring for the spotlight again. Think what a glare of publicity for her and for Zambaldi were they to be credited with the discovery of a supreme artist? They would be acclaimed. The triumphs of the glorious Fanfani would be recounted the world over. She would emerge from the sanctuary to which she fled, when her voice gave out during a performance."

"If Old Stone-face Calvin could have unclamped his mouth long enough I am sure he would have bitten the Contessa and Zambaldi. He was rigid with disapproval all evening."

" He would be. He is a religious fanatic. He was the last man in his church organization to hold out against unity. He lives on a mental island — remote, wilfully ignorant of the fact that this age takes its religion practically, is building up a faith which combines the old understanding and the new, that it demands surcease of waste in effort and funds in the church life. He is feared and kowtowed to because of his financial influence. He's a wizard in business. I know little about technique but to me Christopher Wynne's voice is remarkable. By the way, what did he mean when he said he would see you tomorrow."

Jean slipped a cajoling hand within her father's arm.

" Sorry, Hughie, I didn't want you to know. This afternoon the Terrible Twin suggested a dashing entrance into Garston. I speeded down Main Street. A traffic-cop held up his hand. I kept on. How could I know that the clergyman had dropped his robe for khaki. He stepped in front of the car. I thought for one horrible instant there would be a crash."

" And then? "

" He jumped to the running-board and ordered me to the curb. I told him who I was. It made no difference. I smiled my traffic-cop special and — "

" And didn't get away with it. Unfortunate that the Terrible Twin — are you never to give her the slip, Jean — selected this special time to butt in. Excitement is seething under the surface. The workmen claim that there is discrimination in automobile discipline, that the rich slide by with fines, that the poor are punished. I'm sorry it happened, but, I'll go to court with you tomorrow and make things easy."

A sense of humiliation so rare as to be unrecognizable for what it was ruffled Jean's voice as she protested:

" No, you won't. I will go by my lonesome. I'm no short-sport. Having gotten myself into this mess I won't drag you in with me. I'll crash through. Just the same, I'll make the Reverend Christopher hate the day he turned traffic-cop. If there is any being on earth I can't stand it is an earnest young man."

Chapter III

THE end had justified her confidence in herself Jean exulted, as she ran down the steps of the court house at exactly ten minutes after ten o'clock the next morning, hands thrust deep into the pockets of her white tweed coat. The Judge had dismissed her with a smile and the suggestion that in future she obey traffic regulations — incidentally he told her that he was an old friend of her father. Christopher Wynne had appeared promptly to make his report not only in regard to her defiance of authority, but as a witness against two men who succeeded her in front of his Honor's bench, the men who were responsible for the car with " a curious sag to its back axle," she judged. She had felt rather than seen the scowling inspection of the other two law breakers as the Judge smilingly waved her toward the door. Being at peace with the world, and quite pleased with herself, she had been tempted to intercede for them, but Caution, the sprite who occasionally — so occasionally as almost to be a myth — perched on the hillocks of her common sense, whispered:

" Go while the going's good! "

Behind the wheel of her roadster she drew a long, ecstatic breath. Gorgeous air! Crisp. Tingling. Life-giving after the stuffy atmosphere of the court. Even in the middle of town she smelled the aromatic breath of pine and spruce. A blue and gold day. What should she do with it? Christopher Wynne came down the court house steps. She regarded him triumphantly, mocked gaily:

" Well, Mr. Policeman! "

Hat in hand he stopped beside the car. Something deep in his eyes made her heart stumble. Darn! Why should she feel like a poor, miserable sinner every time she met him? Was it because he was a clergyman and she knew as little of the profession as of the fourth dimension? There was nothing ministerial about his clothes. He was dressed as any man of her acquaint-ance might be, soft shirt, a smart tie, irreproachable in cut and color, grey sack suit, tan shoes. No clerical collar. No hint of a better-than-thou complex. He smiled as he answered her taunt:

" I'm bloody but unbowed. You should have been fined and put on parole. That Judge has no back-bone."

Jean's indignation flared:

" Thank you. Lucky for poor motorists that you selected the church and not the law as your profession."

She had that sense of being set down hard in a corner as he answered:

" Poor *motorists!* How about poor pedestrians? You and your kind set a bad example."

Jean's eyes blazed into his.

" My kind!   And what kind may that be? "

He replied with disconcerting promptness:

" Selfish.   First, last and always — selfish.   You draw a line, shrug and say, ' My responsibility goes no further,' and wrap yourselves in self-complacency. Good-morning."

He bowed with exaggerated formality — was he laughing at her — and swung down the street.   The two men who had succeeded her at the Judge's desk came down the court house steps.   Soft hats drawn at cocky angles.   One had a moth-eaten mustache which accentuated the mocking twist of his mouth.   They shifted their gaze quickly as they caught her glance, looked after Christopher Wynne maliciously.   Yesterday must have been his busy day, she thought impenitently.

What should she do now?   Too early to call on the friends with whom she had kept in touch through their frequent visits to New York.   Her father had gone to the Plant before she was up.   No use attempting to see the Contessa until afternoon.   The Country Club?   A perfect day for tennis.   She started the engine, stopped it as a gay voice hailed:

" Yoo-hoo! "

A girl all green and gold jumped on the running-board.   Jean greeted her in kind:

" Yoo-hoo yourself, Fanchon.   I was thinking of calling on you, decided you wouldn't be up."

" Up!   I'm up with the lark these days.   Isn't he

supposed to be the world's earliest bird? I'm doing Day Nursery work."

"Don't look so smug about it. Jump in and I'll take you anywhere you want to go. I haven't a thing to do. I'd love to chauf."

With one stubby, smartly shod foot on the running-board Fanchon Farrell hesitated. She looked down the street. Jean's eyes followed hers. Was she watching Christopher Wynne who was walking slowly beside a girl? She put two and two together. Fanchon, never positive, always hovering between the affirmative and negative, propitiating, eager to please, had acquired poise, decision. Fanchon and service. Naturally as far apart as the poles. Was the Reverend Christopher the magnet which had drawn them together? She looked at the girl's big blue eyes, slightly wistful now, at her really golden hair. Quite the type for a minister's wife. She was like a delicate pastel. Jean, conscious of her own rich sun tan, her almost black hair, felt like a splashy oil painting beside her. The comparison hurt. It sharpened her voice as she inquired:

"Coming, Fanchon? Even if I have nothing to do I can think of a better way of spending my time than parking in front of the court house steps."

Fanchon reluctantly withdrew her gaze, stepped into the yellow roadster. Sighed:

"No use waiting to speak to Christopher Wynne if Sue Calvin's buttonholed him. She has the Ancient Mariner beaten at his own game of holding up the Wedding Guest. Recently she's been made President

of the Woman's Association of his church. She's got
the inside track against the rest of us. Met her yet? "

" Last night at the Contessa's."

" She's mad about Christopher Wynne. Calls him
' Dominie '."

" She barely spoke to him all evening."

" She wouldn't. Her father was there, wasn't he?
Cat and mouse stuff. The pious Luther being the cat.
He doesn't like the minister of the Community Church
of Garston. Snappy car, Jean. You're stunning in
that white ensemble. Imagine being able to afford to
wear white! You must have a million white suits, they
always look immaculate."

" Doubt if I have more than nine hundred and
ninety-nine thousand," Jean responded drily. " Where
shall I take you? "

" If you really want to help, to the Day Nursery on
the East Side. I ought to walk, I'm putting on flesh,
but I'm late."

Jean gave her entire attention to driving until she
was out of the traffic. Then she leaned back and
suggested:

" Tell me something about the divine Christopher
who can get you out of your bed before noon."

Fanchon's laugh was downy. Her unrouged lips —
Jean had marveled at their natural color in an era of
war-paint — smirked self-consciously as she explained:

" Divine Christopher is right. Wait till you've been
here a week and you'll be going to church." Her meaning giggle set Jean's eyes and temper ablaze.

"I! Going to church. Because of a man. When I do, Fanchon Farrell — I'll — I'll give you this car."

" Honest? "

" Cross-my-throat an' hope to die."

Fanchon looked the roadster over with a maddening air of appraisal.

" When it's mine I'll have it painted green. Yellow doesn't become me. You've lost it, Jean. You can't expect to be different from the rest of us. Every girl in town goes to church regularly and fairly laps up what Chris says whether she understands it or not. No radio fans among the younger set on Sunday morning."

" Do they call him *Chris?* "

" I do. You see, Father being one of the pillars of the church, he's at the house a lot. And I manage to be about. I've a dead open and shut on most of the girls — except Sue Calvin whose father is chairman of the Standing Committee."

" I hate a man who under the guise of church caters to a lot of silly, sentimental women."

" He doesn't cater to the women. He is the most independent person alive. The men are mad about him too — most of them," she qualified honestly. " The church is packed at every service. And when he stands up in the pulpit and sings I feel as though my heart were being put through a wringing machine."

" Given up cards and dancing and smoking, most particularly smoking? "

" Of course not, but we have given church work the right of way. We do that first and tuck the other things in when we can."

" Angel girl! You don't care for yourself a little bit, do you? What's the Reverend Christopher's fatal charm, besides his voice? "

Fanchon regarded her with maddening condescension.

" You'll find out for yourself soon enough."

They were out of the business zone, bowling smoothly through the choice residential district along a hillside avenue, bordered by leaves, scattered, swirled into flurries of color by the crisp breeze, performing a ritual dance of autumn on crimson and golden tips. Past homes set far apart on spacious lawns, spruce hedged; the shining river a silver frame beyond. Mellow and imposing many of them, new and charming a few of them, built by the young scions of the old stock on the home acres. The broad road twisted, descended. Houses were smaller, fantastically varied, less important. Lawns shrank to pocket-handkerchief dimensions — relatively. Fences, like rows of white teeth with occasional gaps where the dentist Time had drawn a tooth or two, leaned languidly. Against the horizon bulked factories. The air grew heavier, the sunshine seemed not so clear.

" Do you know Miss Wynne? " Jean inquired apropos of nothing at all.

" Not well. She's not a knowsy person. She frightens me. When I talk to her I feel as though she were peeling layers of silly conventions from my mind to find out what's in it. She cramps my style. She's a wonderful home-maker besides keeping her partnership in an interior decorating firm. She spends three days a week in New York. She's really artistic — not arty. Hollyhock House, the parsonage, is charming, but then, think what she had to start with. After he had seen her, knew that she was to be the housekeeper, your father left the large pieces of priceless furniture which belonged there. She has preserved the old-time atmosphere. Not a discordant note."

" Do the Wynnes live alone? "

" Except for two Swedish servants and Sally-May."

" Who is Sally-May? "

" Their niece. Aged thirteen and a terror. She's a born mimic. Our crowd is scared to death of her. Queer, thin, big-eyed child. Will be pretty some day. Lost both parents in the flu epidemic. Adores her uncle. She and Flo Calvin and three other girls their age have formed a club. The W.Vs. The Wise Virgins. Can you beat that? Their insignia is a little silver lamp. Christopher Wynne had the pins made. They've organized into a sort of protective society for him. It's a scream."

" Does he think so? "

" Good heavens, no. He takes them seriously. Has them in his study at the church once a week for tea — or its equivalent. Translates the parable for them into terms of preparedness in honor, courage, — I've forgotten the other three qualities — anyway, each of the five lamps represents a — a — oh well, call it a virtue. Some of the older girls who can't cajole a minute out of him are furious with those kids. Here we are. Come in and enroll among the Earnest Workers."

"No thank you. I have my faults but I'm not a hypocrite. When I go into charity work it will be for the Cause, not for a man."

Fanchon's giggle registered skepticism.

"You won't be so upstage when you've been here a week, Jean. We all fall. I'll bet you my jade ring against that gold thing you have about your neck that you'll be playing the organ in Christopher Wynne's church before the new year."

"Thanks, but I've bet enough on a sure thing."

"Don't be snooty about it. Thanks for the lift. See you soon." She hesitated: "You're likely to see a lot of the Wynnes. Your father is quite crazy about the sister." On the sidewalk she paused to scrutinize the roadster through half closed eyes. "I'm mad about my car," she giggled, before she ran toward the building from which drifted the voices and laughter of children. The Day Nursery, obviously. Jean shrugged her disdain as she started the engine.

"Silly to have bet this car. Of course I can't lose, but I hate to do stupid things. Thank heaven, I didn't fall for the second wager. Play the organ in the Reverend Christopher's church! That would be amusing. He'll find that there is one girl in town who won't kowtow to him." Her thoughts traveled back to Fanchon's insinuation. Hugh Randolph and Constance Wynne. An interior decorator! Then she was responsible for the powder-room as well as for the jeweled bracelets. Hughie's voice had deepened when he spoke of her. And he had a wife. Not much of a wife

to be sure but one who never would divorce him in spite
of her threats. The notoriety which would follow
would hurt her with the public. What a mess. Why
couldn't her mother have been a sport. Anyone would
hate living in a small city, but, once in by marriage,
why not make the best of it? Silly to contend that the
environment cramped her genius. She would be careful herself — not — to get caught in a backwater town.

" Extra! Extra! " shouted a newsboy. He intoned
sentences in which Jean caught the words, Community
Church. What had happened to it. She drew up to the
curb. Bought a paper. In large type on the front page
blazed the headlines:

LA CONTESSA DI FANFANI, THE GLORIOUS
FANFANI, MAKES LARGE GIFT TO COMMU-
NITY CHURCH FOR SOCIAL CENTRE ON
CONDITION THAT PARISHIONERS DOUBLE
AMOUNT BEFORE CHRISTMAS EVE.

Chapter IV

IN a morning frock as softly yellow as the feathery chrysanthemums on the middle of the breakfast table, Constance Wynne, from behind the silver coffee urn, thoughtfully regarded her brother. With arm on the mantel he looked unseeingly down into the sociable little fire which blazed, sputtered, cast flickering shadows on the delicately tinted walls of the old room, on the soft-toned linen hangings.

The sun dappled her with colors as it shot its rays through the glass arranged on the shelves against a great, many-paned window behind her. It shone through a bit of mulberry Stiegel, a fat Chinese bottle of yellow quartz; set aglint a Venetian flagon gay with enamels, a priceless bit of ruby Bohemian, an eighteenth century example of Persian sapphire; lovingly touched a tulip-shaped piece of royal purple, a goblet of clear green. Through lemon yellow, amethyst, dark amber, blue and russet brown, it flung its light lavishly, gorgeously.

With a shrug as though ridding his shoulders of a burden Christopher Wynne turned his back to the fire, thrust his hands hard into the pockets of his tweed coat. His sister inquired solicitously:

" Does the inexplicable gift of the Contessa worry you, Chris? "

" Perplexed, yea, perplexed, but not worried." He smiled as he paraphrased the words of the apostle Paul.

" Will the responsibility of raising the money fall upon you? "

" No."

" But Christopher — "

" Forget it, Con. I'm to meet the Standing Committee at eleven. If I am to realize my purpose to make our church a spiritual force in this community, if I am to be something more than a highly paid executive, I've got to take my stand this morning. My back will be against the wall. No turning nor side-stepping. If — here's the late Miss Wynne — " he laughed, as a young girl catapulted into the room followed by twin red setters who flung themselves on Christopher. Her boyishly slim body was clothed in a straight frock of brown jersey. The white collar was fastened by a shining silver pin. Her eyes, shell rimmed, shone clearly blue in her tanned face as she thumped Christopher vigorously on the chest, hailed him affectionately:

" Morning! Old lamb pie."

" Go easy, Sally-May. You and the Rover Boys are as tempestuous as a cyclone." He smoothed her short, wavy hair. " This is the fourth time you've been late for breakfast this week. What are we going to do about it? "

"Sorry. I had to 'phone Flo. Thought I'd never get her. Central was catty on purpose. I'm starving." She scowled at the table. "Only one pop-over left! I'll say you had appetites."

"Helga is baking some for you, dear," Constance encouraged.

"She's a peach!" The girl flopped into a chair. The dogs, one on each side of her, cocked their silky, red heads, opened their mouths expectantly, followed every movement of her hand with beseeching eyes. She attacked a grape-fruit with a force which sent a blinding, smarting spray into one eye.

"Hell!" she exploded as she dabbed at the afflicted member.

Constance Wynne swallowed a startled protest. She met her brother's eyes. They had decided that the best way to meet Sally-May's present phase in language was to ignore it. She was conscious of one shell-rimmed eye watching for the effect of the exclamation. Christopher saw it too. He laughed.

"One drop of juice in the eye is worth a dozen on the tongue for power." His voice deepened, gravity submerged the smile. "There are some words your Aunt Con and I don't care to have brought into this sunny parsonage. Courtesy as well as charity should begin at home. Get me, Sally-May?" He left the room. The dogs started up to follow, regarded the pop-over which the girl was buttering lavishly and settled back on their haunches, motionless as listening posts. She tossed each of them a morsel.

" You boys'd better stick round for the finish. I'm sorry, Aunt Connie, that word just slipped out. I'll bet Uncle Chris's rippin' mad."

" Not mad, Sally-May. It hurts him to have the child upon whom we've spent years of our lives like cheap ways and company."

" Cheap company! I suppose you mean Flo Calvin. She isn't cheap. She's a re-re-acshunary. Her father's all hell-fire and brimstone, she just has to get relief some way — so she swears. He's terribly rich. Flo says he could buy and sell Uncle Chris. He's one of our S. Cs. and — "

" S. Cs.? "

" Standing Committee. You know, the men who run our church. Flo says that her father could put Uncle Chris out of his job, if he wanted to."

Constance saw red with green polka-dots. That insufferable Calvin child! Was her father behind this drive for money? Always she had the feeling that he was biding the time, when factions in the Community Church should clash, each to demand its own altar and gods back again. She sternly regarded her niece who was watching her with big, solemn eyes, even as she kept an uninterrupted supply of food moving in the direction of the demand.

" Sally-May! Do you discuss your Uncle Chris with Flo Calvin? "

" Discuss him! Of course I do. She's as mad about him as I am. Says she'd walk over red-hot waffle irons for him. That's going some. I could die eating Helga's pop-overs." She helped herself to a puff of golden brown crust, hollow as a balloon, from the plate a flaxen-haired, trim maid proffered.

"Watch your step or you will," Constance warned drily. She waited until the servant had left the room before she inquired:

"Has Flora heard of the gift for the Community Church?"

"She's all excited about it. Pigs!" she hissed at the dogs who none too gently had laid reminding paws on her shoulders. She fed them before she went on:

"Flo says, she'd bet her father'd give one of his gold teeth — you've noticed 'em haven't you, one on each side glittering like nice gold tusks — to know why the old Contessa loosened up. Usually she's tighter than a banana's skin and you'd have to go some to beat that. Why is she crashing through now? Flo and I mean to snoop till we find out."

Why indeed, Constance wondered in troubled uncertainty. When at the Contessa's dinner Hugh Randolph's eyes had seemed to burn deep into her heart she had decided that this was the psychical year to spend abroad. Her partner had been urging her to go in the interests of their business. But — how could she desert Christopher now? He would stand like a rock for what he believed and he believed that a clergyman should not spend the time, strength and energy so needed in his church work on the business side of it. Sometimes, devoutly she wished that he had stayed in medicine. He was not appreciated where he was and —

"Seen the Randolph girl? Flo and I are mad about her. She's a knock-out," approved Sally-May through a barrier of pop-over and marmalade.

"Dear, don't talk with your mouth full. You'll never be a lady if you don't cultivate table manners."

"Don't want to be. Ladies bore me to tears. Pre-war stuff. Look at the Contessa with her wigs and her lorgnon. I suppose you'd call her a lady?"

Constance side-stepped.

"I have met Miss Randolph. She is lovely."

"It's all over town that she got pinched for speeding the day she arrived."

The day she arrived! The day Christopher had taken Carter's place at the Crossroads. Curious he hadn't spoken of it. Sally-May went on:

"I guess the older bunch doesn't like her. Jealous. Flo and I were scrunched behind the couch in the Calvin living-room when Sue was having her bridge-club — her father was in New York on business — she has to do it on the sly, he won't have cards or dancing in the house — if the girls hear a step in the hall they pull out Parchesi boards — As I was saying, we'd been helping ourselves to candy and we knew Sue'd be rippin' mad if she caught us — they were talking about the Randolph girl. Fanchon Farrell giggled and said — "

Constance thrust temptation behind her and protested sternly:

"Sally-May, don't repeat what you overheard while *scrunching* behind that couch."

"*Overheard!* Gee-whiz! Guess 'twas lucky I was there. Somebody's got to be little long-ears when there's a minister in the family. Aren't I a W. V.? Doesn't that mean that I'm to keep my lamp trimmed and burning so I can see danger to Uncle Chris?"

"Danger! What do you mean?"

"I thought you wouldn't be so upstage when you knew they were talking about him. Fanchon Farrell, the giggler, was saying that she told Jean Randolph that she wouldn't be here a week before she'd join the rest of the bunch in social service work and be going to church. And Jean was mad and bet her sporty yellow roadster that she wouldn't. Sue Calvin cut in in that voice of hers which scrapes along your backbone like walking on sugar:

"'What's the big idea, Fanchon? You've taken the best way to start Jean Randolph after Christopher.'

"And Fanchon snapped, 'Well, if she gets him, you won't, Sue,' and then the whole bunch cut-in on a regular cat and parrot fight."

A stifled sound at the door. Christopher Wynne stood there.

His eyes blazed as he announced sternly:

"Sally-May, if you listen-in on any more of those big-girl talks and repeat what you hear, you'll — you'll lose that silver lamp."

The girl clasped both hands over the shining pin at her collar. Protested breathlessly:

"He never would take it away, would he, Aunt Connie?"

Constance laid her arm about the too thin shoulders.

"He would if he thought it would teach you not to gossip, Sally-May."

"But, that isn't gossip. I *heard it*. I haven't told a soul that Fanchon said that Jean said that she hated a man who under the guise of church catered to a lot of silly, sentimental women."

Constance never had heard her brother's voice so stern, as when he thundered:

"Sally-May ——"

Fingers tapped on the French window. Unceremoniously Sue Calvin stepped into the room. Good heavens, had she begun coming to breakfast to be sure of way-laying Chris, Constance wondered indignantly. She was too meticulously groomed and dressed to seem human. Looked as though she had been taken from a mold. Not a thread of her red sports suit, not a wisp of the brilliantined hair visible beneath her toque, was out of place. She ignored everyone but Christopher who had retreated to the fireplace with hands behind his back, the slight line which indicated annoyance between his brows. Her voice was as hard, as clean-cut, as her personality as she exulted:

"Thank heaven I've caught you before you got away, Dominie. You keep office hours at the church more strictly than any business man I know. I came to warn you to look out for storm."

Christopher drew out a chair.

"Have a cup of coffee, Miss Calvin?"

"Why don't you call me Sue? I've breakfasted,

thank you, Dominie. Father rises early and drags the family up after him. You are to meet the Standing Committee this morning, aren't you? "

" Yes."

" They are to discuss the best method of raising money to meet the Contessa's gift, aren't they? "

" So I understand."

" Don't be so communicative, Dominie, you're garrulous." It was evident that Miss Calvin was finding difficulty in controlling her irritation. " Well, when they put a certain proposition up to you, don't be pig-headed."

Christopher colored darkly. Sally-May slipped her arm within his. Frowned primly. Constance recognized the W. V. expression as her niece protested:

" What's the big idea, Sue? Why are you trying to boss Uncle Chris? Anyone'd think you were married to him."

Spark to tinder. Miss Calvin's pallid skin flushed hotly. She turned angrily on Constance.

" I wonder if you realize that everyone in town is talking of the rotten manners of your niece! At a meeting of the Woman's Association she dashed into the room when I was speaking — "

Sally-May's face was red with fury as she interrupted stormily:

" Well, I like that! Who was with me? Flo! Your own sister! Pull yourself together! If you're going to lecture on manners you'd better begin with her! Uncle Chris says, ' Courtesy begins at home.' Dashed *into* the room, did I! Watch me leave! "

With astonishing dexterity she propelled herself to the door by a series of perfectly executed handsprings. Upright once more she mimicked:

" ' I've breakfasted, thank you, Dominie.' " Giggled. Added, " ' Why don't you call me Sue? ' " In her own clear, fresh voice she informed: " I've got to exercise the gold-fish in the bath tub, Aunt Connie. F-f-fish, boys! " she hissed at the dogs. With one bound the red setters were at the door, tore after her up the stairs.

Constance Wynne's face burned with mortification. Sue was right. Sally-May's manners were atrocious — but — if you came to that so were those of Flo. Was Christopher's dark color due to his effort to strangle back laughter? Sally-May's exit had been funny, her imitation perfect. Why make a tragedy of it? Sue Calvin pulled on an immaculate glove as she observed venomously:

" The proverb that ministers' sons never come to a good end in this case may be applied to a niece." She met Christopher's steady eyes. A miracle! Vinegar turned instantly to sugar. She temporized in her best sporting manner:

" Don't think me unsympathetic, Dominie. I know what you're up against. Haven't I a little, motherless girl to discipline? But, about the meeting this morning. I came to help. Father's all purple patches because, when he talked the gift over with Contessa di Fanfani, he got the impression that she knew you wouldn't help raise the money. You will, won't you? "

"That's a matter for me to discuss first with the Committee."

"Polite for 'none of your business.' Well, I've warned you. I hear that Mrs. Hugh Randolph is furious with her mother for giving away her money. Not that she's suffering especially. I heard that for *one* short story she got three thousand dollars which she immediately sank in *one* emerald. They say, that when she refused to come back to Garston, her husband stopped her allowance. They say also, that her daughter is as extravagant, as pleasure-daft as she is. We have tried to draw her into our church activities, but she won't help."

Constance was conscious of her oblique, calculating regard before she went on.

"Remember, Dominie! Storm signals out! I ought to know! I live in the house with the Chairman of the Committee. I'll go this way. Thank you."

She looked straight up into Christopher Wynne's eyes as he opened the French door for her. Nothing subtle in Sue's methods, Constance told herself. That last look had made her hotly uncomfortable. Had there been venom in her reference to Hugh Randolph's wife? Were people beginning to comment on his frequent calls at Hollyhock House? If only she could run away. Well, she couldn't. She was selfish to think of it when her twin needed her. What was he thinking as he followed Sue Calvin with his eyes? As their late caller disappeared behind the shrubbery Constance patted his sleeve tenderly, confided gaily:

"If Sue had said 'Dominie' once more I would have screamed. Don't mind her, Chris."

Christopher Wynne's thoughtful eyes flashed into laughter.

"Mind her! Do you know what I was thinking? That there went one little, motherless girl whom I would like to discipline."

Chapter V

FROM one end of a long mahogany table in the plate-glass and gum-wood seclusion of the director's room at the Bank, Christopher Wynne faced the Standing Committee of his church. Six men. Six against one, he decided as he looked from one well-groomed member to another. Luther Calvin, chairman, occupied the ponderous arm-chair opposite him. With a nice sense of theatric values a shaft of sunlight, alive with shifting golden motes, shot through the window, played up the patent-leather glossiness of his black hair, the hard lines about his thin lips. He cleared his throat, observed in his metallic voice which made Christopher think of a saw drawn across wood:

"The Contessa di Fanfani has been most generous."

"She hasn't given the money yet," reminded the rubicund Farrell, whose waist-line was burdened with considerable undistributed flesh. His daughter Fanchon would look like him as she grew older, Christopher decided irrelevantly.

"Don't be a pessimist, Farrell," reproved Calvin

caustically. "Of course we can easily fulfil conditions."

"I agree with Farrell that one hundred thousand dollars is a lot to get out of people — before Christmas of all times — who, today, want something for their money. Most of them don't consider the things of the spirit tangible," sighed a gaunt man with apprehensive eyes.

"This meeting was called to discuss ways and means of doing it. The best, most effective method of promoting a drive." Calvin leaned forward. His agate eyes were at their stillest, profoundly inspective as he inquired, "What's your idea about it, Mr. Wynne? If you will start off with a letter — "

Christopher sensed the man's antagonism. Sue had been right when she had warned him to look out for a storm. He thrust his hands hard into the pockets of his gray coat.

"Here's where I burn my bridges," he told himself. He hated a row but he would stand back of his convictions. His voice sounded unnaturally harsh to himself as he declared:

"The method is for you, gentlemen, and you alone to decide. I have nothing to say except to remind you of the agreement made when I came to the church. My time was to be devoted to services, to intimate, personal contact with my people when they needed my help in time of trouble, in their restless groping for a sustaining faith, for a personal religion; to the boys of the congregation; to study which would make this church a spiritual force in the community. I was not to be called upon to give a moment to the business side."

Luther Calvin's thin face hardened. He drummed corrugated finger-nails on the table. Demanded:

"Do you mean, Mr. Wynne, that when we have a chance to substantially increase the value of this half-million dollar property, you won't help?"

Christopher was aware of six pairs of hostile eyes regarding him. He kept his voice well in hand as he answered:

"I mean, Mr. Calvin and gentlemen of the committee, that I will take no part in this drive for money. I can't do it and do justice to my work. To prepare a sermon which matters, which is interesting, which throws a bridge from the mind of the preacher across to the minds of his congregation, which reaches their vital concerns, takes reflection, thought, time, a refreshed, vigorous outlook. Work for this drive would take me out of my study at the church during the hours which I want — and intend to devote to my parishioners. You would be surprised at the number who drop in for help, sympathy, who feel that they are up against an unyielding wall. Now appeals are coming from my radio congregation, which knows no caste, no creed, no sect. It is my job to help these troubled souls find a gate, which will open, if not upon peace and security, at least upon courage."

Calvin leaned back in his chair.

"Can't you understand, Mr. Wynne, that people will give more generously if you ask for the money?"

A surge of indignation brought Christopher to his feet.

" If the people in this community want this church and all that it stands for to endure, if they care for the intangible things of the spirit, they will support it, no matter who asks for the money. I repeat, I cannot do the work I came here to do and put my time and strength into speaking and writing to procure this fund." Christopher could smell the smoke from his burning bridges. Now that the conflagration had started he would throw on fuel he had been eager for some time to contribute.

" And that isn't all. I protest against an appeal for money for it from the pulpit. Many a man — who, as boy had church-going forcibly fed to him — who comes edging back for that help and spiritual stimulation the world alone cannot give, has been repelled by the weekly intrusion of the contribution plate."

Luther Calvin regarded him stonily.

" And you call yourself a religious leader! "

Christopher felt the blood drain from his face. He clenched the back of his chair with white-knuckled hands as he repeated:

" A religious leader! It depends upon your definition of the term. If you mean that I am trying to re-create, not exhort, to work out a means by which a man may approach the future along the broadening road of faith, with a sure sense of the beauty and challenge of the divine in him, I am. This church was founded on the basis of Christian unity. No matter to what sect he belonged a man's religious belief was to be respected, the fact that all sects were working together was to add vitality to the whole. With that understanding I became the minister of the Community Church of Garston. And I mean to minister. Day by day the conviction strengthens that my thought, my time, my strength, should be devoted to making this church — the very atmosphere inside the walls — a spiritual force, to helping my parishioners over rough places in the road of life, to helping them acquire a faith which will bring them in contact with God. The greatest need of the country today is personal religion. If I take part in the business of this organization, my mind, my heart, my soul will be squeezed dry. Understand, I am not belittling the church's need of money — I am defending my position against the pressure of its perfectly legitimate problems. Remember old Dryden warned:

" ' The province of the soul is large enough
   To fill up every cranny of your time,
   And leave you much to answer, if one wretch
   Be damn'd by your neglect.'

" That is where I stand, gentlemen, in regard to my part in this drive for money. Good morning."

Riddled by critical, condemning eyes Christopher backed from the room. He crossed the marble and bronze foyer of the bank unmindful of the friendly recognition of depositors and clerks. He caught a glimpse of his white, set face as he passed an ornate mirror.

"Look as though you'd met up with a threshing machine," he told his reflection. What would they do to him, he wondered as he strode along the main street. He wouldn't return to his study. He would be unable to concentrate on his work. Better walk till he'd thought things through. He cut across a field. He would get out of the town, his thoughts burned clearer in the open.

He pulled off his hat and drew a long breath as he entered a wooded road. It bordered the river which shone with the burnished brightness of a Crusader's shield. Hemlocks bent tall heads as though to glimpse their stately, dusky beauty repeated in its stillness. A single shaft of scarlet sumach, lingering long beyond its time, flamed near the water's edge. Leafless maples waved to glassy reflections which waved back again. Christopher paid tribute softly:

" ' All space is holy; for all space is filled by Thee.' "

The calm beauty of his surroundings relaxed his taut nerves. He could get a fair perspective now. Word by word he recalled the conference, visualized the men about the mahogany table. Curious how that bit of Dryden's had shot up to the surface of his mind. He hadn't thought of it since he'd learned it in English A in college. Some of the faces had been set and hostile, two of them calculating. Farrell's had been faintly sympathetic. But weather-vanes all, set to turn with the wind of Calvin's approval or disapproval.

Had he himself been stubborn? Was his attitude wrong? Would the controversy bound to follow his stand break up the Community Church? No. It had not been founded upon perishable stuff. In the admixture, the representatives of different creeds had undergone a spiritual change, never again to return to their original beliefs. Should he have consented to work for the money? Convinced as he was that his stand was justifiable should he have offered his resignation? His thoughts traveled back over the crowded week just passed. It had been packed to the brim with services, visits, conferences, reading, in the hope of gaining something to pass on to those in trouble. Where would he have found a moment to devote to the business of the church? " You cannot live skim milk and pray cream," Beecher had said. What motive had loosed the Contessa's purse strings — purse strings which had before this been drawn tight for everything but luxurious living? In answer memory broadcast Vittoria di Fanfani's voice:

" Do not be discouraged, Luigi. There is more than one way to get what we want."

Christopher stopped in his long stride. Would she spend one hundred thousand dollars in an endeavor to force him into opera? Too absurd to consider — and yet, the idea had become an obsession with her, such a fool obsession. If he were to give up the ministry he would practise medicine. Knowing his determination not to give his time to church finances, had she concluded that he would resign his pastorate before

he would consent to work for the money needed to secure the gift? Incredible and yet — never before had
she shown the faintest interest in the public good.

He walked on slowly, thinking, weighing, doubting.
Did her son-in-law know of the Contessa's strategy —
always supposing that it was strategy?

Hugh Randolph had held aloof from the church.
Even after he had given the carillon in memory of his
mother. Why? He must realize its true relation to the
community, that it was a permanent necessity. Faulty,
of course, but one didn't stand aloof from politics, in-
dustry, education, because they were faulty; one put
his shoulder to the wheel and helped. Randolph must
believe in a power stronger than himself. Everyone
believed that. Some called it Destiny, others Force,
still others Luck, some called it the Infinite, some called
it — God.

Perhaps now that his daughter had come to live with
him — his daughter! Christopher's memory flashed a
close-up of Jean Randolph in her yellow and black
roadster at the Crossroads. Once he had seen a great
spectacle spring into life at the light touch of a man's
hand on a button. It had been that way with him.
He had known that she was frightened by the dilated
pupils of her brilliant dark eyes, by the quiver of her
mobile lips which she had tried to steel to haughty
disdain. The hint of terror had sent a whole new set
of emotions thrumming through him. Anger at her
criminal recklessness, a leaping response to her beauty,
an outrageous desire to hold her close till her shaken

nerves quieted. And she had said that she hated a man, who under the guise of church catered to a lot of silly, sentimental women. He would make her take that back.

Catered! To the women of his congregation! A laugh swept the thoughtful shadows from his eyes. The absurdity of the charge. As a whole they were neither silly nor sentimental, he liked them, *but*, if only she knew how he manœuvered to escape them; how he tried to treat them with equal courtesy and attention. It was growing increasingly difficult. They demanded so much of his time. Immensely as he enjoyed tennis and golf he couldn't spend all his leisure on those two sports, nor was he physically able to drink gallons of tea. Lately Sue Calvin had kept fresh flowers on his study table at the church. They were beautiful, always pink, carnations, roses, snap-dragons, chrysanthemums, but, whenever he looked at them he felt an uncomfortable, premonitory prickle. Several times he'd given them away, only to find the slender vase freshly supplied the next morning. He wasn't dumb enough to think that she or any of the others were in love with him — it was just — what the dickens made them run after him like a lot of silly sheep?

He turned into a trail which wound through woods up to a shoulder of the hill. From there he could look down upon the river with its twin isles, upon fields striped by narrow brooks, far off to the white fall of the dam, to loping hills, up to the spreading Randolph home looming above Hollyhock House like an overlord.

It was his retreat. The only place in which he was safe from interruption. Flat on his back, arms under his head, the blue sky over him, he could think things through. Or, he could lock himself into the nestling log cabin to which Hugh Randolph had given him a key. To be sure he shared the retreat with Sally-May and her pals, but the children were at school when he wanted it. It had been Jean Randolph's play house when she was a little girl. Jean — he stopped. Stared down at the wisp of rose and white georgette in the path as though it had been an adder. A handkerchief — of sorts. Rose and white! That meant Sue Calvin. She affected red shades from pale pink to deepest crimson. Once in the early days of his pastorate he had told her of the lure the cabin had for him when perplexed. She had known that his conference with the Standing Committe would bristle with opposition. Had she divined that he would come here? He couldn't, he wouldn't talk with her in his present frame of mind. This ensemble age had its uses. Like knights of old a woman was recognizable now by her colors.

He wheeled. With the caution and delicacy he might have observed were he tip-toeing over a field of eggs he descended the trail. Even as he neared the road he maintained his stealthy tread. He stopped as a soft voice hailed:

" Yoo-hoo! Why are you gum-shoeing down the hill, Chris? "

Fanchon Farrell was watching him from her shabby

sedan. Christopher swallowed an exclamation of exasperation. Laughed.

" In the exercise of due care, as the courts call it. The last time I came swinging down the trail I stirred up a hornet's nest."

Fanchon giggled.

" All hornets are not winged. Methinks I hear some buzzing like mad this minute in the directors' room at the bank. Never mind how I know. I wasn't born yesterday. Jump in and I'll give you a lift." As he hesitated she added:

" Sue Calvin's roadster is parked ahead. I suspect that she's enjoying the view from the cabin. Coming? "

Christopher met her laughing eyes. He liked Fanchon Farrell. Grinned in response. Confided as he stepped into the car:

" I've walked enough today to preserve my boyish figure. I'll ride."

Chapter VI

WITH speculative eyes Jean Randolph regarded the Contessa as she reclined among pale blue cushions on a *chaise longue* in her boudoir. Did she never slip out of the rôle of the Glorious Fanfani? Two Marguerite braids of auburn hair — her morning transformation — lay over the shoulders of her exquisite lace negligee. Her face was tinted to harmonize. The one human exhibit in a museum of memories, the girl thought as she looked about the room. Strong sunlight, which might have proved betraying, sifted through rose-color net became a lovely, flattering light. Photographs of the diva, sketches in color, in black and white, lined the walls. She was pictured in all the great rôles of opera. Juliet; Astrofiammante, Queen of the Night in the Magic Flute; Tosca; Fidelio in male attire; Butterfly; Carmen, dark as a gypsy, a blood-red cassia flower in her laced bodice; Rosina in black mantilla, were but a few of the characters. Enclosed in glass was a high-heel gold slipper from which a Crown Prince had drunk the singer's health. A case of exquisite fans, presented by adorers, royal all of them, was topped by a gold loving cup inscribed with names world-famous. Charmingly framed " Verses to Vittoria " — " To the Glorious Fanfani," composed and signed by poets, Italian, French, English, Spanish, crowded one another in friendly rivalry. Gifts from all over the world, tributes to the voice and charm of the woman lying among the cushions with a suggestion of languor, filled shelves and tables. Over the mantel hung a highly colored portrait of a highly colored personality, the late Count.

Jean thought of her father's comment:

" Were she anyone else, I would suspect that the Contessa is frightened."

Something furtive, like a hunted thing peering from behind cover, lurked in her dark eyes. Tragic for a woman with a young spirit to grow old in body, the girl sympathized. She glanced at the photograph of the youthful singer as Violetta in La Traviata, the opera in which Vittoria Fanfani had made her debut. Then she had been younger than she herself was now, Jean remembered, as she glimpsed her own slim, white figure in the mirror which two plump cupids — unclothed except for gilding — held in chubby hands. The thought softened her voice as she reminded:

" You sent for me, Contessa? "

" Yes. I want to know what the girls with whom you are playing round — Sue Calvin and her coterie — say about my gift."

" Nothing — that I hear. They may be buzzing like bees but they shut up like clams when I appear. Something tells me that I've mixed a metaphor. Perhaps the girls can say nothing complimentary so they're dumb about it."

"Why can they say nothing complimentary?" snapped the Contessa. "Is it not a munificent gift?" Indignation intensified the rouge on her cheeks.

"If you want me to be honest, I'll say that any gift all tied up with pink and blue ribbon conditions is a darned poor gift."

The Glorious Fanfani sniffed.

"What do you know about philanthropy? Nine times out of ten bequests have strings to them. Do you ever go to church?"

"Sometimes."

"Only sometimes! *Dio mio!* Then why criticise me when I turn pious?" She chuckled, "Object to my giving away my money? When your mother hears of it there will be a row. She will get none of it, anyway. She has enough. I have a plan — what is it, Carlotta?" she demanded petulantly as a swarthy woman in black with an apron resplendently embroidered in colors appeared on the threshold.

"Mr. Wynne to see you, Madama. He say you sent for him."

The Contessa re-arranged her braids, approved her complexion in a hand mirror framed in an elaborate filigree of silver, unfolded a laced handkerchief which gave out the sickish fragrance Jean remembered.

"Tell him to come up, Carlotta." As the maid left the room Jean rose. "Sit still. You are not afraid to meet a clergyman, are you?"

The girl sank back with an angry flop.

" I'm not afraid of anything."

The Contessa regarded her like a malevolent bird preparing to peck and peck hard.

" Then why are you so red. Come in, Mr. Wynne."

Did he hesitate on the threshold an infinitesimal part of a second as he saw her, Jean wondered. Imagination. He wouldn't smile and nod like that if he had. He was dressed in the same unclerical suit he had worn the day he had met her at the court house. Somewhere she had picked up the impression that ministers wore funereal frock coats. He drew a chair near the *chaise longue*, his back to the light. The Contessa regarded him triumphantly. Demanded:

" How is the drive for money going? "

His eyes, clear, gray, slightly amused, met hers.

" Page the Women's Association and the Standing Committee for information."

Her brow crinkled in assumed annoyance. Jean knew her well enough to detect gratification in the quirk of her lips, in her stilted use of words, her voice, as she inquired:

" Why do not *you* know about it? Is it not a part of your *duty* to head that drive? "

His steady, quizzical eyes met hers.

" You knew when you hobbled your gift with conditions that I wouldn't consider it so, didn't you? "

The Contessa parried:

" I had supposed that you would be glad of anything which would increase the efficiency of the church plant. Did not you, my child? "

Before Jean indignantly could refute an opinion, Christopher Wynne interposed:

"We'll leave Miss Randolph out of the discussion." He leaned a little forward in his chair, hands clasped about one knee. " I am glad of anything which increases the efficiency of the church plant — but — at the same time I intend to keep my efficiency to help my people untrammeled by business problems."

" *Dio mio!* Help who? Help a lot of silly women who only go to church because they are head over heels in love with you."

Jean never had seen anything whiter than Christopher Wynne's face as he rose. He loomed above the Contessa as he deplored:

" I am sure I have tired you talking and — "

She flung off her languid pose. Sat erect as she stormed:

" You know that you have not. You know that it is your *damnable* pigheadedness. You could be famous, rich, adored and you — you — " Her voice caught curiously. Her lips were blue as she sank back against her pillows. Her frightened eyes met Jean's. She mumbled weakly, " It is — my — heart." She clutched at Christopher Wynne's hand as he slipped his arm under her shoulders, her jaw sagged loosely, she whimpered: " Do not let me die! I cannot — I — I am afraid."

He held her closer, one hand on her wrist, glanced over his shoulder.

" Call her maid! " He looked down at the face

against his arm, as he comforted, sustained: "You're not dying, Contessa. Already the color is coming back to your lips. Even if you were there's nothing to be afraid of, more than if you were stepping into the next room."

Did he really believe that, Jean wondered, as she pressed the bell. By the time the Italian woman reached her mistress she was lying back on the cushions, white, shaken, but her malevolent self. She looked up at Christopher Wynne bending over her.

" I — did not go — that time. I will still have — you where you belong, enchanting — thousands with your voice — if — if the Lord will give me time."

Fingers on her wrist, Wynne laughed.

" That's the way with you egotists. In your extremity you appeal to the Lord. Why shouldn't He be on my side as well as yours? " He took a glass from the maid, held it to the Contessa's lips, tenderly, solicitously. A born physician, Jean thought. Why in heaven's name had he turned aside into the narrow road of the ministry.

" Take every drop. Now lean back and go easy for a few hours. Take care of yourself. My friendly bouts with you are the spice of life. Send for me any time you want me."

" I hope — you will be so busy raising — that money that you will have no time for — visits." Her voice strengthened with each halting word.

" I shall have all the time to give that my parishioners need, Contessa."

Her eyes came brilliantly alive.

" Will you not work — for that money? "

" No."

" Then Luther Calvin — will force your resignation." Triumph in her voice, inflexibility in Christopher Wynne's as he countered:

" I shall not resign." He added more lightly: " You are unjust to Mr. Calvin. He is narrow but I'm convinced that he honestly believes what he professes."

" *Dio mio!* You see good in every one! "

Wynne laughed. His voice was teasingly affectionate as he countered:

" Don't you wish that you did? Think how much richer my life is because I do. Don't let her tire herself talking, Miss Randolph." He paused on the threshold. " You wouldn't appreciate this in English so I'll say it in Italian, *Andate con Dio.*"

He looked back and smiled before he stepped into the hall. How unmoved he had been by the Contessa's persistence. She herself had met with the same result when she had defied the traffic law of Garston, Jean remembered. Some day she would match her strength against his. He invited opposition. She might get smashed in the encounter — but — consciousness of the Contessa's intent regard pierced her absorption. Why was she staring at her? A faint violet tinge still lingered in her lips, her eyes were feverishly brilliant as she sniffed:

" H'mp! ' God be with you,' he said. If the Deity would be with me long enough to get that young man into opera, I would build a church — of sorts — as a thank offering. I staged that heart-attack," she boasted and regarded the girl narrowly for a hint of contradiction. " Use the clinging-vine rôle sparingly when you have a husband, Jean, but never, never resort to tears to get what you want. A languid body in his arms rouses the protective instincts of the male, tears make him fighting mad."

She sat a little straighter, regarded herself in the mirror in its frame of silver filigree.

" I used this when I acted Violetta." She laid it down. Sang enchantingly:

"' *Ah fors' è lui che l'anima* ' —

" That is the begining of the aria in the first act of La Traviata, in case you do not know. You young Americans are so ignorant of music," the Contessa explained and thrust in the same breath. Jean did know but made no sign.

Back on her cushions, eyes clouded by memory, she reminded the girl of a broken doll discarded, flung down by a child eager for a newer toy. The Contessa sniffed avidly at the crystal flagon on a small stand beside the *chaise longue*. Rebelled:

" *Dio mio*, it is absurd for the doctors to declare there is something wrong with me. I am fitter than ever I was in my life. You heard me sing." She demanded petulantly: " Why do you not agree with me? You are as dumb as a Dresden figurine."

" Do Dresden figurines come in modern sports clothes? " Jean evaded gaily.

The magnetic needle in the Contessa's mind swung back to the subject of greatest attraction.

" I found out what I wanted to know. Luther Calvin will force Christopher Wynne's resignation if he does not obey his orders. He is powerful enough to swing the other members of the committee to his way of thinking. Then our young clergyman will be so bitter against church and its dictators that he will go to the other extreme, opera — and we will have him."

Jean was startled by her fanatical exultation. Hughie was right, she was obsessed with the idea. It was getting greater and greater hold of her. Was her exceptionally strong mind weakening with her heart? She tried to hide her concern as she said lightly:

" Why should Mr. Calvin make him resign? Isn't he filling the church every Sunday? I thought that was the great qualification in a minister."

" Filling it! He is packing it. Luther Calvin was against unification in the beginning — I hear that he is restless under Wynne's modern interpretation of the Bible — and — he asked Constance Wynne to marry him and she turned him down. He is of the mean, get-even type. He will take his revenge on her brother."

" Strange that such an attractive woman never married."

" Early love affair. Fiancé killed in the war. If he had lived and she had married him she would doubtless be wishing now that he had been killed in the war. It is easier to remain true to a memory than to a live man, my child," caustically proclaimed the Contessa as through narrowed eyes she glanced at the portrait of the late Count. " How old are you, Jean? "

The girl crossed to the French window. Looked down upon the garden touched with frost.

" Twenty-five."

" *Dio mio!* Standing where the river and ocean meet," paraphrased the Contessa with a wicked chuckle. " The ocean is a big, lonely place on which to embark alone. Have you never been in love? You should have been with those ardently curved lips." She had probed till she touched the quick. Jean flamed:

" In love! I! I've had a great incentive to marry, haven't I? I'd call Mother and Father a horrible warning."

" Your Mother! Love! *Dio mio,* Madelaine does not know the meaning of the word. She never will plumb its depths, she might be hurt. Love is ecstasy, agony, suffering, giving, until self is forgotten. She never forgot herself for you — she never wanted you — for her husband. Little passions! Little passions content her. She is like her father, but I — I — have loved magnificently." Abruptly she folded her dramatic pinions, swooped to hector:

" I had expected that long before this you would have gone the way of all flesh — all female flesh in this town — would have been up to your ears in church work."

" Church work! I? What could I do? "

" You might play the organ — or," as though inspired, " you might play the bells, they are an allied art. That would take you to the church — Christopher Wynne has his study there. You would have the advantage of the other girls. What is it, Carlotta? " she demanded fretfully, as her maid appeared at the door with a tray. " A caller at this unholy hour! You know I never receive till tea-time."

" Not for you, Madama. For the Signorina."

" For me? " Jean took the card. She tried to control the pleased widening of her lips as she read the name. The Contessa rebuked testily:

" Do not stand there like a cat licking the cream off her whiskers. Who is it? "

" Harvey Brooke."

" That southern man who was at your heels Walter Raleighing for you last winter, usually slightly tipsy? "

" He isn't at all a Walter Raleigh and he isn't usually tipsy. You happened to see him so once," Jean protested indignantly. Then realizing that nothing pleased the Contessa more than the assurance that she had pricked, she laughed and mocked:

" He has come in time to save me from a spinster's grave, or to use your metaphor, embarking upon the great ocean of single-blessedness."

The Contessa disliked repartee — except her own. She waxed peevish, and — in the light of her knowledge of Jean — indiscreet.

" And I had counted upon Christopher Wynne's falling in love with you to help pry him from the ministry. He is just the man for you to marry."

Jean rebounded from the shock, explosively if not grammatically:

" Me! — *Me!* — marry a clergyman! I would as soon think of playing around with the Angel Gabriel. When I step out and find myself a Prince Charming, he'll be an honest-to-goodness lover, advance model."

The Contessa snickered, turned malicious eyes toward the door. On the threshold stood Christopher Wynne. Slightly white. Eyes coolly amused. Jean wrenched her startled gaze from his. Opened her compact. Intent on the mirror smeared her lips with color till they looked like a bloody gash in her face. There was a slight vibration in Wynne's voice as he declared: " I accept your challenge, Miss Randolph."

" Challenge? "

" To prove that a man may be a clergyman and an honest-to-goodness — that was the term, wasn't it? — lover." He turned to the Contessa who was regarding him with triumphant malevolence. " I came back to tell you — it seemed only fair — that your scheme is working to perfection. The Standing Committee of the church has delivered its ultimatum. Before a specified date I am to decide whether I will give time to this drive or sacrifice my pastorate the first of the year."

" Well? " In her eagerness the Contessa sat erect, for once the arrangement of the Marguerite braids forgotten. " What will you do? "

Christopher Wynne laughed.

" The time isn't up yet. Miss Randolph, there is a glittering roadster pawing impatiently at the door."

Jean roused from the state of coma into which his declaration that a man might be lover as well as clergyman had plunged her. What had he meant? There had been a quality in his voice which had licked along her nerves like fire. She dropped a dutiful kiss upon the top of the Contessa's henna transformation and made a blind attempt at exit.

"Not that door, Miss Randolph. That's a closet. This way."

The Contessa chuckled. Furious, humiliated, Jean looked defiantly up at Christopher Wynne as she passed him. Two tiny flashes burned behind the laughter in his eyes as he reminded:

"Don't forget! Like the lady from Missouri, you're going to be shown."

Before the entrance door of the Left Wing Harvey Brooke, blond, smiling, a tweed model of the well-dressed man, greeted gaily:

"Here I am, Jean, as per schedule, to rescue my sleeping beauty from the spell of the magician. Good Lord, but this is a dull burg. It reminds me of a merry-go-round. Lots of action but it doesn't get anywhere. I've been here one hour and it's seemed a thousand — without you. Hop in."

In the luxurious perfectness of the roadster Jean drew a long breath. Almost she felt as though she had been under a spell——with the Contessa qualifying as witch. As Christopher Wynne stepped from the front door she raised her voice that it might reach him:

"Harvey, you're an angel to come to my rescue. This is the deadest spot in the universe. Not a real, flesh and blood man in the place."

Chapter VII

S UNDAY hush. Jean sensed it as her yellow and
black roadster shot between the gate-posts of Hill
Top. Curious how the world stilled on the Seventh
Day. She looked back. It seemed as though the
myriad eyes of the spreading white house regarded
her with stark disapproval. She wrinkled her nose at
them defiantly. Was New England conservatism
getting in its work that she should imagine criticism
in a lot of silly windows? Defiantly she glanced at the
golf-bag, tennis rackets, conspicuously displayed on
the seat beside her. She glimpsed her white sports
frock with its yellow jacket in the windshield mirror.
Nothing wrong about that.

Gorgeous day. The late October air was tinged with
frost, fragrant with the smoke from wood fires, the
aromatic breath of pine and spruce, musical with
the high, light sound of distant bells, the croon of
nearby branches shaking off their last leaves, tenderly,
lingeringly, like mothers sending their youngest children to school for the first time. Overhead spread a
sky, beautifully, clearly blue, its brilliance streaked
with cloud drifts, evanescent as opaline mists. The

ribbon of shining river might have been dropped from overhead to tie up the bonny russet fields, so translucently it reflected the dome above.

Jean reduced the speed of her car as she entered the main street. A challenge to the World and his Wife. If anyone inquired her destination she was prepared to answer gaily:

"To the Country Club of course. Why not? Imagine sitting in a stuffy church this glorious morning."

She nodded and smiled radiantly at acquaintances. Every girl in town was bent decorously churchward. Hypocrites! How long would they desert the Club for the Church were Christopher Wynne to be given his congé? The month was creeping on. Had he decided to give in, to work for the money? She had heard fragments of dispute between her father and the Contessa. He hotly resented the dissension she had started. His mother-in-law was exultant. The congregation of the Community Church was splitting into factions, some members were bolting the ticket, as it were.

Was it the fashion to walk to morning service in Garston? Everyone was doing it. She passed Sue Calvin and her father. He frowned disapproval, set his thin lips, lifted his silk hat grudgingly, his daughter gave her an oblique, calculating stare. Fanchon Farrell, a green and gold vision, hurried by pulling on her gloves. She sighed theatrically, called:

"Another gown!" Giggled. Cast a possessive glance at the roadster, added:

" Mad about my car! "

Constance Wynne, smart as a model in her simple
cloth frock, her fox scarf, nodded, smiled. Sally-May,
beside her, pursed her mouth in conscious rectitude,
regarded the sports-laden roadster over the tops of
her spectacles. Prim little thing, Jean resented hotly
and sent the car ahead. A hush descended as though
the whole world were waiting, then from the church
tower was scattered a lovely shower of sound, followed
by great chords like the notes of many organs.
Melodiously, majestically the bells petitioned:

"O God, our help in ages past."

Jean accompanied the notes with the words of the
hymn as the carillon pealed on.

A sweetly solemn " Amen! " and the vibrant bells
were still in fact. In fancy they beat and throbbed
and crashed through Jean's consciousness as a picture
of Christopher Wynne standing by the piano of gold
inlay in the Contessa's drawing room flashed on the
screen of her mind. He had sung this very song after
having explained the influence it had had on his life.
Her face flamed. Why had she flaunted her indifference
to church in this cheap, stupid way? The Terrible Twin
again! Her shamed color burned deeper. No. No
longer would she hide behind that childish double.
Jean Randolph had deliberately driven her sports-laden
car by the church in the hope that Christopher Wynne
would hear of it. She wanted to hurt him. Why?
As though he would care. It was increasingly evident
that he had only contempt for her. Then why had he
said in a voice which had caught at her breath:

"I accept that challenge."

She stepped on the accelerator in a vain attempt to escape her thoughts. If only Sally-May hadn't seen her. Before this the child had stared at her with frankly admiring eyes, this time there had been prim disapproval behind the shell-rimmed spectacles. How much responsibility had one toward the rest of the world? Was she wrapped in self-complacency, as Christopher Wynne had accused? What had happened to her? From the day she had returned to Garston her code of indifference seemed to have been put into reverse. She had thought more of life and its meaning as translated into terms of daily living than in all her carefree years before. Good heavens, was her Randolph blood getting the upper hand? Was she narrowing into a tight, little conservative?

She had been gay, light-hearted, defiant when she had started out this morning. The deep, solemn bells had shattered her complacent mood. What was there about church to attract the people whom she had passed? Not all of them were young. Not all of them were of the sex to find Christopher Wynne alluring. Spiritual values? She had heard the term. Of course she had stood for honor, loyalty, truthfulness — a liar was such a coward — those qualities were a Randolph inheritance. What influence had woven them, like the red thread of courage, into the character of the first of the family?

Deep in her sub-consciousness the question persisted even after Harvey Brooke joined her at the links.

Blond, gay, affectionately tormenting he followed her.
They played eighteen holes of golf — all the while she
was visualizing the dim interior of a church, Christopher Wynne in his black gown — perhaps he didn't
wear one — perhaps —

"Snap out of it, Jean!" Brooke protested as they
returned to the club house. "Your game's slipping.
You've been as responsive going round as a wax man-
nikin. What's on the little mind?"

"Nothing, Harvey."

"Truthful Jean. She realizes her mental limita-
tions." He tucked his arm in hers, cajoled, "'Bout
fed up on this town? Chuck it. Marry me and we'll
do anything, go anywhere you say."

"I can't, Harvey."

"I've found an emerald for you, Sweetness — I'll
produce it the minute you say the word — that will
knock the spots out of that gorgeous one your mother
wears on her little finger."

Harvey couldn't know, of course, that that ring was
hateful to her because she had loathed the story which
had brought the check which had bought the ring. She
shook her head.

"You can't bribe me with an emerald. I promised
my father I would stay through the winter."

"A sacrifice! Yea, a sacrifice on the altar of filial
affection," Brooke mocked gaily. "Well, if you won't
fly with me — I mean that literally — I've ordered a
new plane, a seaplane, thought I'd experiment on the
river, I'll try anything once. This town is up to date

in one respect, the flying-field is a corker, with its big
river frontage, its beacon. — Let's eat. I've reserved
a table. There's always a big crowd here Sundays."

" I'm surprised. I thought they were all at church."

Harvey regarded her solicitously.

" Meow! This town is getting you. I never heard
you sound catty before."

" I'm sorry, but they do go to church, don't they? "

" They sure do, in hordes. May drop in myself some
day, just to find out what Wynne talks about. I'll
give him credit for being human. Gave him a lift one
Sunday afternoon when I was coming home from the
links, car full of golf clubs. Sort of apologized for
playing. He laughed. Said, ' Why not? The Sabbath
was made for man. I contend that the person who
attends morning service is entitled to do anything he
likes in the afternoon. He won't go far wrong.' —
Kind of wished I'd been at church."

Jean stopped suddenly.

" I won't stay for lunch. I'm going home."

" Home! What for? "

" I'll have luncheon with father and the Contessa,
they lunch together on Sundays, they call it breakfast
and keep open house. Come if you want to."

" Sure, I'll come. Do you think I'm in this dead
town for any reason but to be with you? I'll join you
at Hill Top after I've had my shower."

Why had she grafted Harvey Brooke on to her day,
Jean demanded of herself impatiently as she entered
a woodsy road. She wouldn't go through the town

again. The river looked dreamily peaceful. Made her think of a lioness asleep. She had seen it rage and roar during a spring break-up. That narrow path up the hill had worn bare since the days when she had her playhouse half way up, or, half way down, if one approached from Hill Top. Was the log cabin still usable? She would investigate. Harvey and luncheon might wait.

She parked her car among some bushes. Swiftly ascended the trail. Sombre shadows skulked under the pine trees, checkers of sunlight quivered in the open spaces. She stopped once. Curious feeling she had of not being alone. Had a dim shape slipped from tree to tree? Silly. Imagination. She couldn't call it nerves. She had none.

In the clearing before the cabin she mounted a huge boulder — a meteorite cast off by some flaming star millions of years ago, doubtless. Above her, mysterious, illimitable blue. Below, fields, the isle-dotted river, gray in spots with floating logs, cliff-like banks surmounted by cottages — almost she could look down the chimney of one — the distant town, the bell-tower, silent now, no longer singing. Walls marking off fields. Even as a child those laboriously piled stones had spurred her imagination. What hidden life went on between the boulders and cobbles, gray, moss-patched, rust-streaked, mica-bright which formed the stone walls of New England?

To the north loomed the dark bulk of the Plant, the white dots which were the houses of the workmen.

Infinite space. It rested her. Rested! Why should she be tired? She, who did nothing but amuse herself from morning till night — she was bored to tears. Mysteriously restless, she seemed always to be longing for something — she didn't know what. A purpose in life? Perhaps she missed her organ practice. It had been her one serious interest. In New York she had dabbled in philanthropy. All her set did that with more or less sincerity. That was not what she wanted now. She might offer her services in the Day Nursery — she adored children — perhaps because in her rather lonely childhood she had so longed for play-mates. No, if she tried to help there would be winks and I-told-you-so-nods behind her back. " A victim to the ' fatal charm ' ? " Fanchon would giggle. All such avenues of escape were cut off. She would mud-dle through the winter on society and books and Harvey Brooke's devotion. She wouldn't lunch with the Con-tessa. She was not in the mood to bear her cynicism.

The church tower shook out its treasure of sound. Aerial harmonies. Trills. Runs. Silvery notes. Majestic chords. An element of mystery. The car-illon. She loved it. The Contessa's mocking sug-gestion echoed through the corridors of her memory:

" You might play the bells, they are an allied art."

Jean's imagination quickened to the thought. Why not? They were played from a key-board. Her organ training would help. Something to do! Something worth while to do! The Belgian carilloneur would teach her. Hughie paid his salary, how could he refuse?

Her elation took a tumble. Would Fanchon and the girls accuse her of interest in Christopher Wynne? She stiffened. Was she to allow them to take *all* the joy out of life with their suspicions? Not a chance. Even if the clergyman's study were in the church, need he know what she was doing? He need *not*. Why need anyone beside the bell-master know? She would interview him tomorrow, swear him to secrecy. She would work like a beaver. Then some day when she had acquired a fair amount of skill she'd surprise her family and friends. A purpose! Something interesting to do in this dead town!

Thrilled, happy, humming lightly she approached the log cabin. It had been kept in excellent repair. She tried the door. Padlocked. Eyes shaded by her hands she peered through the bars which protected the windows. Someone was using it. It had chairs, a table with an old-fashioned blue and red checker cloth, logs ready for lighting in the fireplace, five old-fashioned lamps on the mantel, polished, shining, filled to the brim with clear oil. In gold letters on each crystal bowl, was a word. She pressed her face against the bars. Could she make them out? Yes. HONOR. COURAGE. GRATITUDE. FAITH. RELIABILITY. The lamps must belong to the W. Vs. Had her father loaned the cabin to them? Across one end of the long room was her boat. In it were the very cushions she had used when with a governess she had rowed on the river. Her father had stored it here all these years! He did care for her.

A sound behind her! Someone else on the hill? She turned. Her heart did a cart-wheel and righted. Between the boulder and the log cabin stood a man staring at her with green eyes from beneath the brim of a rakish hat. One of the men whom Christopher Wynne had had haled to court. She remembered his moth-eaten mustache, which didn't quite conceal the mockery of his twisted mouth. She gave back his glance steadily as she demanded:

"What do you want?"

He thrust his hand into a pocket, as he reassured:

"You needn't be afraid, Miss. I'm lookin' fer the parson. He uses this cabin to work in, don't he? Every time I've come there's be'n a skirt a-sittin' an' waitin'. I want to consult him about — about my salvation I guess he'd call it."

His tone and eyes mocked. What did this man really want of Christopher Wynne? Jean tried to keep her voice indifferent as she inquired:

"Why don't you go to his study at the church?"

He showed his white teeth — beautifully white — in a satiric grin.

"Now that's an idea, too! But, likely there'd be interruptions. I want to see him alone. He had me pinched fer a little bit of law breaking, it's kinder put a crimp in my business." His eyes narrowed, opened wide again quickly, as he added — "Thought he might advise me — how — to be honest an' get a livin' now — now that machines have taken my job."

He was lying, Jean told herself, trying to deceive her

as to his real motive in seeking Christopher Wynne. Too much humility in his voice, too much sparkle in his eyes, too much mockery in his smile. What was his real motive? Revenge? Why should he think the clergyman came to this hill? She suggested:

"You really would better go to his study. This is my cabin and — and as Mr. Wynne and I are not friends, he is not likely to come here."

"Gawd! I remember. You're the girl he had up for speedin' the same day he grabbed my car. Say — "

He stopped to listen to the sound of running steps up the trail, voices young, high-pitched, the jangle of keys. With cat-like agility he slipped behind a tree, stole to another, then another, vanished like a wraith as Sally-May Wynne and fat Flora Calvin puffing like a porpoise, dashed into the clearing. They squealed satisfaction as they saw the girl, reproached in unison:

"Why didn't you go to church?"

Jean stiffened with indignation. She would put these children in their places for keeps. She inquired in a voice spiced with ridicule:

"Does the Reverend Christopher send you out after strayed sheep?"

After one horror-stricken second Sally-May got into her stride.

"Send us after you! Gee whiz! Can't we come to our own club room for a conf'rence? Lot he cares about you since I told him you said that you hated a man who under the guise of church catered to a lot of silly, sentimental women."

Jean could have cried — had she been the crying sort — from humiliation and fury. She caught Sally-May by the shoulder, shook her lightly as she demanded:

" How dared you tell him that! Who said I said it? "

Fat Flora drew a thread of gum from her mouth, retrieved it before she drawled:

" Fanchon Farrell and — "

" I guess you didn't know that Flo and I are W. Vs., did you? That's our headquarters." Sally-May nodded toward the log house. She looked at Flora fixedly before she explained more genially:

" Your father lets us use it. He won't allow us to take the boat out, said that he was keeping it till his own little girl came back. Did he mean you? Perhaps you'd like to see how we've fixed up the cabin? "

Thoroughly ashamed of the shake she had administered — after all these were children — Jean smiled her appreciation.

" I would. It was my play-house for years before I was as old as you are."

She watched as Sally-May inserted a key in the padlock and threw open the door. The two girls stood aside for her to enter. She forgot them as she crossed the threshold. There was the bench with crooked legs she had made, she felt again the pain of her pounded thumb, pounded five times for every nail she had hit fair and square. A bunk was built on one side of the cabin. On the wall was a shelf of books. She smiled as she recognized an old, tried and true friend, The

Swiss Family Robinson. She must have thrilled over it an hundred times. The sight of the boat contracted her throat. If only she had realized before the depth of feeling beneath her father's reserve. She had had a happy childhood, if a lonely one. Always there had been the Terrible Twin for company. Had Sally-May a twin? Sally-May! How quiet she was. She turned. Four hands gave her a vigorous push into the room. The door shut with a bang. The padlock clicked. She ran to the window. Pounded on the glass. Called:

" Let me out! "

Sally-May's pointed face with its spectacled eyes looking preternaturally wise and owlish, peered in upon her. Beside hers, slashed with a grin which would have caused the Cheshire Cat to hang its head in shame, snuggled fat Flora's.

" Promise to go to church every Sunday? " the two chorused.

Jean saw red with fury. So that was it. Those fiendish children were attempting coercion. She regarded them levelly. Spoke close to her own side of the glass.

" I'll not promise to go to church if you keep me here forever." She struggled with a window. Sally-May grinned exultantly.

" Pull yourself together! You can't get out even if you open it. Hoboes came up here and broke the glass so they could get in to sleep. Mr. Randolph barred the windows so they couldn't. Promise an' we'll let you out."

" Promise an' we'll let you out," echoed Flora, her curiously speckled brown eyes impish with triumph.

In answer Jean drew a chair toward the fireplace, searched on the lamp-laden stone mantel for matches. From the corner of her eye she saw the two heads close together in consultation, saw two heads nod, saw two figures steal away.

She ran to the window. The girls were disappearing into the upward trail. Should she call and parley with them? Tell them that she would consider going to church? Not if she remained a prisoner forever! She foraged in a cupboard, found a tin box of matches. Struck one and tossed it on the kindling. A tiny flare. A flame. A crackle as the wood took fire. What should she do now? She glanced at her wristwatch. One o'clock. She realized that she was hungry. Ravenously hungry. Her father and the Contessa would be at luncheon soon. Would they miss her? Ridiculous situation! Locked in by those abominable children! She returned to the cupboard. Did the W. Vs. keep provisions here? Yes, there was a tin of crackers, ancient but edible. She wasn't ravenous enough to eat those — yet. A bit of cheese so hard that no self-respecting mouse would attempt a nibble. A jar of jam. Mouldy on top but still jam. She could go without food for some time before she touched that. Quite suddenly she became thirsty. She couldn't stay in the place. She wouldn't. She pushed up one of the windows. Shook the bars. They had been screwed on to withstand wrenching. She could call, but who would

hear her?   Except for the household at Hill Top the
residents of Garston dined at half after one on Sundays.
No one would hear unless — the face of the man who
had been waiting for Christopher Wynne flashed upon
the screen of her mind, the mockery of his twisted
mouth, the insolence of his green eyes.   Not so good.
Soundlessly she drew down the window.   Suppose he
were still lurking about?   He would see the smoke of
her fire.   Gently she parted the burning logs, watched
the young flames die out.   That was that.

She tiptoed to the bookshelf.   Stopped to read the
beautifully illuminated script in a frame on the wall:

**Then shall the kingdom of heaven be likened unto ten
virgins which took their lamps and went forth to meet the
bridegroom
And five of them were wise and five of them were foolish.
They that were foolish took their lamps and took no oil
with them;
But the wise took oil in their vessels with their lamps.**

Jean read the parable to the end.   Fanchon had
said that Christopher Wynne translated it into terms
of preparedness for the W. Vs.   That explained the
words in gold on the crystal bowls of the lamps.   Her
smouldering anger flared.   He would better instruct
them in the matter of common courtesy.   They needed
lessons in that more than anything else.   Seething with
indignation she took down the battered copy of The
Swiss Family Robinson, seated herself in the boat,
tucked the cushions about her and began to read.

The story held her interest as it had when she was

a little girl. She followed the castaways through their
adventures. The case of hams increased her thirst,
the descriptions of potted pigeons made her ravenously
hungry. She read on and on. How blue the sea was!
How green the palms! The boa-constrictor! She
must rescue the donkey. If she screamed would she
frighten the monster? Horror roused her. She sat up.
Rubbed a hand over dazed eyes. She had been asleep.
Dreaming. Thank heaven! That serpent had been
horribly real. How long had she been shut up? She
looked at her wrist watch. Half after three. The
cabin was getting spooky. Purple dusk in the corners,
shifting shadows on the log walls caused by skeleton
tree-arms waving against the reddening sky, the effect
was chillingly uncanny.

Locked in and night coming on. Curious that no
one had missed her. Those detestable girls! Had
they forgotten her or didn't they dare tell what they
had done? Unless she wanted to spend the night in the
cabin she must shout for help. She hated to have
anyone know that she had been tricked. The story
would spread like fire on run-away oil. Fanchon
would giggle — Sue Calvin would look superior — she
detested them all! As for that abominable Sally-
May —

Words were too feeble to express her fury. She
ran to the window, shoved it up with a force which
rattled the glass. She pressed her face against the cool
iron bars. Opened her mouth to shout. Closed it with
a snap which sent her teeth sharply into her lip as a

face almost touched hers, a face with green eyes, a moth-eaten mustache above a twisted mouth. She dragged her voice up from the depths to demand imperiously:

" What are you doing here? "

The man chuckled malevolently; set his soft hat at a more rakish angle, answered:

" Still hangin' on 10r that promise of salvation."

Chapter VIII

CHRISTOPHER WYNNE paced back and forth in the living room of old Hollyhock House, now the parsonage. A charming room of early nineteenth century design. The doorways with ornamental features modeled in low relief, the soapstone lining of the fireplace, the floor boards of painted pine, the portrait of a woman in yellow satin, massive topaz earrings and necklace, set into the woodwork above the mantel, had been in place to welcome the first Randolph bride to Garston. The only modern touch was the piano in one corner.

From beneath veiling lashes Constance Wynne watched her brother. His restlessness was out of character, especially on Sunday afternoon when he was apt to be relaxed after the morning service. Sally-May reading near the window was out of character too. She couldn't remember an hour since they had come to Garston when the child had sat so still. Only once had she stirred and that was to answer the telephone. Flora Calvin had been on the wire. Sally-May had been somewhat snappy in answer. Constance had caught the inflection if not the content of her reply.

A tiff probably, which accounted for Sally-May's presence at home. She spoke to her niece:

"Stop reading by that poor light, dear. You will ruin your eyes."

To her surprise the girl obeyed without protest. Constance regarded her uneasily. What did her unusual docility mean? Was she ill? At sound of the closing book the red setters, stretched on the hearth-rug, backs to the fire, languidly raised observant heads, languidly thumped inquiring tails. Christopher stopped his restless pacing to smooth Sally-May's short hair, to demand affectionately:

"How does it happen that you're at home? Thought that the W. Vs. met in the cabin on Sunday afternoons."

His niece avoided his eyes as she answered:

"Days are so short that Flo and I had our conf'rence after morning service. The big girls go up on the hill to snoop on us. We fooled them today."

"Which girls?"

"Fanchon Farrell, Sue Calvin and their crowd."

"Does Miss Randolph go?" Christopher inquired casually, too casually, Constance decided. Lately she had begun to suspect that Jean Randolph interested him. She had sensed his keen attention whenever her name was mentioned. Suppose he were to care for her seriously? It couldn't happen. It mustn't. Charming as she was she was inherently selfish, worldly, altogether pagan. She the wife of a minister! The suggestion would be laughable — if Christopher were not the minister in question. Sally-May's voice recalled her wandering thoughts.

" Gee whiz! You'd been rippin' mad, old lamb pie, if you'd seen her driving along the street just as the bells were ringing for church. She had golf clubs and tennis rackets hanging all over her yellow and black roadster and she was nodding and smiling to the other girls as though she were thinking:

" ' Poor boobs! Running after the minister.' "

" Sally-May! " thundered Christopher, " Didn't I tell you never to refer to that remark of Jean's again? "

So, he thought of her as " Jean," Constance reflected. Oh, it was unbearable that out of thousands of parishes, he should have settled in Garston, that out of millions of girls in the world this one should have interested him. If only she would return to her mother. Mother! Hugh Randolph's wife. She had to keep reminding herself that he had a wife. Sally-May's reply to her uncle's stern question switched Constance's train of thought back to her surroundings.

" Pull yourself together, Uncle Chris. If you knew of the missionary work Flo and I — " the shrill call of the telephone interrupted. She dashed to the door. The two setters anticipated her exit by a second. " I'll answer. I'm sure it's for me. Flo said she would call again." In an instant her voice drifted back from the hall:

" Hulloa! — Yes — No! I don't." Followed a few indistinguishable words as though her mouth were close to the receiver. Then scathingly; " Don't be a quitter. Haven't the W. Vs. a mission? I'll bet you're scared. Jelly fish! No stiffening in the spine. You belong with the Foolish Virgins. Better give your courage lamp to someone else. — Well, perhaps, before dark. You should worry. It's her own fault. Better stick round for the finish. Got to go. Helga's going to teach me how to make scones for tea. Goo'-bye! "

Running steps kitchenward. The joyous yelps of dogs. Christopher looked at his sister.

" What's up? Why should Flo be scared? Fee — Fi — Fo — Fum! I smell mischief. What the dickens has Sally-May up her sleeve now? "

" Something. I'm ashamed to acknowledge it, but, she's been too good to be true ever since she stole in for dinner like a nice, sleek pussy-cat purring for her cream."

" Didn't she come home with you? "

" No. You heard her say that she and Flo had a conf'rence after church." Constance felt the color burn in her cheeks as she ventured hesitantly:

" Chris — I don't mean to be a pest, to meddle in your life, but — but — I am uneasy about you. You — you aren't becoming interested in Jean Randolph, are you? "

The old room was still. To the woman eagerly awaiting her brother's reply it seemed to be listening, listening for one more story to be added to the files of a century; the tick of the tall clock in the corner seemed to echo rhythmically:

" Are you? Are you? Are you? "

Christopher Wynne leaned an arm on the mantel, looked down into the red coals as he asked gravely:

" Suppose I am? "

Constance in a deep chair before the fire clasped her hands about her knees. That low answer of her brother's had set them shaking. A premonition of disaster? The burning logs cast witch-fire shadows across her eyes, her voice was unsteady as she warned:

" You'll be unbearably hurt, Chris. Shut her out of your heart before it is too late.

" No use in closing the door now, Con. She's in."

" Chris! Chris! Why did you let yourself care for her? "

" Let myself! She was in before I knew it. She took possession the day I held up her roadster at the Crossroads."

" Have you never tried to put her out? "

" Not very hard."

" You have always said you would not marry a girl with money, and she is heir to all the Contessa has, to all her father's wealth, to all of her mother's."

" I know it. I still think it a mistake. But — I'm not exactly a pauper. I have a small income beside my salary — though I may not have that last long."

" Then you mean to hold out against taking part in raising this money? "

" I do. I have been here a year, I have put the best of myself into the work, I feel that I am beginning to make good. It will be a terrific wrench to give it up, especially to be asked to resign. I may be wrong in my attitude — but — it seems right to me and I'll stick to it."

" Then you are right to stick. A wobbler takes two steps back for one ahead. But, about Jean Randolph, she never will marry a clergyman — perhaps if you persist in refusing to raise that money — you will give up your profession — then you might have a chance with her."

" Do you think I would marry a girl who would want me to give up my profession? When I began to consider entering the ministry I consulted the wisest man I knew, a man who had spent his life in the work. I asked him how I might be sure that my desire was a steady sea of determination, not a wave of impulse set in motion by my war experience. His reply is burned into my memory:

" ' If you have a profound conviction that the things of the mind are of enduring satisfaction, a keen sense of the high privilege of seeking for truth on which to feed your soul; if you are really human in your life, sympathies and attitudes; if you have a genuine interest in men and women for their own sakes; if you live consciously, eagerly, gladly in the intimate relations of life with God and spiritual realities and from these experiences endeavor to lead men to God and God to men — as all true artists, poets and thinkers do — then, my son, I counsel you to enter the ministry if you feel deeply urged to do so. The modern drift is along the broadening road of faith. That " road that leads through dust and heat to hilltops clear." ' "

" Even after that I turned the matter over in my mind for weeks. Then I decided. I shall not retreat.

You are unfair to Jean Randolph, Con. You don't
look below the flippant surface. I know by the fine,
sweet line of her mouth that she isn't the sort who
would pry a man from his life work, force him into
something more pleasing to her."

"My dear, she is! She is! You are the one who
won't look below the surface. Everyone says that she
is engaged to Harvey Brooke, that she is merely waiting until the visit she promised her father is over before
she marries him. He is distinctly her kind, Chris.
Young, rich, good-looking enough, with an easy-going
tolerance of unethical practices — I've talked with him.
He calls it being progressive, liberal, freedom of
thought. Who was it said that freedom of thought
becomes absence of thought? "

" Brooke is all right fundamentally, Con. Most men
have a double. One who questions, perhaps jeers, at
the simple virtues of restraint, integrity, dependability,
idealism, which form the basis of the better self's code
of living. One who grips like a sudden flair for ad-
venture into unknown, dangerous countries, who really
isn't a part of him."

"You are generous and understanding, Chris, but
— try to put Jean Randolph out of your life. If you
don't you will be horribly hurt."

Christopher laid his hands on his sister's shoulders,
smiled whimsically down into her eyes.

"I will be horribly hurt if I do, Con, so there you
are. If she really is engaged to Brooke that settles it.
But I'll keep her in my heart and take the con-

sequences." He listened. " Someone coming up the front walk. In a hurry. The visitor is not for me or he would have come to the library door. I'll let him in."

He went into the hall. Constance heard him say: " You, Mr. Randolph? "

She swallowed her heart which had begun to make merry in her throat. Who was she to counsel Christopher when the sound of a man's voice — a married man at that — set her pulses hammering? She clasped her unsteady hands tight behind her as Hugh Randolph entered. His grave eyes betrayed his smile as he announced without preamble:

" I know that I've come on a fool's errand, of course she wouldn't be here, but, I'm trying to locate Jean. She played golf with Harvey Brooke this morning. He promised to join her at Hill Top for luncheon. He saw her start off in her roadster. I judge from his confused apology that he was drawn into a game of poker at the Club which lasted till about twenty minutes ago. Then he came pelting after Jean to explain. She didn't come home. We can't locate her. Came here as a last resort. Of course nothing has happened to her but the memory of that college girl who disappeared — Couldn't get you by 'phone. Your line is out of order."

" Our line out of order? Sally-May was using it only a few minutes ago. I wonder — " Constance ran to the hall. The telephone transmitter dangled on its cord. Of course Central couldn't make connection.

A sudden suspicion wriggled into her mind. Had Sally-May left it off to stop Flora Calvin's insistence? Insistence about what? She recalled her niece's impatient protest:

"I'll bet you're scared. Jelly-fish! No stiffening in the spine. — Well, perhaps before dark. It's her own fault — "

What had she meant by "It's her own fault?" Whose fault? Could the two girls be responsible for Jean's disappearance? Hurriedly she returned. Christopher, white, cool, steady, Hugh Randolph, flushed and anxious, were near the door. From the threshold of the library which opened from the living room, Sally-May peered inquiringly through the strong lenses of her shell-rimmed spectacles. Suspicion crystallized to conviction as Constance looked at her. She accused sternly:

"Sally May, have you seen Jean?"

Christopher and Hugh Randolph on their way to the hall stopped. Constance suggested sharply:

"Don't go yet Chris." She repeated:

"Have you?"

The girl assumed the air of conscious righteousness which always maddened her aunt as she parleyed:

"I saw her after church."

"Where?" chorused the men.

"In the cabin on the hill."

"Good Lord, her old playhouse. Stupid of me not to think of looking there. Then where did she go?"

The veins on Christopher Wynne's forehead stood out like cords as he repeated Randolph's question:

"Where did she go from there, Sally-May? Answer. Quick."

The girl's voice lacked some of its smug assurance.

"She — she didn't go."

"What do you mean, didn't go?"

"Don't grab my arm like that, Uncle Chris. I mean that I suppose she's in the cabin. Flo and I went there for a conf'rence. When we spied her near that big boulder we said to each other, ' Now's our chance! ' We told her she ought to go to church — Flo's father calls it laboring with a sinner, when you tell a person what she ought to do. She laughed at us, said a lot of other things, hateful things about you, Uncle Chris, then we locked her in — and she — well, she said she'd never promise to go to church if we kept her there for ever. So we left her —"

Christopher's face was ashen as he demanded:

"You left her locked in?"

"Of course." There was a hint of tears in Sally-May's bravado. "Flo got scared — jellyfish — 'phoned to ask if we wouldn't better let her out — but, you never let me off, Aunt Con, till I've promised to be good — now, where's he going," she demanded as her uncle started for the door.

"I'll bring her here for tea, wait, Mr. Randolph," Christopher flung over his shoulder. Constance heard his sharp whistle to the dogs, heard them rush through the hall. Quite suddenly the stiffening departed from her knees. She caught the chair back to steady herself as she commanded sternly:

" Sally-May, go to your room. Don't come out until I call you."

" But, Aunt Connie! I've made scones. They're in the oven. Helga say's they ben good. I can't . . ."

" Sally-May! "

Constance spoke in a voice she never before had used to her niece. The girl flung her one indignant glance, tossed her head in injured dignity. She paused on the threshold to hurl over her shoulder:

" There ain't no justice! You said yourself that Jean Randolph was selfish, undisciplined. Oh, you didn't know I heard you. Then when I try to help train her I get the sack."

She departed whistling. Constance turned to apologize to Hugh Randolph, who with arm on the mantel was staring down at the red coals of the fire. Her heart rushed out to him. Frightened by the tumult of emotion she had to steady her voice before she re-assured:

" If Jean is locked into the cabin of course she's safe. Chris will have her out before it is really dark. He has a key. But, wouldn't you better go too? You know, she — she doesn't like him."

" Even if she doesn't, Christopher as a rescuing party will be all that is necessary. Her mother and I haven't been a success as parents I'm afraid, and a broken home hasn't helped, but, even if Jean is spoiled, as you say, Constance, I know that she is sound and sweet at heart. Now that I'm at ease about her, I'll relax. For a few horrible minutes . . ."

He stopped and squared his shoulders as though throwing off a burden. Never had he called her brother by his first name, Constance remembered, never before had he mentioned his wife to her. Why now? How the advent of this girl had turned lives upside down. What would be the end? She met his steady eyes as he asked:

"Will your brother give in to the Standing Committee in regard to raising that money?"

Constance shook her head.

"No, he thinks that the time he would be obliged to give to it would cut-in on what he considers his real work. Sometimes I wonder if the ministry is his real work. He would have made such a wonderful physician, strong, tender, with an uncanny insight into the working of men's minds. He has generations of medical men behind him. And now — and now, Hugh, he's hopelessly in love!"

She hadn't realized that she had used Randolph's Christian name until she saw the light flame in his eyes. His voice was husky as he answered:

"Hopelessly? I can't connect the word with your brother, particularly when I remember the slavish adoration of almost every girl in town."

She shouldn't have betrayed Christopher's secret. Suppose Hugh Randolph were to suspect the truth, suspect that it was his daughter whom Chris loved. She must say something to mislead him. She implored hurriedly:

"Forget what I said, I am so troubled about Chris

that I betrayed his confidence. He has been in love with the girl for a long, long time."

Was there a tinge of disappointment in Randolph's voice as he asked:

"Someone he knew before he came here?"

How one good lie begat another! After an instant's hesitation Constance answered:

"Quite a while before."

"He'll win her in the end. He will make an indomitable lover. Defeat will slink to the other side of the street when Christopher comes marching on. Don't question the wisdom of his choice of a profession, Constance. That very background, generations of men who have ministered to human bodies — and those old physicians ministered to sick souls as well — has flowered into something high and fine, with a suggestion of the superman, in Christopher. He has everything to make a life of value. Abounding physical vitality, a glorious voice, a superb mental equipment, balanced judgment, just enough of old Plymouth Rock to help him withstand the breakers of opposition; a sense of humor which revivifies, like a freshening shower after a heated day; sympathetic understanding, tenderness, which is so much more than kindness, and more than all this, a deep and abiding faith in the living God, in the divine in man. I wish — I wish that I might believe as he does."

Constance's voice was unsteady as she asked softly:
"Can't you?"

"No. The old argument. If there is an all-seeing

God, why does he permit the Infernos of life? Discipline, of course. Well, I've had, am having mine. Why should it continue? For the last year I have fought my passionate longing for divorce. I won't have Jean's future wrecked by our mistakes. The child of divorced parents starts off on the wrong foot. My wife is content to let conditions remain as they are. Modern as she is, she realizes that unless she could pose as a martyr — I refuse to be branded as either libertine or monster that Madelaine may gain her freedom unsmirched — she would lose some of her public. For Jean's sake I feel that we should hang together any old way — but — there are times — " he took an impetuous step forward, caught her hands.

" Constance — "

She interrupted passionately:

" Oh, no! No! Please — I — "

His hold tightened till it hurt.

" You have answered my unspoken question."

He released her, crossed the threshold. Stonily Constance watched him go. She tried to call. Her throat contracted, shut off her voice. She heard the outer door open. Into the room stole the rhythm of bells. She glanced at the clock. The carillon recital was beginning with Verdi's Jerusalem. It had been Christopher's inception to take the place of afternoon service. He had insisted upon a varied program when Luther Calvin had fanatically insisted upon hymns. Chris had won out with his plea that the carillon should be made an artistic as well as a spiritual force in the community. The square in the midst of which towered the church, the streets leading from it like spokes radiating from the hub of a wheel, would be lined with parked automobiles. People came from miles about to hear the bells.

Constance opened the window, stood motionless, listening. The bells chimed the prelude to an old song. She hummed the words softly to their accompaniment:
" ' Tell me the tales that to me were so dear,

Long, long ago, long, long ago.

Sing me the songs I delighted to hear,

Long, long ago, long ago.' "

"Do you remember the path where we met?" the bells pealed on. Constance's breath caught in a sob. She dropped to her knees, rested her head with its dusky crown of satin-soft hair upon her arms folded on the window-sill. Why, why was life so hard? A second sob followed the first. It wrenched open the gate behind which she kept her emotions locked. She cried as she had not cried since the World War had brought her life crashing down about her.

Chapter IX

S TILL hangin' on for that promise of salvation! "
Jean's surprise merged into defiant anger before
the mocking suggestion in the voice of the man whose
green eyes glinted beyond the bars. Thank heaven
they were iron. Impregnable as Gibraltar they would
resist attack. Good old padlock. She could rely on
that too. She'd rather be locked in than out in this
predicament. She opened her lips to reply, closed
them as from the sky came a shower of enchanting
notes which woke the echoes. The bells grew in power
till the universe throbbed with their magic and their
music. Far off she could see a tiny light in the church
tower where the carillonneur sat at his mighty key-
board. It was like a beacon by which to steer her
course. Her voice reflected her sense of security as she
suggested:

" You really are wasting your time. The parson, as
you call him, won't come here." Faintly, delicately
rippled the bells, deepened into chords. The man
laughed.

" I'll take my chance — "

" Yoo-hoo-o-o!   Jean!   Where are you?   It's
Harvey! "

Jean's heart leaped in relief.   Harvey Brooke!
Thank heaven.   The man crushed his face against the
bars, whispered hoarsely:

" Who's that? "

" Didn't you hear him say, ' Harvey ' ?   I suggest
that you get out of the way before he comes.   He
wouldn't fall for that ' salvation ' stuff.   Not after he
had seen your eyes.   He might — "

He had gone, thank heaven.   She was talking to
space.   She drew a long sigh of relief, called eagerly:

" Harvey!   Harvey!   I'm here! "

She saw Brooke emerge from the green gloom of the
trail, look about in perplexity.   His hat was on the
back of his head, a wavy lock of light hair stuck to a
forehead damp with perspiration.   His face was deeply
flushed.   Not too steady on his feet, was Harvey.
She hated him like that.   He was still in the sports
clothes he had worn in the morning.   Curious that he
hadn't changed to lunch with the Contessa.   She
pressed her face close to the bars and called again:

" I'm in the cabin."

He sprinted toward her, stopped as he met her eyes.
Accused indignantly:

" For Pete's sake, what are you doing in there? "

Jean matched his indignation.   Why didn't he let her
out?   She countered flippantly:

" Came here to meditate on my sins, angel boy."

He flung his hat on the ground before he perched on

the boulder and pulled out his cigarette case. He grinned tormentingly.

"Yeh, you did. Well, go to it, I won't interrupt. You need meditation and then some. Better concentrate on the lousy way you treat me."

Jean capitulated.

"Don't be a crab, Harvey. Do you think I'd stay in this stuffy place unless I had to? I'm locked in."

Brooke slid off the boulder.

"Locked in! Honest? How come?"

"That detestable —" Jean bit off the sentence, she wouldn't tell tales on Sally-May and Flora Calvin — "lock snapped. I was looking about my old playhouse and before I knew it I was shut in." The truth. Skillfully juggled to meet the situation, but, still — the truth.

Brooke produced his keys. Tried one after another, not too steadily. Growled:

"It's one of those infernal Yale locks. Perhaps I can work a window bar loose. Try on your side."

As Jean pulled and pushed he caught her hand. Drew her close to the bars. Exulted:

"I've got you! You'll kiss me before I let you go."

"I can't imagine a more unsatisfactory way to kiss," suggested a cool voice behind him.

Christopher Wynne! At the entrance to the upper trail with two red setters as still as two bronze dogs beside him. Jean's recoil from the surprise of his appearance was expedited by the sudden loosening of Brooke's grip on her wrist. His grin was sheepish as he faced the man standing behind him. He acknowledged boyishly:

"I'll say it is, Mr. Wynne. But, the situation isn't quite so raw as it seems. I've been wild with anxiety about Jean. When I saw her car parked on the river-road relief went to my head. She won't say she'll marry me till she leaves here — she won't let me kiss her until the engagement's announced. Not so good."

Jean seethed with hot embarrassment. To be caught in such a ridiculous situation was bad enough, without Harvey's apologetic explanation. She mocked:

"You ought to be called the Babbling Brooke, Harvey. If you must tell the story of your young life leave out my part in it. Now that — that Sir Galahad has arrived perhaps I'll get out of this fiendish place."

"How can he do better than I if he hasn't a key?" demanded Brooke aggrievedly.

Jean noted the keenness of Wynne's eyes as they rested on his face. There was a thread of steel in his friendly voice as he announced:

"I have a key. I will let Jean out. Hustle off to Hollyhock House in your car, will you, and reassure Mr. Randolph?"

Brooke hesitated.

"But, Jean — "

"Her car is parked on the river road, you said. She will have to drive that back, anyway. Even though Sally-May assured Mr. Randolph that Jean was here, he'll be anxious until he knows that she is safe."

His voice had hardened when he spoke of Sally-

May. Did he know that his detestable niece had
locked her in? How was he going back to Hollyhock
House? Not with her, if she had to stall her engine to
avoid taking him. Of course her father ought to be
reassured, but she could get there quite as soon.

" Harvey — " she called through the bars.

Without waiting for her to finish the sentence
Brooke answered:

" I'm going, Sweetness. I'll burn up the road."

He plunged down the darkening trail. Jean retreated to the fireplace. She could hear a dog snuffling
about the cabin, from a distance came the frenzied
yelp of his twin. Christopher Wynne approached the
window.

" Sally-May confessed — not voluntarily, the truth
was wrung out of her — after your father and Brooke
had turned the town upside down in their search for
you. She's a naughty child at times. She will apologize for this and in some way make restitution.
Meanwhile — Sir Galahad, you do me too much honor
— will let you out, that is," he laughed, " if you'll
promise to be good."

Jean returned to the window. Inquired crisply:

" Does that mean that I'm to promise to go to
church? I won't. I'll never go to church. Never — "
" Under compulsion," she qualified to herself.

Chrisopher Wynne stepped back. Did he mean to
desert her? Her breath caught in her throat. A key
clicked. The door was flung open. His voice was
grave as he assured:

"You are free."

She crossed the threshold into the fresh, spicy air. Drew a long breath. Turned her back upon Christopher to look at the western sky, all crenelated pink walls, mauve tipped pinnacles of clouds.

He asked gravely:

"Why do you think that I'd force you to church? Not to mine. You would be a distracting element."

She faced him to demand indignantly.

"Distracting to the congregation?"

"Possibly, though I was not thinking of that. It is growing dark. Let's go."

"Thank you. I shall be quite safe. You may go back up the hill, the way you came."

His laugh sent curious little prickles quick-stepping along her veins.

"Oh no, I'll see you through the woods. Do you realize how the scorn in your voice sets your eyes shining? They are like brilliants. Are you angry because I sent Brooke off? It was my chance to talk with you. The moment I enter a room you slide out of it. Remember I told you that there was no reason why a man in my profession couldn't be an honest-to-goodness lover — and lovers from time immemorial have been granted a certain latitude. I — Hear the Rover Boys? They have treed something."

Had he changed the subject on purpose or had he really heard the dogs? Jean listened. A stealthy stir in the underbrush? Her heart stopped. Pounded heavily on. Had the dogs treed the man who had been hanging round the cabin? His explanation that he was after advice had not rung true. He was shadowing Christopher Wynne! Why? Much as she disliked the man beside her, nothing should happen to him when he had come to her rescue. He would be safe as long as he was with her. Would he think that she was as silly as the other girls were about him if she tried to keep him with her? It couldn't be helped if he did. She caught his sleeve. Implored breathlessly:

"Let's go! Quick! I heard a queer noise. I — I'm frightened."

She hated that acknowledgment — he would think her a short sport. How else could she hurry him? He would be investigating the dogs' quarry next. His concern as he took her hand strongly, reassuringly in his increased her self-contempt.

"Of course we'll go, but, I can't see the word fear in your vocabulary." He whistled sharply. Impatiently she drew him forward.

"Never mind the dogs. Hurry!"

Before he could take a step the two setters had flung themselves upon him. They dashed toward the trees behind the log house, returned to look up at him with beseeching brown eyes. Mouths wide open, tongues dripping, throats growling they begged. Christopher gently pulled their long, silky ears.

"No you don't, Rover Boys! You've cried 'Wolf' too many times. You've treed a poor little red squirrel a hundredth part of your size, haven't you?"

The dogs yelped in answer. Started for the trees. Christopher whistled. Called:

" Heel! "

Heads down, tails dropping, they followed dejectedly as he crossed the clearing. He waited for Jean to precede him. With the lurid vision of an enemy stealing upon him from behind she protested:

" Go first. I'll follow."

" Certainly not. Go on. The trail is clearly defined."

She was burningly conscious of his nearness as she hurried down the path. She strained her ears for fear she might miss a sound in the underbrush. There were hundreds of them. A dead limb creaked. A tree toad shrilled with startling suddenness. Retiring birds twittered. A leaf floated eerily to the moss below it. Was that the glint of green eyes behind a naked shrub? What was that? She stopped to listen. Christopher Wynne laid his hand gently on her shoulder.

" You are nervous, aren't you? Sally-May has upset you with her silly trick. You are quite safe — Jean." His hand tightened. " Listen! The carillon! "

Side by side, the man and the girl unconsciously bent forward. With an effort Jean threw off the spell. Started down the trail. Observed crisply:

" It's getting horribly spooky among these trees."

" We haven't far to go. Your car is in the road. We'll be in front of the fire at the parsonage before you can say Jack Robinson."

" Don't talk to me as though I were a frightened child! I'm not going to the parsonage."

" Oh, yes, you are, for tea. Con expects you. I asked your fahter to wait. She will keep Brooke too."

In her indignant haste Jean stubbed her toe against a root, stumbled. Wynne caught her. Held her close. His voice was curiously breathless as he demanded:

" Turn your ankle? "

She twisted herself free.

" Old stuff! The twenty-seventh dramatic situation. Lovely maiden sprains ankle in lonely wood — hero carries her miles in his strong manly arms."

" You are lovely. Was that a suggestion? My arms are strong."

Jean's face burned to her ears. She countered furiously:

" How could you think I meant it? Have you no sense of humor? Here's the road and thank heaven there's my car! This trail has seemed a million miles long," she added for full measure. After that he surely couldn't think that she had joined the swarm of his admirers. She pulled open the door of the roadster, stepped in.

" I'll take you as far as the highway," she offered magnanimously.

With his hand on the windshield he regarded her with a whimsical light in his eyes.

" I'm not going to the highway. If — I go alone I'll go up the trail. I go back and forth to the Carters' via the hill three or four times a week   You could throw a stone down the chimney of their little white house from the cabin."

With a defiant tilt of her head Jean reached for the clutch. The dogs suddenly stopped snuffling in the underbrush. Stiffened. Made a sudden dash for the trail barking madly. Did they hear the man who had been waiting for Christopher Wynne? He must not go back alone with that menace shadowing him. She capitulated ungraciously.

"Have it your own way. I'll take you to Hollyhock House. I forgot — the parsonage. I never can remember its new dignity."

He whistled to the dogs, watched them return, slowly as though contemplating mutiny, before he persisted:

"And stay for tea?"

"Yes. Plenty of room for the Rover Boys in the car."

"Better for them to run." As he stepped into the roadster and closed the door she added furiously:

"Tyrant. You expect everyone to obey you, don't you?"

The car slid smoothly forward. Wynne answered irrelevantly:

"If you were in love with Brooke you would want him to kiss you."

Amazed, breathless, Jean assured defiantly:

"I *hate* to be kissed! It's a silly practice."

"I'll make you change your mind about that — unless — " There was no trace of laughter in his voice as he demanded:

"Are you engaged to Brooke?"

In her surprise at the sudden question she stammered the truth.

"Not exactly — I — I'm waiting — " Furious with

herself for her confession she added indignantly: "You've no right to ask such a question. I am not one of your — your flock."

"You have no idea what you are missing by remaining outside." Gravely he added, "Neither have you a conception of the load you have taken from my mind by that word 'waiting'."

Chapter X

CHRISTOPHER stopped on the threshold of the living room of Hollyhock House with an exclamation of consternation. What had happened to Constance? Her face was as colorless as the walls behind her. Her eyes had the drenched look of dark pansies beaten by the rain. Where was Hugh Randolph? Gone? Had he brought that expression to her eyes? Had Harvey Brooke, standing with one arm on the mantel looking up at the portrait of the lady in yellow satin and topaz? His color was normal. Evidently the effect of his afternoon party had worn off. Surely he had not frightened her. He laid his hand on his sister's arm.

" Con? "

She patted his fingers. Laughed shakily.

" Don't look so concerned, Chris. I'm quite all right again. Of course I've been crying, in spite of a lavish application of cold water one has but to look at me to know that. It was the bells. I haven't cried for years and years. Once the lid was off I indulged royally. I got all the tears out of my system at once. Modern efficiency, isn't it, Miss Randolph? " she asked gaily as she greeted the girl who entered, the yellow and white of her costume becoming at once an integral part of the room. " It is wonderful to have you here," she welcomed cordially.

Wonderful! It was a pale word to express all he felt as he looked at Jean for the first time in his home, Christopher told himself. Not engaged to Brooke — yet. If he couldn't make her love him before she left Garston —

" Come back to Hollyhock House, Chris! " His sister's warning voice shattered his vision. " We couldn't keep Mr. Randolph. He — he had things he wanted to do once he knew that his daughter was safe."

She touched a match to the lamp under the fat silver kettle squatting among Lowestoft cups and saucers on the tea-table. Sally-May appeared in the library doorway. Her eyes behind their strong lenses were red-rimmed. She hesitated as she saw the visitors, then with a convulsive sob, ran across the room. She flung herself upon Christopher.

" Go easy, Sally-May," he warned, breathless from the shock of her attack. She wailed:

" Don't look at me as though you didn't love me any more, Uncle Chris! "

Tenderly he laid his arm about her thin shoulders.

" If I didn't love you, you couldn't hurt me. What have you to say to Miss Randolph? "

Jean protested:

" *Please* don't — "

Sally-May gulped. Apologized:

"I'm sorry that I locked you in, but — you were horrid to — "

"No self-justification," Christopher reminded. "Either you are sorry or you're not sorry. Which is it?"

"I'm sorry."

"Don't say anything more, please. Really I enjoyed the afternoon. I re-read Swiss Family Robinson. Like the story, Sally-May?" Jean inquired.

The girl capitulated to her voice and charm. Who wouldn't, Christopher demanded of himself turbulently. She was utterly lovely when her lips curved in that adorable tip-tilted smile.

"Like it! It's a corker. I get horribly sick at my stomach though when the boa-constrictor swallows the donkey. What's that sound outside?"

Christopher recognized the jingle of silver-plated harness. There was but one person in Garston, in the state so far as he knew, who used horses. Contessa di Fanfani was arriving for tea. He opened the hall door to a dapper footman in a long, blue coat which swung to give a hint of cream breeches. The man touched his tall silk hat, mumbled, hurried back to the brougham. A rosy-cheeked coachman, liveried to match his seat-mate, held the reins over a high-spirited pair of roans which pranced and coquetted daintily. The footman solicitously helped the woman in velvet and sables from the carriage, accompanied her to the door. She tipped her head sidewise, looked up at Christopher from under the brim of her picture hat, with eyes as bright as those of an impertinent bird as she exclaimed:

"*Dio mio!* Am I really arrived? We drove through the middle of town. Swarms of automobiles. But, the police held up traffic for us to pass. Take my wrap, Mr. Wynne. You here, Jean?" she demanded as she crossed the threshold of the living room. "Where did you find her, Harvey?"

Brooke's answer was lost in the stir of greeting. Constance pushed forward a ladder-back chair. Jean arranged a foot-stool for the Contessa's absurdly small feet in their buckled, ridiculously spike-heel pumps. The cover of the silver kettle jiggled up and down in welcome, the spout sent up a white spear of steam which spread into an irregular, fretted arc of mist. Christopher's lips twitched in a smile as he looked at Sally-May who was staring at the Contessa as though she expected to hear her command:

"A pumpkin and six white rats!"

She did look as one imagined a fairy godmother might look. A worldly-wise godmother. Superlatively worldly-wise. She raised her jeweled lorgnon, glanced from one face to another.

"*Dio mio!* How serious you are! I have interrupted obsequies perhaps? You *asked* me to come for tea any Sunday afternoon, Miss Wynne."

"Asked you! We've been begging you to come for weeks and weeks, dear Contessa," Constance confirmed fervently. "You haven't been in the old house since the day we moved in."

Lorgnon raised, Contessa di Fanfani sent her eyes on a tour of inspection. They locked for an instant with the brown eyes of the portrait above the fireplace; dropped to the ornamental features modeled in low relief on the mantel; traveled to the gilt cornices with their hangings of yellow damask; to the mahogany secretary with its labeled pigeon holes; dropped to the Turkey carpet. Come back to Constance.

"You have kept the atmosphere of the old house. It is a museum piece. I suppose Jean will want it when she marries," she suggested with her usual lack of tact — or was it her mischievous desire to prick, Christopher wondered.

"There are other ancestral homes in the country," resented Harvey Brooke.

The Contessa inspected him through her jeweled eyeglasses, snickered:

"A southern county heard from. Mr. Walter Raleigh with a landed estate under his arm. If — "

Constance interrupted:

"Sally-May, bring in the tea and scones. The maids go out Sunday evenings, Contessa, so we serve ourselves."

Jean linked an arm in Sally-May's, proposed gaily:

"Let me help. I'm an experienced waitress."

Harvey Brooke caught the young girl's other arm.

"I'm a bear at buttling. Take me on, Miss Sally-May?"

Abreast the three crowded through the doorway. Their laughter, Sally-May's high, excited voice diminished to a distant murmur. Christopher answered a ring at the front door. Luther Calvin's cold, agate eyes were at their stillest as he stepped into the hall, announced:

"I came to protest against your statement in the pulpit this morning that it was impossible to accept the story of the Creation as told in the first chapter of Genesis."

Christopher felt his color deepen. Contact with Luther Calvin had much the effect of stepping into a bed of nettles. With an effort he kept his reaction to the man's personality from his voice as he corrected:

"I said that it was impossible to accept the story if — measured by a twenty-four-hour day. That 'And the first day' referred to a period of time. Surely you will admit — "

Laughter pealed from the kitchen.

"Having a party — on the Sabbath?" With the question Calvin set his silk hat with meticulous care on the brass-bound sea-chest in the hall.

"Not in the slightest degree a party. Sally-May and — and friends are preparing the tea-things." Luther Calvin lingered. Directed his eyes kitchen-ward as though contemplating a wet blanket charge upon the merry-makers. Christopher suggested:

"My sister is in the living room."

With a sound which would have assayed fifty per cent. growl, fifty per cent. snort, Calvin crossed the threshold. Constance greeted cordially:

"We are honored! First Contessa di Fanfani and now you, Mr. Calvin."

"*Dio mio!* Too much red meat for one day, or to change the metaphor, ' Two stars keep not their motion in one sphere.' How is the drive coming on, Signor Calvin? "

Christopher caught the malicious gleam between the Contessa's artistically mascared lashes. Was she setting a little fire to ignite Calvin's always smoldering resentment? She knew that he detested that Signor prefix and she delighted in using it. Before the tight-lipped man could answer, Harvey Brooke entered with a pot of tea in one hand, a laden muffin-stand in the other. Jean followed with a plate of cakes. Her face was alight with laughter. Never before had Christopher seen her without the mask of scorn and indifference which she wore for him. He swallowed hard. If it were humanly possible, he would crush that mask under his foot, have that lovely face against his shoulder — where —

" Look at those, Uncle Chris! I made 'em." At the imminent risk of scattering her *chef d'oeuvre* to the four corners of the old room Sally-May waved a plate of scones, each delicately crisp morsel indented with a tiny well of ruby strawberry jam. " Aren't they luscious? Jean filled them."

Luther Calvin visibly congealed. The Contessa, who was regarding her granddaughter through raised lorgnon, set flint to powder.

" Jean filled them! Jean domestic! *Dio mio!* Preparing to be the wife of a poor man, my child? "

Constance promptly extinguished the spark.

" My waitress is leaving. Would you consider a job with every Sunday off and outrageously high wages, Miss Randolph? "

The color which had surged to Jean's face at the Contessa's jibe, faded to a lovely pink as she protested gaily:

" Thank you, but I never accept a situation without my butler. You'd have to take Harvey too."

Brooke agreed exultantly:

" Yes *mam!* Me and — and the wife works together."

The Contessa snickered.

" *Dio mio!* Has it gone so far as that? "

Jean flamed:

" Don't be absurd, Contessa! You know that I'm not married." She flung a scornful glance at Harvey Brooke. " I never will be. I hate men! They're too darn idiotic. I wouldn't take a chance with one of them."

The quirk of the Contessa's rouged lips registered her satisfaction. She philosophized with maddening suavity:

" What is marriage without the element of risk, my child? How far would we get if we waited for certainties? If you are afraid — "

" I'm not afraid of anything," defied Jean.

" In this case the element of risk would be for the man," cut in Luther Calvin frigidly. " One couldn't expect a sense of permanency in a young woman who brazenly drives by an open church on her way to the

Country Club. She would be incapable of maintaining the high principles on which all marriage should be based."

"Here endeth the first lesson," mocked the Contessa.

"Good Lord! I —"

"If you will leave the door unlatched you must excuse visitors for walking in unannounced," Sue Calvin interrupted Brooke's indignant protest. Her red costume clashed into the charming room like a discordant note in a spring song.

Constance stepped quickly forward. Luther Calvin frowned portentously. The Contessa raised her lorgnon. Said *sotto voce*, though well she knew that her words were audible to everyone:

"The plot thickens." Aloud she explained sweetly: "You are just in time to contribute to our symposium, Miss Calvin. Subject, 'The effect of non-church attendance upon prospective wives.' Have I stated your contention correctly, Signor?"

Her victim growled an inarticulate response. Constance protested:

"We've been talking a lot of nonsense, Miss Calvin. Join us at the tea-table. We have a fascinating new butler. Chris, this influx of service is spoiling you. Put your thoughts in your pocket and pass the scones."

Christopher shook off his absorption in the human drama — inhuman some of it — and took the plate his sister forced into his hand. Her eyes were grave with warning as they met his. The Contessa imperiously indicated the piano, commanded:

" Sing for me! "

He kept his eyes on the plate of scones he balanced in one hand.

" Not this afternoon."

" Why not? "

" I can't sing when I see people hurt."

" And who has been hurt? "

" Jean."

" I suspect that you are in love with our Jean."

" Irrevocably."

" *Dio mio!* You are a one-woman man. Of course, you being you. You gave me a vicarious thrill. Many men have sworn that to me and meant it, meant it magnificently — for the time." Voice and eyes seemed to lose vitality as she added; " Do not delude yourself with the hope that she will marry you. A clergyman! Never. There is too much of her mother in her. Now if you were in another profession — in the world — "

Christopher's indignation cooled into a laugh. How transparent she was. How obsessed with one idea. He inquired lightly:

" You mean — in the world of opera? "

She rose. Christopher noticed with concern the whiteness of her face. How easily she tired.

" Ingrate! Signor Calvin, may I take you home? There are one or two details of the fund drive I would like to discuss with you."

The atmosphere seemed to tighten with suspense. The Contessa sighed theatrically:

" The clamor for us to remain is heart-rending, Signor, but, alas, I must go. Coming? "

Luther Calvin was rigid with disapproval as he followed down the path. Bare headed Christopher stood at the door of the brougham. The Contessa kept him there as she proposed one date after another for an evening of music, while the shining roans champed at the bit no whit more eager to be off than was he.

" Very well! If you do not want to come! To the house of Mr. Calvin, Beppo! " she snapped. The footman closed the carriage door, sprang to the box. The horses pawed and pranced, dashed down the drive.

Christopher watched them out of sight. Life was a curiously webbed plot. The day that he and Constance had moved into Hollyhock House, he had been singing lustily as he placed his books. His sister had flashed into the room, had beckoned him to the window. A brougham and pair were before the door. Contessa di Fanfani had heard his voice, had stopped to invite them to dine with her. She had flippantly acknowledged that clergymen were quite outside her aura but that she commandeered a fine voice no matter to whom it belonged. He had liked her, later had admired her valor as desperately she fought her losing fight for health. Suppose she had not heard him singing? Certainly she would not have made the gift to the Community Church, which was tearing the parish to shreds. He might not have met Jean — Jean! Jean was in his house and he was philosophizing over plot-webs outside. He sprinted up the path. In the living room Constance was clearing away the tea-things.

" Where are the others? "

" Miss Randolph and Harvey Brooke slipped out by the library door. Jean admitted that she'd had quite a day. Sally-May disappeared when you went out to the carriage." She lowered her voice. " Sue Calvin's in the library waiting to talk with you."

" Why — when for the first time Jean came to the parsonage, should there have been an influx of visitors? " Christopher demanded. Constance put warning fingers to her lips. His eyes were stormy as he entered the library. Sue Calvin, as cool as though she had just been taken from the ice, looked up at him.

" You're frightfully glum, Dominie. Because I waited? Close the door. I have something very special to ask you."

What was it now, Christopher wondered warily. His taut muscles relaxed. The old room with its unpainted pine-wood paneling, time-softened to a mellow brown, its great fireplace, its cupboards and its books, never failed to charm him. He perched on a corner of the large flat desk, took one knee in his embrace as he asked:

" What is it this time? A speech of welcome to a visiting association? A song for a benefit? "

Her eyes, cool, controlled, quenched the laughter in his.

" A suggestion for you to consider. I hope you'll agree with me."

With an inexplicable impulse to ward off her confidence, Christopher protested:

" A suggestion.   Agree with you?   Do you think that the same thought inserted in both our minds at the same instant would come out the same?   It would be colored by our individual philosophy, twisted by our experiences, prejudices, enthusiasms, and emerge shaped by our individual conclusions."

" Was that impromptu or an extract from a coming sermon? "   Sue Calvin's thin lips so like those of her father tightened: " Does that mean that you won't listen? "

" Of course it doesn't.   Go on! "

" I — I — wish that you'd sit in a chair.   You realize that I'm a modern of moderns, don't you, Dominie? "

A premonition of something unpleasant to come brought Christopher to his feet.   His nerves hummed like taut telegraph wires.   He crossed to the fire, poked it till a charred log sputtered into flaming protest.   It sent curious licking shadows against the iron fire-back.   The poker fell with a clatter as he replaced it.   Bending to recover it he heard Sue Calvin say:

" Why shouldn't a girl ask for what she wants as well as a man?   Will you — marry me, Dominie? "

Chapter XI

THE music of the bells still stirred the air as the clock in the tower ponderously struck four. Jean Randolph, on the bench before the manual clavier of the carillon, each key of which was connected by lever and wire with the clapper of its corresponding bell, dropped her hands into her lap. In spite of gloves and finger protectors they felt rough and bruised. Had she made a mess of her first attempt at playing? Daily for two weeks she had put in hours of practice on the dummy console, which was so like the organ that she had had no difficulty in learning to use keys and pedals. The bell-master had insisted upon her playing the carillon today. Fortunately he had given her a selection which had called for the lighter bells; she had been unprepared for the amount of strength both in hands and feet necessary to make the big ones respond.

As she rose from the bench the carillonneur pulled himself from the depths of a capacious leather chair. His blue eyes sparkled, his teeth beneath his heavy black mustache had the effect of a thin line of breakers against red reefs as he approved:

"Vera good, vera good, Mademoiselle. You have the touch."

"Then it wasn't a flop? To me it seemed as though the bells must be wrangling and jangling horribly."

"You were nervous. It showed in the *arpeggios,* there was hesitation in the crossing over of the hands. That will come right, Mademoiselle. Every day now, you must play the carillon."

"It will be a horrible infliction for the townspeople."

The bell-master shrugged.

"How much do they stop to hear? How much do they feel? My bells are majestic, simple, sublime, tender, their timbre sweet, their harmony including all the notes of the voice, yet these peoples go honk! honk! honking by or stop with screeching brakes. You need not be afraid, Mademoiselle, those below have ears to hear, yet they hear not my bells. You will play them tomorrow at the same hour, yes?"

"Of course, I'll come, and thank you for your interest, Monsieur Bélique," Jean responded cordially as before a mirror she crushed on a soft felt hat of the vivid blue shade of her crêpe frock. She slipped into a matching broadcloth coat with rich fox trimmings.

In the bell-chamber where a great company of bells, mounted upon a frame-work of wooden beams, extended in parallel rows, tier upon tier, the small ones hung high, the big ones just clearing the floor, she stopped to look out over the city, its outlines softened, its crudities beautified in the November haze of afternoon. The slanting sun was lining a cloud with gold.

From the high tower the world below seemed curiously still, an enchanted city.

From a case hanging on a hook, among a motley collection of old coats and hats, she took a pair of powerful field glasses. Raised them to her eyes. How they magnified! How near they brought the log cabin nestled in the hillside, the white cottage below it on the river bank. It seemed as though her outstretched hand might touch the dormers of the house. Here and there jewels of light flashed on; far away the white dam gleamed like a silver clasp on the river which girdled the golden-russet fields. A speck appeared in the western sky. Larger and larger it grew until its wings were visible. A plane! It came nearer. It floated down, down, down, till it rested lightly on the shimmering water.

Harvey Brooke in his sea plane! With what assurance he handled it. Once when she had protested against his flying, had suggested, she hoped tactfully, that sometimes he was not clear-headed enough to be a pilot, he had replied indignantly:

" I may be a fool, but you can take it from me, I'm not fool enough to fly when I'm not clear headed."

This was the first day she had seen the sun since the afternoon she had had tea at the parsonage. Two weeks! Two weeks of almost constant rain. She hadn't been in Hollyhock House before for ten years. She had forgotten its charm. Constance Wynne was an ideal home-maker for — for a minister — for anyone. No wonder Hughie admired her inordinately.

He had been away since that Sunday. Had he been
responsible for her tears? How — how human, how
like any other man Christopher had seemed in his
home. Always she had imagined, when she'd thought
of it at all, that a clergyman would be quite different.
How detestable the Contessa had been. Hinting that
she, Jean, wouldn't marry a poor man. Pity that
Harvey wasn't poor that she might prove her wrong.
Old Stone Face Calvin had taken the little joy out of
the afternoon which the Contessa had left. He had
glared as though he would bite her. Sometime she
would blaze at him, tell him what she thought of him
and his obnoxious piety. Meanwhile he was whetting
his knife to get Christopher Wynne. Would he
succeed? Could Chris — Christopher — be forced to
anyone's will? Could he force one to his? His husky
voice echoed through her memory.

"I'll make you change your mind about that unless — "

Her pulses responded and set up a clamor. Curious
the effect he had had upon her from the moment he had
jumped to the running-board of her roadster. Fright?
Aversion. Just natural aversion. Else why should she
feel an irresistible impulse to run? To slam a door between them? Lock it? Bar it? When all the other
girls in town — according to Fanchon — ran toward
him. Silly! It didn't get her anywhere to stand here
thinking how cordially she disliked the man.

She forced her attention back to the plane she had
been watching unseeingly. The great bird floated

lightly down stream. Lifted gigantic wings. Soared. Dimished to a speck. Jean slipped the glasses into their case. Drew a breath of relaxation. She hadn't realized how tensely she had watched the rise from the river.

Could she arrange to play the carillon every day, she wondered as she descended the steep, iron steps which connected the bell-tower with the floor below. It would mean cutting out afternoon festivities. Already Fanchon and her set were registering curiosity as to the reason of her absence from many of their parties, were accusing her of being upstage. She'd have to explain sometime. She would side-step their comments as long as possible. Even if they discovered what she was doing they couldn't justly accuse her of interest in Christopher Wynne. She hadn't run across him once in the church during the time she had been coming for practice.

She stepped into the elevator, started it. Her thoughts trooped on.

Rather curious that they hadn't met. She had to pass his study door on the entrance floor each time she came. But then, why should she see him? Hadn't she taken the precaution to ascertain that he was not in the church between two and four? Hadn't she arranged to practice during that time?

The elevator lighted as noiselessly, as gently as a feather. She pulled back the flexible lattice. As she opened the outer door she heard Fanchon Farrell laugh. Her voice stopped Jean as effectively as would the transfixing red eye of a silent policeman.

" What gorgeous carnations! " She giggled, " Sue's color. I heard that the President of the Woman's Association considers the flower supply of your study, part of her job, Chris. What happened to the bells this afternoon? Heebes jeebes? Is Monsieur Bélique slipping? "

Had it been as bad as that, Jean wondered. She listened for Wynne's answer.

" Probably the bell-master's pupil experimenting. He told me that he had taken one on. It wasn't so bad. We will have to endure it for the sake of art. Where's the rest of your committee, Fanchon? Leave the door open. I want to speak to Monsieur Bélique as he goes by."

Swiftly Jean stepped back into the elevator, soundlessly closed the two doors, gently but firmly pressed the button for the third floor. She wouldn't pass that open study door and be pounced upon by Fanchon Farrell — not for a thousand dollars.

She laughed as the car rose slowly, said under her breath:

" Caught In the Act, or the Escape of the Beautiful Carillonneuse! 'Twould make a corking movie caption."

What would Monsieur Bélique think if she appeared in the bell-chamber again? Why go all the way up? That was an idea. She pressed the button. The elevator stopped. She looked at her wrist watch, the diamonds in the setting blinked at her with the eyes of a conspirator. Better allow the committee five minutes in which to assemble, then the study door would be closed. She would slip by. The committee. Was Sue Calvin a member of it? She kept Christopher Wynne's study supplied with flowers. What comics those girls were making of themselves over him. If he weren't terribly pleased with himself he would hate them all.

She listened. Music. The organ? Heavenly sweet. How far away it seemed. A man's voice rose in song. Choir practice. The sound of shoveling coal — Ezry Barker's assistant stoking the furnace — how out of date not to use oil — some of Luther Calvin's economy perhaps. She looked at her watch. Had it stopped? Only one minute gone? She held the jeweled timepiece to her ear. Ticking. Ticking. Time wasn't even crawling. It was standing still. She was due at the Contessa's this afternoon. She had been so busy with practice that she had neglected her grandmother of late. It seemed absurd to think of the glorious Fanfani as a grand —

The car began to rise. Who had started it? Monsieur Bélique? He would think her mad if he discovered that she had been riding up and down, would tell Christopher Wynne about it in his excitable way. Gently she pressed the red " Stop." As the car stood still she soundlessly slid back the flexible lattice. The elevator couldn't move unless both doors were tightly closed. Now let them try! Clicks. Impatient clicks. Shouts from above! Feet coming down the stone stairs. Stump! Stump! Stump! She knew by the sound that the bell-master's always simmering temper was about to boil over. The moment he reached the ground floor he would burst in upon Christopher Wynne with his grievance. What a mess! She would better go back to the top and take the stairs down. Soundlessly she closed the lattice. Lightly pressed the button. Why didn't the car move? Her heart jumped. Suppose, suppose she were really caught! Caged! Between floors! Horribly warm. Suppose she were to faint? Figuratively she shook herself.

"You never fainted in your life. If you get panicky you never will get out!"

She gripped her imagination. Held it steady. Touched the button again. Pressed. Pressed hard. Nothing doing. Loud voices rose from below. Someone was trying to move the elevator. Devoutly she hoped that it wouldn't start. Doubtless Fanchon and her committee were at this moment packed in the corridor giving suggestions. How they would stare and giggle were she to descend into their arms. She wouldn't go down. She would go up. What had she done to the tricky thing to make it stick?

Carefully, firmly she pressed the button. No response. She frowned at the lattice. Pushed it gently. It clicked! In her caution she had not quite closed it. Could that have been the trouble? Heart thumping hopefully she pressed the button. Slowly the car rose. Clicked by one floor. Stopped. Cautiously Jean pulled open both doors. Closed them soundlessly. She tiptoed past the iron steps which led to the bell-

chamber, to the stone stairs. She stopped. Facing her
panted Christopher Wynne. Had he run up all the
way? His face was darkly red, his eyes like black
coals, his voice was husky as he stormed:

" I thought you were caught between floors! You
ought to be spanked and spanked hard! "

Jean's heart which had flopped like a fish out of
water steadied. She laughed from sheer nervousness,
mocked:

" Spanked! That dates you! " With maddening
condescension she inquired:

" Were you trying to get the elevator? I'm sorry!
I was — I was experimenting. You may have it now."

He made a futile grab at her as she brushed by him.
She ran down one flight after another — she had the
sense of having done this before — in a dream perhaps
— it was the best thing she did in dreams, running
down stairs. The car clicked by her. Downward.
Would Fanchon and her committee be waiting in the
corridor for an explanation of the trouble?

She stopped. Ahead of her was a sign ' Balcony.'
She would go down by the church stairs and out
through the main entrance. Soundlessly the green
baize doors swung behind her. She hesitated in the
soft gloom. Felt her way along. Turned a corner.
Stopped and caught her breath. Beneath her, velvet
aisles, like the spokes of a wheel, sectoring mahogany
pews brightened by the rich crimson of damask cushions, led to the chancel where candles burned in massive
sticks. The spear-heads of light which blossomed from

the silver branches on the altar vivified the color of the sumptuous red roses in a silver bowl. Through the interstices of an exquisitely carved reredos filtered soft tints from a great window — lilac and rose and green and amber — above in slender, tall, illuminated text was inscribed:

Peace I leave with you, my peace I give unto you. Let not your heart be troubled, neither let it be afraid.

The notes of the organ rose and swelled, the invisible choir at practice chanted softly:
  " The lord is in his holy temple:
    let all the earth keep silence before him."

Jean dropped to her knees, rested her chin upon the broad ledge of the balcony. She closed her eyes for a second, opened them. The faces and hands of the few persons sitting motionless in the pews in the nave gleamed austerely white. A lambent glow illumined the dusky shadows of the transepts. How hushed. How still. How — how consecrated the place seemed. Where had that last word come from? Never in her life before had she used it. Something seemed to be reaching toward her from out the silence and beauty of the altar, something strong, human, sustaining like an outstretched hand.

With an impatient murmur at her own absurdity, she rose from her knees and groped her way to the stairs. Stopped with one hand on the rail, held her breath that she might miss no note of the distant voices as they chanted the *Nunc Dimittis*:

" Lord, now lettest thou thy servant depart in peace."

She threw back her shoulders as though ridding them of a spell as she waited at the curb for a taxi. As it shrieked and rattled its way to Hill Top, she tried to throw off the sense of having come from a strange country far removed from the sweating, laboring, fighting city she was jiggling through. Curious that the world she had left seemed the more real of the two.

Chapter XII

THE Contessa in a sardonic humor and green velvet, sat in regal, lonely state in her palace chair in the drawing room with its old paintings and embroideries. In the background two men in blue and cream livery awaited her orders. Her afternoon transformation was a little masterpiece of color, a little masterpiece of undulation. Her dainty feet on the foot-rest were slippered in gold with sparkling buckles. The collar about her throat was of lustrous pearls, one enormous pearl gleamed softly on her finger. The expression of furtiveness was more marked, Jean decided, as she greeted her.

" Sorry to be late, but — "

" Do not tell me that you have been flying with that Brooke boy," the Contessa interrupted fretfully. "I heard him on the river. He woke me from my nap with his noisy plane."

" No. I've been up with him but I'm not as yet entirely air-minded. Didn't he make a beautiful landing. I watched him from the church tower." Jean could cheerfully have bitten out her tongue as the

Contessa snapped up the admisison with the avidity of a voracious trout rising to a fly.

" What were you doing in the church tower? "

No use in longer trying to keep the secret of her practice. Monsieur Bélique in his excitement doubtless had spread the news by this time. Christopher Wynne knew now the name of his pupil. Jean helped herself to a delicately rolled anchovy sandwich from the silver tray which the servant obsequiously presented before she admitted:

" I'm ravenous — I'm learning to play the carillon."

" *Dio mio!* were you making those hideous sounds on the bells this afternoon? Between those and that plane — "

Jean laughed. Tea and sandwiches and the Contessa's mood were restoring her sense of proportion and humor.

" Was I that bad? Monsieur Bélique assured me that I was ' vera good.' The duplicity of man! Now I know that he praised me to spare my feelings. It takes one's family to relentlessly hold the mirror up to one's failings."

" Or this modern fad of self-analysis. Introvert? Extrovert? Cat or dog nature? I suppose like others of your generation you spend half your time at it. *Dio mio!* What a waste. In my youth we did not need psychology. We had our women friends to tell us the truth — as they saw it — about ourselves. I have experienced all brands from the I-think-you-ought-to-know variety to the feline who purrs one's age to every man she meets. The more I see of women the better I like men."

"Miss Calvin!" announced the majordomo and bent impressively from the waist of his cream and blue striped waistcoat which always made Jean think of a bumble bee.

"Introvert! Enter pussy!" murmured the Contessa with a diablerie which set Jean's lips twitching. The great mirror in its ornate Florentine frame reflected the girl's approach, her vivid red coat with fox collar and cuffs over a black satin gown, the matching red felt hat, the luster of pearls at her throat, the calculation and dislike — indubitably dislike — in her eyes as they met Jean's. She nodded to the looking-glass girl in her blue frock. Bent over the Contessa's regally extended hand. Intoned conventionally:

"So glad to find you at home."

Perched on the edge of a chair, she declined tea and its accessories. Afraid of extra calories, Jean wondered, and set her teeth deep into the luscious icing of a delectable cake. Miss Calvin requested in her acidulous voice which when she strove for graciousness, suggested lemon juice masked, lightly masked, in honey:

"Will you attend the concert which the Woman's Association of the Community Church is sponsoring to raise money to help meet your generous gift, Contessa? I know that you have subscribed for tickets but your presence would add incalculable distinction."

Would the glorious Fanfani swallow that large

offering of applesauce, Jean wondered. It slid smoothly down. Her consent dripped gratification.

" I will if possible. Is the fund growing? Will the conditions of my gift be met by Christmas Eve? "

" Undoubtedly."

" Has Mr. Wynne consented to help? "

" No."

He had held out against them. Jean watched the Contessa. No mistaking the victorious light in her eyes even as she clasped deprecating, jeweled hands, sighing melodramatically:

" *Dio mio!* Then he has been asked to resign? Poor boy! "

Miss Calvin looked down at the glittering clasp on her black antelope bag. Glanced up, confided with studied hesitation:

" I've begged the committee to give him more time. You see — I — we — "

" What do you mean, I — we — " prodded the Contessa mercilessly. " Are you intimating that you and Christopher Wynne are to marry? "

Miss Calvin's assumed confusion vanished like a light frost before the sun. Eyes and voice were direct, hard, as she confirmed acidly:

" How quick, how discerning you are, Contessa. Can't we work together? I know that you want Christopher to take his place in the great world outside this backwater town. So do I. What can we do — together — to force him out? "

Christopher Wynne and Sue Calvin! Married!

Jean's mind whirled, sent off sparks of protest, with the
rapidity of an emery wheel in action. Impossible!
— two weeks ago he had said — she mustn't think of
that — marry a hard-boiled girl like Sue — the Contessa's exultant voice — what had she up her sleeve as
she leaned forward, bright red spots accentuating her
fashionable pallor, malevolent mischief brightening
her eyes.

"A bit of publicity would help us." She tapped
her jeweled lorgnon thoughtfully against her carmined
lips. "An interview with me in the morning paper
— I am at my brilliant best in an interview — have
you influence with the editor? "

"My father is the majority stock-holder."

"*Dio mio!* Signor Calvin holds this city in the
hollow of his hand! Have you a pencil? "

In answer Miss Calvin opened her smart bag.
Jean estimated the writing equipment exposed. Preparedness and then some. Everything there but a
table-desk and a typewriter.

"As President of the Woman's Association of the
Community Church I go prepared to take notes."
Pencil poised, with a professional air which would have
caused a real reporter to shrivel with envy, she encouraged:

"Ready."

Fragile hands gripping the palace chair, the golden
coat of arms on its back making a nimbus about her
worldly head, the Contessa dictated slowly:

"In an interview graciously granted last evening

Contessa di Fanfani — known to all the world as the Glorious Fanfani — announced that she would double her gift to the Community Church — if Mr. Wynne resigned — the pastorate."

The last dramatically emphasized word splashed into the fragrant stillness of the room as a flung pebble splashes into a still pool. Its meaning spread in slowly widening circles. Reached Jean. She sprang to her feet. Protested breathlessly:

"Oh! *No!* Contessa!"

Two steel gimlets drilled into her consciousness. Sue Calvin's eyes! A chill voice taunted:

"So — Fanchon's prophecy has come true! You have joined the horde of Christopher's worshipers, have you?"

Fury choked Jean for an instant. Only for an instant.

"I have *not* joined the horde. I like fair play. You two sitting there smugly conspiring to pull a man out of his church make me sick. One of you because of vanity, the other because of infatuation. You will never, never do it!"

"Infatuation! You're insulting!"

"Oh, you can't call it love, Sue. Love helps, it doesn't hinder. If you loved Christopher Wynne you'd be proud of what he has accomplished!"

Sue Calvin's laugh slashed.

"How do you know so much about love? Crazy about Chris yourself, perhaps?"

The intimation set Jean ablaze. Above the clamor

of her emotions she heard her own light laugh, heard
her own voice say:

"How do I know so much about love? I'm — I'm
mad about — about Harvey Brooke, that's why."

"Cat and parrot stuff, what?" observed a voice
from the doorway.

Sally-May! What ill wind had blown her into the
room just in time to hear her senseless declaration?
How much had she heard? The young girl's short-
sighted eyes under her drooping, brown beret were
fixed speculatively on Sue Calvin for an instant before
she approached the Contessa who was regarding her
through her jeweled lorgnon as she might a protoplasm
beneath a microscope. Slim and straight in her brown
jersey frock, with an orange kerchief knotted about
her thin shoulders, Sally-May bobbed her best dancing-
school curtsy, presented an envolope to the Contessa.

"Aunt Connie sent this." Her errand accomplished,
she tipped her head sidewise, pursed her lips, frowned
at Sue Calvin, warned:

"If you put that in the paper about Uncle Chris
resigning I'll — I'll tell the world you proposed to
him!"

Silence. Deep. Abysmal. Electric currents. A
malevolent snicker. A spark. An explosion:

"Detestable child."

Sue Calvin shook Sally-May to emphasize her fury.
The girl twisted free.

"Gee whiz, Sue, you hurt. Pull yourself together!
You know you asked Uncle Chris to marry you the

afternoon the Contessa was at our house for tea. When you told Aunt Connie that you must see him alone in the library I had a hunch he'd need help. I said over the motto of the W. V's.:

" ' But the wise virgins took oil in their vessels with their lamp,' and then I crawled under the big desk in the library and you talked and he talked a lot of stuff before you said:

" ' You realize that I'm a modern of moderns, don't you, Dominie? ' "

Had Jean's eyes been closed she would have sworn that it was Sue's voice.

" Sally-May Wynne! If you say one more word I'll — I'll — " threatened Miss Calvin.

" Going to publish that interview? " persisted her inquisitor.

" *Dio mio!* What interview? What *do* you mean? " demanded the Contessa ingenuously. Sally-May regarded her with poorly veiled contempt.

" Good, but not good enough. That man in the fancy wrapper who opened the door told me I'd find you here. I've been listening to everything you said. Have to be little long-ears, when there's a minister in the family." She transferred her short-sighted gaze to Miss Calvin.

" Going to send that drool to the papers? Because if you do — "

Her victim tacked.

" You're such an amusing child. Good afternoon, Contessa."

Sally-May took a determined step forward, continued as though there had been no interruption to her threat:

" Because if you do, I'll tell the world that Uncle Chris turned you down and turned you down hard."

With a furious exclamation which might have meant defiance or subjection Miss Calvin crossed the threshold. Sally-May stared belligerently at her back. Jean slipped an arm through hers, approved:

" Good for you, Sally-May."

The girl shook off her hand. Glared at her accusingly.

" There's no fish in that chowder! I thought you liked Uncle Chris — Flo and I'd decided that if we could get you going to church we'd make a match — now I'll tell him that you're mad about that silly Harvey Brooke! "

Chapter XIII

S EATED on the mauve and silver bench in the powder-room Jean critically inspected the starry-eyed girl reflected and re-flected. Her dark hair had the sheen of satin. The yellow velvet of her frock accentuated the rich beauty of her brunette skin tinted delicately by the pink light from the lamps.

She fastened long old-fashioned garnet earrings to her ears, shook her head that the light might bring out their ruby sparks. Not gay enough. Somewhere Sue Calvin had seen the statement of a psychologist that red and yellow had an hilarious effect upon the human spirit. She was to test its truth at the dance she was giving tonight. As flasks were taboo — Sue knew her Woman's Association — she was experimenting with color as a stimulus to gaiety, had asked her guests to wear one or both of the primary colors. Also she had requested that there be no dinners before the dance, she didn't want the fine edge of the color effect worn off before the party.

Jean removed the earrings, clasped a string of pearls about her throat, held an open fan of stiffened, lacquer-red georgette leaves against the front of her frock.

That would do, that with matching bag and slippers. She nodded to the looking-glass girl, approved aloud:

"You look happier than when you first stared back at me. You are busy, that's the answer. Too bad there is no one here to admire you. If Hughie were at home he would give the little girl a hand."

She absent-mindedly rubbed her already brilliantly polished nails on a pink palm. He was coming home tonight. Did he know that her mother had planned to leave New York? Nothing particularly strange in that, except that usually she remained in the city until after the holidays. She picked up an open letter on the dressing table. Her brow crinkled as she read the last lines in Madelaine Randolph's dashing hand:

"As New York seems a barren desert without you, I'm running away tomorrow for a month with friends, closing the apartment. Will be back in time for us to have our Christmas together. I hope your father will be human for once and let me have you that day. Send letters to my literary agent. He will forward them."

Jean looked at the date of the letter. Her mother had already gone. The apartment would be closed. Why hadn't she said where she was going, with whom? "Little passions!" the Contessa had mocked. If only she could forget the words. They flashed on like an electric sign whenever she thought of her mother. She met her own troubled eyes in the mirror. Should she have stayed in New York? She rose impatiently. Waste of time to question her decision now. She had threshed out the pros and cons before she had written her father that she would spend the winter with him in Garston. Hughie would be back tonight. Perhaps he would know his wife's plans. She had a curious feeling that she was in some way responsible for his absence. Rosa, pink-cheeked and black-frocked, entered with a sumptuous ermine coat over her arm.

" Meester Ezry's waiting for you, Signorina."

Jean paused in the process of sheathing her slim self in the snowy garment.

" Why is he driving? "

" He deedn't tell me, Signorina. He say, ' Tell Mees Jean I wait.' "

Jean smiled at the Filipino boy who opened the door. She liked her father's servants. They were as quiet as mice. Absurd comparison. One never heard a mouse when it wasn't making some sort of racket.

On the broad porch she stopped for an instant to look up at the star-spangled sky. Toward the east the moon was throwing off a cloud mantle fringed with tattered silver, much as might a danseuse, preparing to take stage centre, fling off an enveloping wrap. She drew a long breath. The air was glorious, but it smelled of rain. More rain! There would be a deluge if the weather did not clear. A shaft of light slashed the sky. The beacon at the flying field.

"Goin' to stand there all night, Jean, 'cause if ye are, I'd jest's soon be in bed as here," Ezra Barker's drawl came from the lighted limousine. She ran down the steps. Beside him on the front seat she condoled:

"It's a crime to keep you up. How do you happen to be driving?"

"It's the only chance I get to talk with the little girl who used to be always a-tagging at my heels." His voice was gruff.

She patted his sleeves.

"Ezry, you're a dear. Let's go."

"Where to?" inquired Barker as the engine purred softly.

"To the Calvins'. Sue is giving a dance."

"A dance! By mighty! And she president of the Woman's Association! Do the members approve?"

"Why not? They dance themselves. Keep step with the times, Ezry."

"I don't disapprove of dancing. I was thinkin' of Mr. Calvin. He's dead set against them kind of goings-on, ain't he?"

"He is, but, he has gone to Chicago for a week. Sue planned this party a month ago, hired a jazz orchestra and sent out invitations by an underground route."

"That don't seem quite fair an' square to me."

It hadn't seemed quite fair and square to her when first she heard the plan, Jean remembered, but, here she was on her way to join the festivity. She defended:

"He's such an old tyrant, Ezry, he invites deceit. Why should Sue stand for his antiquated, iron-hand stuff?"

" If she don't like his ways she'd better git out into the world an' earn her own livin'. She's twenty-one, ain't she? She don't have ter stay in his house. While she does, seems ter me, she'd oughta consider his feelin's. But then, I'm old fashioned I guess, me an' Chris Wynne."

Jean, who had laid her hand on his arm to administer an approving pat, withdrew it quickly at his last words.

" Mr.Wynne! He's as much of a tyrant in his way as is Stone Face Calvin."

At the imminent risk of ditching the limousine Barker squared round in his seat to look at her.

" Say, Jean, what you got agin the minister? He's the salt of the earth."

" I don't like that kind of salt."

She felt his eyes appraising her in the dim light of the limousine. He sniffed.

" You mean the Turrible Twin don't. An' if you mean by ' I don't like that kind of salt ' that you don't appreciate the qualities that make Chris Wynne what he is, yer oughta be — yer oughta be — well, kinda swished round in boiling oil."

" Ooch! Not *boiling* oil, Ezry. It sounds frightfully hot."

" Go on an' giggle, if you want, but I tell you, the person, man, woman or child, who don't appreciate Chris Wynne, ain't more'n half there. He does more in one day to help in this town than the rest of us does in a year. His influence for good on the young folks is immeasurable. They're crazy about him, he's so kinder jolly and human and understanding. He has time fer every one an' his troubles. He must get terrible fed-up on folks' worries, an' pocket-aches, an' heart-aches. Take Luke Carter's wife. Of course she's terrible sick — that's her trouble — but she gets het up every little while thinkin' she's dyin', claims it won't be hard to go, if she kin take tight holt of Chris's hand while she's passin'. She sends fer him any old time day or night an' he goes. I tell ye, there aren't many young men his age would be so patient. Many's the time I've seen him cuttin' by my place — it's half way between Hollyhock House and Hill Top — he says he kin go faster down the hill. It's several miles by the road even in his car. Lucy Carter's dyin's gettin' to be sort of joke in the neighborhood, but Mr. Wynne don't see anything funny, he goes whenever she sends." A worried note crept into his voice as he monologued on:

"I wish't he'd stop trapesin' over thet hill alone nights. There's them who think he meddled in their affairs when he was directin' traffic — I don't suppose they'd hurt him mortal, but — "

As though projected by a mammoth lantern the face of the man with the moth-eaten mustache flashed on the screen of Jean's mind. In spite of his explanation that he wished to consult Christopher Wynne professionally, she had distrusted his motives that Sunday afternoon in front of the cabin. The diabolical glint in his green eyes, the malevolent twist to his already distorted mouth had roused her suspicion. She had

told her father of the meeting, should she tell Ezry
Barker? Evidently he was uneasy. To encourage
his confidence she mocked:

"Hurt him! I thought everyone in town adored
the Reverend Christopher."

"Now, don't git fresh, Jean. Thet's the Turrible
Twin speakin'. Use yer bean. Did ye ever know any-
body, everybody liked. Even that Man who come
to save the world most two thousand years ago had
his enemies, hadn't he? Chris Wynne has his. The
minister who never arouses criticism ain't likely to
kick up much enthusiasm. Luther Calvin — Stone
Face you called him — it suits him fine — is agin him.
That little wizened-up man may be a whale of a
fi — financer — but he's as crazy as a loon over religion
— howsomever that's his trouble. Here we are! By
mighty, ain't the house handsome all lighted up! I
kin hear the band. Say, it sets my boots to goin'! "

He kept time with his feet to the rhythm and swing
of the music as the door opened and let out a blare of
saxophones, shouts of laughter. Barker chuckled as
he stopped the car:

"By mighty, what they all yellin' so for? Watch
your step, Jean, don't tumble. Wouldn't it be a joke
on Sue if her pa stole back unexpected. Calvin's a sly
old fox if ever there was one. I'll eat my hat if he
don't suspect how she's tryin' to pull wool over his eyes
with her Parchesi boards an' the like. The whole
town's laughin' 'bout the way he's fooled by his family.
He'll find out sooner or later an' then I believe he's

capable of taking a cane to them girls, he's that fanatical." He looked up at the sky. Sniffed, " It'll be rainin' before morning. Want I should come for you? "

" No thank you, Ezry, Mr. Brooke will drive me home, won't you, Harvey? " she inquired of the blond giant who materialized from out the shadows of a vine whose dried leaves rattled in the sharp breeze. He slipped his arm possessively in hers.

" That's what I'm here for. Been waiting for the last hour." As they turned toward the door he bent his head to accuse:

" You've given me the stony stare since the Sunday you got locked in that cabin, Jean."

" You had no right to try to — to kiss me. Later before the Contessa and that hateful old Calvin you intimated that we were engaged."

" Well, we are the same as — aren't we? "

" Not yet, Babbling Brooke! " She freed her arm and preceded him into the hall. A man servant obsequiously bowed her toward the stairs. Masses of yellow chrysanthemums, vases of red carnations were everywhere. The girls she passed were gowned in red and yellow, the white shirt fronts of the men were crossed by wide satin ribbons in the same colors. Everyone seemed on their toes with repressed excitement, Jean decided, as a maid reverently removed her ermine coat.

A few moments later she entered the brilliantly lighted, uproariously noisy drawing room and glimpsed her hostess, in a sparkling red frock, standing against a background of green damask hangings that screened the bay window from which one could look down upon the river. Jean knew the broad seat behind them. Many a time when she had been dummy, she had curled up there to watch the swift flowing water, to escape the incessant chatter at the card-tables about Christopher Wynne and his perfections. Yellow chrysanthemums were massed as a background for the negro orchestra in red coats which occupied an alcove at the opposite end of the long room. Ezry Barker's suggestion flashed into her mind.

"Wouldn't it be a joke on Sue if her pa stole back unexpected."

A joke! More like a tragedy.

"Step lively, Jean. Good Lord! I wish you girls would cut out the perfume. Air's heavy with it. I hate the darned stuff! Make your little bow to the hostess. I want to dance," prompted Harvey Brooke behind her as he dodged the revolving, gliding, side-stepping couples. They formed new patterns with every throb of the music. Red and yellow, yellow and red; balloons of two colors attached to wrists and ankles; onyx and ivory, crystals and rhinestones setting the shifting mass agleam. Black coats and white shirt fronts accented the maelstrom of color. Brooke whispered:

"You look like a million dollars, Sweetness." As Sue Calvin greeted them with her metallic smile he approved gaily:

"You've landed a knock-out this time, Sue. The party's a wow. Your old psychologist had the right dope if it's noise he wanted. All you need is the Reverend Chris with a big red cravat and yellow waistcoat to lead round and you'd have pulled off the sensation of the centuries."

Jean caught her breath as she remembered Sally-May's taunt: " I'll tell the world you proposed to him! " With an effort she averted her eyes from the face of her hostess. Slipped her arm in Brooke's. Reminded:

" We're wasting this perfectly gorgeous music." As he swung her into the dance she whispered:

" Harvey Brooke! Didn't you see Sue's face flame when you spoke of Mr. Wynne? For the first time since I've known her she looked as though she had blood, not liquid granite in her veins. You'd have babbled on forever if I hadn't dragged you off."

Brooke's arm tightened.

" Your mistake, Sweetness. From now on I do the dragging. I'll pull the cave-man stuff some day and drag you to my lair by the hair of your head. Good Lord, suppose primitive woman had adopted the bob. Long hair was of biological importance in those days, I'll tell a listening world."

Jean smiled up at him with tormenting charm.

" Silly, as though a listening world cared for what you think."

He relinquished her with a muttered protest as a man touched his sleeve. From one pair of arms to

another Jean drifted to the rhythm of strings, the tap
of drums, the blare of saxophones. Try as she might,
she couldn't blot from her mind the expression of Sue
Calvin's face as Harvey had referred to Christopher
Wynne. It had gone as red as her frock — almost.
According to Sally-May she had proposed to him!
And according to Sally-May he had turned her down.
Christopher Wynne led around at this garish party as
Harvey had suggested! He led! It was to laugh!
Her sense of gaiety snuffed out. She stopped dancing
before the hangings which screened the bay window.
Sanctuary. She would slip behind them for a while.
The noise was deafening. Giggling. Shouting. The
pop of punctured balloons. Whoops of excitement.
She would side-step the next color party. She hadn't
realized that she was tired. She had played the large
bells twice during the day. Was that why she felt
limp as a rag? She looked up at her partner to excuse
herself. Regarded him incredulously for an instant:

" You Harvey? I thought — "

" Yeh! You did! You've been going round like a
dancing automaton all evening. Didn't even know it
was I when I took you in my arms, did you? A lot you
care — "

" Sue! Sue! "

The high hysterical shriek rose above the music.
Strings, brasses, drums, stopped with a crash as fat
Flora Calvin in pale blue pajamas followed her voice
into the middle of the room. Her feet were bare and
pink; her short hair stood on end; her speckled brown
eyes were wide, frightened, as she shrilled:

"Sue! Sue!"

With the swiftness of a red bird her sister streaked across the room which had miraculously cleared of dancers, caught her arm, shook her as she scolded:

"Flo, didn't I tell you to stay in bed?"

"That's darned ungrateful. I almost break my neck to tell you father's on his way here—"

"On his way! What do you mean?"

"That makes you listen! I guess he's coming up the steps by this time. Sally-May—"

"Go home everybody, for heaven's sake, go home. If you can't get away, hide. Somebody put out the lights," implored Sue Calvin. She dashed toward the orchestra, the members of which were regarding her with rolling eyes. Their jaws were dropped, their white teeth glistened in their red mouths. She shooed them out of the door as a hawk-shadowed hen might drive her chickens before her. Harvey Brooke caught Jean's arm and drew her behind the hangings. Chuckled:

"Here's where we do a fade-out." The curtains had barely closed them in when a hard voice from some-where outside demanded:

"What's going on here?" The lights flashed on. Sounds of persons moving. Whom had old Stone Face Calvin brought with him, Jean wondered. His voice again:

"They're hiding in the back of the house. We'll—" the sentence dwindled away into the distance. Harvey Brooke whispered close to Jean's ear:

"Hop up on the seat! He'll see your red slippers if you don't."

In spite of anger at her ridiculous predicament Jean laughed. The situation was absurd. Harvey pulled her forcibly to the seat. Standing close beside her he whispered hoarsely:

"Stop giggling! He'll hear you. We can't let Sue down, can we?" He bowed his head to prevent hitting the ceiling. It seemed as though aeons passed as they bent forward listening. Ominous sounds in the distance. Mysterious creaks nearby. Someone coming? Jean lost her balance. A laugh fluted from her lips. To save herself she clutched Harvey tight about the waist. His arm closed around hers as he whispered theatrically:

"Let him come on! I'm sitting pretty. I —"
Words gurgled in his throat as a hand grasped the hangings.

Chapter XIV

IN a low chair beside the fire in the living room at Hollyhock House with the soft pink blanket she was knitting a lovely mass of color against the orchid of her gown, Constance Wynne listened to her brother's voice as it rose and fell in caressing melody:

"'From the desert I come to thee
On a stallion shod with fire,
And the winds are left behind
In the speed of my desire.'"

Were his thoughts on Jean Randolph? The red setters stretched on the hearth-rug pricked silky ears.

The prosaic sound of the rushing water of the shower drowned the next lines, then passionately sweet rose the refrain:

"'Till the sun grows cold,
And the stars are old,
And the leaves of the judgment
Book unfold!'"

Sally-May, sitting under the lamp, elbows propped on the table, removed forefingers from her ears,

looked up from the book over which she had been bending, protested:

"I wish Uncle Chris wouldn't sing that mushy song!
It makes me feel funny in here." She placed her hand
in the general direction of her stomach. Constance
picked up her needles.

"That is a famous love-song, dear. It has made
thousands of persons feel funny — here." She laid
her hand over her heart.

"Love song! Why is he singing a love song? Fat
chance he has of getting the right girl with them all
chasing him. Only one who doesn't, Jean Randolph.
Flo and I had it all doped out that we'd make a match
between her and Uncle Chris — "

"Sally-May! Don't dare to interfere between
those two! You don't know — "

The girl slumped in her chair, stretched beige silk
legs before her. In her gay little garden print frock
she looked not unlike a mammoth nosegay, somewhat
crumpled. She sniffed indignantly.

"I don't know what? That Jean's in love with that
silly Harvey Brooke? I ought to. I heard her say she
was."

"When?"

"Gee whiz! Your voice exploded like a gun.
Yesterday at the Contessa's."

"Who was there?"

"The Contessa, Jean and Sue Calvin."

"Did she admit that before *Sue?*"

"Uh-huh!"

"What did Sue say?"

Sally-May pursed her lips in the pucker which Constance knew portended trouble for someone. Answered darkly:

"She said a lot of things. Has the evening paper come?"

"Not yet, dear. Why this sudden interest in the newspaper? This morning I heard you pattering down stairs in your bare feet to get it."

Sally-May hesitated — explained hurriedly:

"The teacher in Hist. A told us to clip every printed word we saw about the Pan American Highway. We — "

She stopped speaking as a voice coming down the stairs sang:

> "'Under thy window I stand,
> And the midnight hears my cry:
> I love thee, I love but thee.
> With a love that shall not die
> Till the sun grows cold — "

The song ceased as Christopher Wynne reached the threshold of the living room. The red setters charged. He laid a hand on each silky head.

"I hate like the dickens to repress your affection, Rover Boys, but, observe that I'm dressed for dinner." With an apologetic pat he removed their paws from the front of his blue coat. Sally-May thumped him on the chest.

"You're a direct answer to prayer, old lamb pie! I'm starving. Aunt Connie wouldn't go in to dinner until you came."

"Sorry to be late." Constance noted the change in his eyes from gay to grave. "I had a long session in my study at the church." With apparent effort he lightened his voice. "Come on, Sally-May. I'm as hungry as you are. Let's eat!"

From time to time during dinner Constance speculatively regarded her niece. Was the laudable desire to acquire information as to the progress of the Pan-American Highway the only reason for her interest in the newspapers? Was Sue Calvin in any way mixed up in it? Why had she turned the subject so quickly when she had been questioned as to Sue's reaction to Jean's declaration of love for Harvey Brooke?

Later in the living room she watched her as she picked up the sheets of the newspaper as Christopher laid them down, scanned them short-sightedly, her brow knit. No. Great and inspired as was the project, the highway which was to link the Americas would never cause such breathless — expectant, was more appropriate — absorption.

As Christopher dropped the last page and crossed the room to the piano Sally-May caught it up.

"Sports! Nothing there *I* want!" She went to the window and looked out. "Sue's got a peachy night for her party. Eats from New York. Darky band and everybody in town over eighteen and under forty invited. Were — were you, Uncle Chris?"

A strange note in her voice, as though there were an underlying motive in the question, sent Constance's eyes to Christopher's face. It was not her imagination. He had colored darkly. Had he and Sally-May a secret — a secret which concerned Sue Calvin? His fingers strayed over the keys, the improvised melody made a soft accompaniment to his voice as he answered:

"No. Is it a dance?"

Her face glued to the window, the muslin curtains held back by a brown hand, Sally-May answered:

"Uh-huh! Everybody's got to wear either red or yellow. A psy — psycho — psycho — olo — gist told Sue that those colors made people gay. Flo says she bets the roof will lift when the party gets going. Slathers of autos whizzing by already."

"But, I thought Mr. Calvin wouldn't permit dancing in his house?"

"He won't, Aunt Connie, if he knows it. He's in Chicago for a Bankers' Convention — Sue's known of the date for weeks. Planned to throw the party while he was away."

Constance looked at the clock.

"Time for you to be at your home-work, Sally-May."

"Oh, dear, life's just one old lesson after another." She crossed to the piano. Leaned against it, regarded her uncle wistfully: "Mind if I study in your library?"

Fingers still idly touching the keys, he smiled at her, said tenderly:

"I love to have you work there, little girl."

With a strangled sob she flung herself on him. The piano bench lunged precariously for an instant, regained its equilibrium as he rose and put his arms about her. She strangled back a sob as she looked up and reminded:

"This is the first time you've really loved me with your voice since — since that Sunday — " She dropped her head against his shoulder. He raised her chin till he could see her face.

"Sorry now that you locked Jean in, aren't you?" As she nodded without raising her eyes, he went on:

"Never take it upon yourself, Sally-May, to punish a person because he or she doesn't think as you do. Life has a way of taking a hand at all necessary discipline." He walked with her to the door of the library. Threw a kiss in response to hers before he answered the telephone in the hall.

"Christopher Wynne speaking. Who — " A voice hoarse with emotion and fright broke in:

"'Phoning for Luke Carter. Mrs. wants you quick. Doctor says she won't live more than half an hour. She says, 'Tell Mr. Wynne he promised.' "

"I'll come at once."

"I'm going to Carter's, Con," Christopher announced from the threshold.

The rosy mass of wool slid to the rug as his sister sprang to her feet.

"Not down the hill. Remember Hugh Randolph's warning."

"Nonsense. I can make Carter's in ten minutes cutting across lots. It takes twice as long in the car by the road. Lucy is desperately ill."

"Who 'phoned?"

"One of the neighbors probably."

"At least take the Rover Boys."

Recognizing their names the two red setters sat up, sensed the significance of Christopher's coat and hat, dashed for him.

"Down boys, down!" As they flopped in dejection to the rug at his feet, he explained: "I won't take them, Con, they might disturb Lucy by their barking. If I am kept late Luke will bring me home in his flivver. Don't worry."

He closed the front door upon her protest. Outside the house the air was damp, chilly. The moon was making the east to west crossing in leisurely fashion, playing hide and seek behind skurrying clouds. As he cut across the field Christopher glanced up at the stars. Thousands of them looked down upon him unblinkingly. Worlds upon worlds. Sometime there would be interplanetary communication. Would he live to see it? He couldn't believe that the earth was the only body in the great universe which supported intelligent life. The trail down the hill was almost as light as day. He slipped the flash-light he carried into his pocket. The weather-man had radioed a storm warning. Looked as though he'd have to guess again.

His thoughts went back to the afternoon he had found Jean locked in the log house. She had neither affirmed nor denied her engagement to Brooke. If she really loved him would she have admitted that she was — was waiting? Waiting for what? To be sure of herself or to please her father? He might leave Garston long before she went. It was November. His contract with the Community Church ended with the year. He had stood firmly entrenched in his determination not to work for the money to secure the Contessa's gift. The Standing Committee had said nothing about renewal of contract. It wouldn't. He knew now that he was too modern in his viewpoint to suit the majority. Jacob's wrestle with an angel was to them a wrestle with an angel, nothing more. Sue Calvin would see that his term was not extended.

He shut his teeth hard in his lips, hot color burned to his hair as he relived the few moments with her in the library at Hollyhock House. Few, but poignant.

"I'm a modern of moderns, Chris," she had said. "I believe that a girl has a right to ask for what she wants as well as a man. Will you marry me?"

He clenched his hands hard in his pockets as he felt again his keen embarrassment. Did a girl when she turned a man down feel as brutal as he had when in surprise and consternation he had blurted:

"No. *No*, Sue!" Then in a clumsy effort to save her humiliation had added, "I — I — have no thought of marriage at the present."

"Is it because of money? I shall have plenty."

Intense solicitude for her had sharpened his voice. "No. *No!*"

"If we were married Father would be all for you, not against you, Dominie."

"Sue, please——" the situation had been intolerable.

"Then that's that! Good night!"

He threw back his shoulders as though ridding them of a burden. He had had many curious encounters since he had entered the ministry, but nothing which had brought such unbearable embarrassment. Did Luther Calvin know of his refusal to enter his family? He had grown stiller, colder.

Christopher stepped from the trail into the clearing in front of the cabin. The moon touched the tall tree tops, the windows of the log-house with its lovely gleam before it dodged behind a fleecy cloud. Overhead a star quivered and went out. The sudden transformation from light to dark blinded him. He drew the flashlight from his pocket — his hand tightened on it as he heard a stealthy sound ahead. A human sound! Had it come from the entrance to the trail which wound down hill to Carter's? Was it merely the wind soughing through the gloomy pines, rattling a dry leaf? As he strained his eyes to penetrate the dark, his ears to hear, Hugh Randolph's warning recurred to him with startling clarity:

"Keep away from the hill, Wynne. I've been told that those two men you had pinched resent your interference with their enjoyment of life, liberty and the pursuit of bootlegging. They've found out that you use the log cabin. Of course, they wouldn't dare injure you, but, well, keep away from the hill till the feeling blows over."

He had laughed at the warning then — but, he was up against something sinister now, he knew it, he would better not turn on the light.

A clock in a distant steeple solemnly told the hour. The clock in his church. His church! He'd keep it his if it were humanly possible. The last moments of Lucy Carter's life were slipping away. He must go on. Go on! To what? If only the menace lurking across the clearing would come out into the open. He was not afraid. He had no fear of death, only a great curiosity. But, he had so much to do. Life was sweet when one lived in a world packed with possibilities of achievement. Jean Randolph's face flashed on the screen of his mind, the fine sweet mouth, the brilliant eyes, always with a tinge of fear in their depths — he thrust her out. Thought of her set his blood afire and he needed a cold, calm power to judge and weigh now. If he called would the man lying in wait come out into the open, give him a fighting chance? No, he would succeed only in making himself a target. He must go on. Lucy Carter needed him. He must not fail her. He had need of help outside himself. He pulled off his soft hat, looked up at the illimitable, impenetrable dome above him, under his breath murmured a fervent prayer for protection, strength to overcome whatever threatened.

He stood for a moment with uplifted face. Then, fortified, upheld by a sense of close, spiritual companionship, he strode forward, entered the descending trail. The moon cautiously stole out from behind a cloud, silvered the tree-tops, cast purple shadows in his path. Eyes and ears alert he hurried on. Underbrush rattled, scraped, rustled in the wind; from afar came the hoot of a predatory owl, but no human sound disturbed the brooding quiet of the woods. Had that sense of a lurking menace been but an attack of imagination?

He glanced at the illuminated dial of the watch on his wrist as he reached the Carter house on the bank of the river. Ten minutes before he had left the parsonage. Incredible. It seemed as though he had lived hours since he had answered that telephone call. Would he be in time to be of comfort to Lucy? It would be a release for her to slip quietly away. He tapped softly on the door. No lights in the house? Curious. Even if he were too late there would be things to be done — he tapped again. From an open window upstairs came the low murmur of voices. Footsteps. A light flickered. The door opened a crack. A man's sleepy, exasperated voice inquired:

" Who is it? "

" Christopher Wynne."

The door was pulled open. Luke Carter, clutching a lurid, fuzzy bathrobe about his thick shoulders, blinked at him.

" You, Mr. Wynne! What's happened? "

" *Happened!* Didn't you send for me? "

" Send for you! No sir! "

Chapter XV

CHRISTOPHER stepped into the hall with its new art paper, its old art umbrella stand, kept his voice low as he explained:

" About twenty minutes ago someone 'phoned me that Lucy needed me, that the doctor had given her but an half hour to live."

Luke Carter's ingenuous eyes seemed about to bulge from their sockets. He ran his spread fingers through his mop of red hair rampant.

" You came down the hill? "

" Yes."

He collapsed on the inadequate top of the umbrella stand.

" Now what do you know about that! Lucy's been more comfortable today than she's been in weeks. She didn't send for you. She was asleep till your knock woke her. She'd like to see you."

" I won't disturb her. Take me home in your flivver will you, Luke? "

" Sure I'll take you home. Just wait till I get into my pants."

Christopher paced the narrow path outside as he waited. The moon, still at its game of hide and seek, silvered and shadowed the river as it flowed swiftly on its way to sea. The water was higher on the banks than he had ever seen it. Two weeks of rain had swollen the current. Had the fact that the house was so near the water anything to do with Lucy Carter's illness, he wondered. Luke's voice had been vibrant with hope when he had reported her good day. Who had 'phoned that message? Danger had stalked on the hill-top. He had felt it. Had the man who had decoyed him lost courage when his chance to strike had come? Who could it have been? He hadn't many enemies.

As he drove his rattling flivver Carter kept up a running fire of question and conjecture as to the motive behind the summons. Christopher suggested as he stepped from the car at the parsonage door:

" Better say nothing about this, Luke. If there was a plot we'll keep the plotters guessing as to how much we suspect. Thank you for bringing me home. Good-night." When he entered the living room Constance Wynne's voice quivered betrayingly as she rejoiced:

" Thank heaven, you're back, Chris. I was developing nerves. I had a feeling that there was something queer about this call, can't tell why, just felt it. Sally-May went to bed early so I didn't have her to confide in. Did — did — Lucy Carter — "

" No. She is better tonight than she has been in weeks."

" And she dragged you out! That woman is a pest. There is hot cocoa in the kitchen. I thought you would be cold and hungry when you came in."

Christopher poked the fire unnecessarily as he deliberated. Should he tell her that it had been a fake call? No. If he did she would be anxious every time he went out. Better for her to be unfair to Lucy. He suggested lightly:

"Let's forget it." He crossed to the window. "Main Street is alive with cars. Sue's party must be in full swing. Great night for it."

"What a pity that she can't have her harmless pleasure openly. Luther Calvin is a horrible example of the narrow outlook which the rest of the world — if one is to believe current novels and plays and articles — credits to New England."

Still at the window Christopher answered thoughtfully:

"It is the fashion now to laugh at, make light of New England reserve, 'repressions.' 'New England conscience' has gotten to be almost a term of opprobrium; but scoffers forget that Pilgrims and Puritans provided something solid, something enduring, something spiritual upon which to build a great and growing nation. Not many of the middle and western states but have a chunk of Plymouth Rock in their foundations. It's good basic material. Someone's coming up the walk! It looks like — it can't be — it is — "

"Chris! Stop mumbling! *Who* is coming up the walk?"

"Luther Calvin!"

"And that red and yellow party raging at home." Constance's voice caught in a nervous laugh; "To quote Sally-May, 'Better stick round for the finish.' Open the door. Bring him here. While you are talking I'll slip into the library and 'phone Sue. We can't let him walk in on her, even if she has brought disaster on herself."

Before Christopher reached it Luther Calvin had opened the front door. He shut it with a force which shook the house. He leaned forward, hands gripping the crook of a heavy cane as he approved in a metallic, carrying voice:

"Glad to find you at home, Mr. Wynne."

Was that "you" sharpened by suspicion, Christopher wondered. He invited cordially:

"Take off your coat, come in by the fire and have some hot cocoa. The weather man slipped up when he prophesied rain. Great night, isn't it?"

Uncomfortably conscious that he was talking to gain time, Christopher followed Calvin's slight, short figure into the living room. He must be detained until Sue had a chance to clear the house. Of course she shouldn't have had the party, but, just as surely, of course, her father was a narrow-minded tyrant. Calvin bared his teeth with their gleaming gold inlays in the caricature of a smile as he protested:

"No cocoa for me. I never indulge in food after my supper. I dropped in to talk over church matters on which I'd like your judgment, Mr. Wynne."

Constance glanced at her brother, met his eyes. She rolled up her knitting, laughed successfully — though Christopher recognized an undercurrent of excitement — as she suggested:

" Then of course you don't need me."

The urbanity of Luther Calvin's tone was a trifle overdone as he assured:

" We do, very much, as the subject is music." He crossed to the door which led to the library and closed it. Still urbane he explained:

" I felt a draught."

He remained standing between Constance and the door. Christopher, arm on the mantel, regarded him from between narrowed lids. Was he intentionally cutting off access to the telephone? Did he know of the dance at his home? Sue must be warned. Her defiant, " Will you marry me? " flamed up in his memory. Would he ever forget it? Did a girl feel like a criminal when she turned a man down? No, the custom of centuries had made it easy for her, but, for a man to refuse a woman — he forced his mind back to the present crisis. He must get to the 'phone in the library. No use trying the one in the hall, his voice would be audible in the living room.

" You haven't heard a word I've said, Mr. Wynne," accused Luther Calvin. " But as your sister approves we'll call the matter of the new hymn books settled."

" I beg pardon for my inattention. When you launched the subject, I suddenly remembered a parishioner who needed my help. If you'll excuse me for a moment I'll get the matter off my mind."

As he crossed the room Luther Calvin blocked the way. His voice was icy, his words as clear-cut as pelting hail as he combatted:

"Not yet, Mr. Wynne. The parishioner in need of your help is my daughter. She won't get it. Neither you nor your sister will leave this room at present." He backed against the library door.

Christopher's steady eyes met his still, agate glare.

"You forget that you are in my house," he reminded courteously.

"I forget nothing." Luther Calvin's voice rose in fury. "You know that *my* house has been turned into a sink of iniquity, that it's being used as a dance hall and you — you — a minister of the gospel are aiding and abetting my daughter in her deception. I'll wait here until yonder orgy is at its height and then — and then — "

Constance caught her breath in a nervous gasp. Christopher crushed back a laugh. That phrase, "Yonder orgy" might have been lifted bodily from one of the dime novels he had read surreptitiously when a boy.

"You laugh — you — " Luther Calvin's tirade was interrupted by the sudden opening of the door behind him. He turned furiously as a voice inquired:

"What's all the shoutin'?"

Sally-May, with bobbed hair tousled, blue eyes — sans horn-rimmed spectacles — peering short-sightedly, hands thrust into the pockets of the jacket of her striped pink and white pajamas, balanced back and forth on bare, rosy feet on the threshold as she complained:

"Gee whiz! I was sound asleep and you woke me

up when you banged into the house, Mr. Calvin." As Christopher took a quick step toward the door, she went on:

" You won't have to 'phone Sue, old lamb pie, I did it."

" You! You! " Luther Calvin raised his heavy stick. Constance caught Sally-May close as Christopher seized the man's upraised arm, wrenched the cane out of his hand.

" Go easy, Mr. Calvin. It's bad enough to turn a harmless little dance into a sink of iniquity, don't add violence to that mistake. When you have cooled off, I'll go home with you. The party which seems a nightmare to you now will prove nothing more than a girl's foolishness when Sue explains it."

Calvin's burst of fury cooled. Icy calm succeeded it.

" You're right, Mr. Wynne. ' The discretion of a man deferreth his anger; and it is his glory to pass over a transgression.' My car is waiting. I'll hold you to your promise to come with me. "

" I am ready." Christopher looked at Constance who with both arms about her niece replied with a nod of understanding. As he left the room he heard Sally-May's loud, excited voice demanding:

" What kind of a sink is a sink of iniquity, Aunt Connie? "

In a luxurious limousine Luther Calvin bent forward, silent, motionless, boney hands clasped on the crook of his stick. He grunted as the automobile passed a long line of parked cars of every make and description. Rangy cars, stubby cars, shiny cars and shabby cars. A sudden wave of activity swept their ranks. Engines whirred, brakes groaned, wheels turned, horns bleated. Sally-May's warning had taken effect, Christopher decided.

As he entered the house he heard a faint, hoarse whisper, the fragment of a giggle, the far-off crash of a dish. The atmosphere was heavy with perfume, the great hall was gaudy with red and yellow flowers.

" What's going on here? " Calvin demanded in a high, hard voice at the moment he snapped on the lights of the drawing room.

Confusion indescribable. The large rug had been hurriedly dragged to the centre of the room, had been as hurriedly abandoned unrolled. In front of one of the doors lay a scatter of playing cards with the saturnine King of Spades face up. The polished floor was dotted with dark fragments, the remains of once buoyant balloons. It reflected the glitter of the rhinestone buckle on a lonely, little red slipper — Cinderella fleeing at the warning tocsin — the warning tocsin in this case must have been fat little Flo. Christopher choked back the laugh conjured by the vision of the panic-stricken guests. Luther Calvin tapped him on the arm.

" They've evidently fled to cover, these dancing fools who aren't brave enough to face the consequences of their iniquity."

Hating his part in the nightmarish proceeding, Christopher followed him. He might succeed in warning some of the guests in hiding. If Calvin were not humored he might resort to violence — he had been a little mad when he had raised his stick to strike Sally-May.

As the master of the house disappeared in the direction of the dining room, Christopher slipped into the hall. Cautiously he opened the door of a closet. A light flashed on. He strangled a chuckle at its birth. In a corner partially hidden by fur coats hanging from a rod, huddled Flora Calvin asleep. A melting mound of pistache ice-cream in the platter in her lap supplied a sluggish green stream which flowed into a greener pool on the floor. In one hand was clutched a big silver spoon. Christopher caught her by the shoulder, shook her gently, whispered:

" Flo! Flo! Wake up! Go to bed! "

She opened heavy lids, regarded him unseeingly, closed them. The mound of ice-cream plunged gently into the green pool. Christopher listened. What should he do with her? Her father must not find her here. It was she who had given the alarm. Only one thing to be done. Get her to her room. He lifted her in his arms. He had known that she was abnormally fat, but he hadn't been prepared for such dead weight. He carried her upstairs, set her down none too gently in the hall, shook her lightly.

" Wake up, Flo! Go to bed! "

" Did you bring him — for revenge? " whispered a harsh voice.

Bending over the little girl he looked up at her sister. The glint in Sue Calvin's still, agate eyes reminded him of a cobra he'd once seen hooded to strike. How she hated him! From now on her father would have an ally to force the undesired minister from the Community Church. He resented hotly:

"Bring him! He brought me! I tried to keep him at the parsonage till I got word to you."

She looked at him scornfully, still keeping her voice low.

"Harvey Brooke said that all I needed to make the party complete was the Reverend Chris to lead round — he didn't suspect that it was Father who had you on leash."

Christopher regarded her for a tense moment. Luther Calvin's voice below! Dogging his footsteps was of more importance than refuting his daughter's accusation at this exact moment, he told himself.

"Better get Flo to bed and keep out of the way yourself," he advised curtly.

He ran down the stairs. On the threshold of the drawing-room he stopped. A lilt of laughter! From the bay window screened by hangings? Jean! No mistaking the music of that sound. He smiled in sympathy. Luther Calvin must not find her. He was fanatically critical of her. That was his voice in the hall. Now he was bent over the scattered cards, picking them up.

Soundlessly Christopher stole across the great room, slipped behind the hangings. The smile on his lips stiffened. Standing on the window seat, arms clasped about one another's waists, shaking with mirth, swayed Jean Randolph and Harvey Brooke. The girl's lovely neck and arms were like tinted ivory, the light from overhead illumined the satin waves of her hair, deepened the yellow sheen of her velvet frock. Theatrically she spread her lacquer-red fan. Over the top of it her eyes met Christopher's, their laughter changed to mockery as she whispered:

" It is the wish of the majority that the picture be viewed in silence. Do not talk! "

Chapter XVI

MOCKERY faded from Jean's eyes as they met the burning intensity of Christopher Wynne's. Her heart set up a frightened clamor. An amazing, outleaping force seemed sweeping her toward him. For the fraction of a second she fought a wild impulse to fling herself into his arms. Was she quite mad? Had the red and yellow party set her nerves as well as her teeth on edge? She hadn't been her cool, assured self since the day she had been made to bend to the substitute traffic-man's authority. Subconsciously she had been aware of currents, swift, uncharted swirling nearer and nearer. Whenever she was with him she was besieged, threatened by his dominating personality. It was a clear case of hypnotism. Jean Randolph and a minister! The most absurd combination ever. She'd smash his hold on her and smash it hard, if it left her raw and bleeding. She would barricade herself behind her beloved stone walls, she'd pile one upon another — she would —

" Coast clear? " whispered Brooke hoarsely. His arm tightened about her as he leaned forward. Harvey, her first line of defense! The spell was broken. Christopher Wynne looked from her to the man beside her.

"Raise the window gently. Drop to the ground, Brooke. I will help Miss Randolph out."

Cautiously Harvey Brooke followed instructions. As he disappeared into the darkness outside, Wynne put out his arms.

"Come."

Jean shrank against the fine net curtains.

"No! No! Harvey will help me! I — I'm engaged to Harvey!"

For an instant Christopher Wynne's eyes looked straight into hers. Then he caught her in his arms, whispered huskily, lips close to her soft hair:

"Engaged to Harvey! You love me — you darling!"

"Where's the cold air coming from?" demanded a metallic voice beyond the hanging.

"Quick!" Wynne whispered and lifted her through the opening.

Brooke caught her before her feet touched the ground, pulled her forcibly down among leafless shrubs, which scratched and pricked her bare arms. She protested passionately:

"I hate sneaking out like this, Harvey. We — "

"Why is this window open?" rasped Luther Calvin's voice above them. Instinctively Jean crouched, her red fan clutched against her breast.

"I'll close it. I — " The lowered sash shut off Christopher Wynne's explanation.

Brooke stood up with a groan of relief.

"That's that! Let's make our get-away. You're shivering. Here put this on!" He pulled off his coat, laid it across her bare shoulders.

"Harvey, you'll freeze. I have a perfectly good ermine wrap in Sue's room."

"Yeh, you have. How do you expect to get it? Think I'll take a chance with that roaring lion inside? I'm no Daniel. I have a top-coat in the roadster. Come on!"

He seized her arm, hurried her along in the shadow of friendly shrubs. The long tails of his evening coat flapped against her heels. His gleaming car was the only one in sight when they reached it. Jean's sense of humor bubbled through her turmoil of spirit:

"Poor Robinson Crusoe roadster with never a man Friday in sight."

"The Fridays made their get away when old Calvin bellowed, 'What's going on here?' I'll bet some of them are still going. Put this on!" He retrieved his evening coat, swathed her in a woolly rug. With the collar of his top coat turned up about his ears he threw in the clutch. As the car slid smoothly forward he settled back.

"All set? Good Lord, why did Wynne horn in on the party? The old man must have picked him up *en route*. What was he saying to you when he dropped you out of the window?"

Jean's pulses broke into double-quick as Christopher Wynne's husky whisper echoed through her mind:

"Engaged to Harvey! You love me — you darling!"

No! *No!* Even if she did, she told herself passionately, she must stop it. *She* marry a minister! She'd ruin his career! She, conform to life as he lived it! Inconceivable! She had seen what a small town had done for her mother! No narrow road for her! She would not make the same mistake. She was fond of Harvey. She would be happy if she married him. She —

"As you were saying," prompted Brooke.

Jean emerged from a maze of troubled thought. Asked blankly:

"Was I saying anything?"

"You were not, Sweetness. You didn't even answer my question."

"What was — " she remembered, "what was Christopher Wynne whispering to me? I was so excited, Harvey, that I don't remember — exactly."

"He's a good egg. Can't see why he doesn't get married. If he just crooked his finger he'd have a nice little harem all his own. Warm enough?"

She nodded. Had her voice congealed along with her body at thought of that crooked finger? Harvey was absurd as usual, but there were any number of girls who were merely waiting encouragement to fling themselves into Christopher Wynne's arms. She was not one of them, she assured herself passionately, she was *not*. Tomorrow her engagement would be announced. Having already told Christopher Wynne it behooved her to let Harvey know that she had decided to marry him.

The light from the car lamps accentuated the stark beauty of towering trees, flashed the lower windows of houses into flaming lidless eyes. The damp air smelled of dying leaves. Overhead hung a canopy of spongy clouds which looked as though they might burst into tears at any moment. The streets were deserted. Had the whole world of Garston — the Social world — fled to cover? What would happen to Sue? She was afraid of her father. How had she dared plan the party? Lucky that Christopher Wynne —

" You love me — you darling! "

Would that husky voice ever — ever stop echoing through her mind? Once she had demanded of Fanchon:

" What's the Reverend Christopher's fatal charm beside his voice? " and Fanchon had answered:

" You'll find out for yourself soon enough."

Well, she had found out. What should she do next?

" Tired? " Brooke hesitantly put his arm about her. Jean's inner self drew sharply away, but her body relaxed against him. If she were to marry him, she would better commence at once to like his arm about her, she reminded herself bitterly. He drew her close.

" Beginning to like your old Harvey a little? " his boyish voice broke before he added, " love him a little? "

She extricated a hand from her woolly wrappings. Laid it on his on the wheel.

"I've always liked you better — better than any other man, Harvey. I — I — think I'll wear that emerald you have for me." She had said it! A stone wall, unscalable, impenetrable.

The engine stopped with a suddenness which threatened to imperil its too — too mortal interior as Brooke caught her in his arms.

"Does that mean that you'll admit our engagement?" He bent his head, kissed her fully, lingeringly upon the lips. She recoiled, pushed his face away.

"Harvey! Please! Don't do that again. I — I *hate* being kissed!"

The light from a street lamp revealed the amazement in his eyes, the new sternness of his mouth as he declared violently:

"Then you don't love me! If you did you'd *want* me to kiss you."

Christopher Wynne had said:

"If you were in love with Brooke you would want him to kiss you." She thrust back the memory of his eyes and voice. Would Harvey cast her off because she hated being kissed? If he did she might be weak enough to show Christopher Wynne how much she cared, wreck her life and his. She must tell Harvey! She assured eagerly:

"I do love you — only — only — won't you please be just friendly till I get used to being engaged? I've — always hated petting — this is — my *positively* first experience."

The light came back to his eyes, the smile to his boyish mouth as he demanded:

"Honest? I thought every girl had at least two or three affairs before she settled down with friend husband."

"Would you like me better if I had?"

"Like you better! Fishing, aren't you? Here!" From his waistcoat pocket he drew a ring. "Always had it ready in case this chance came. Hold out your hand." He slipped a great emerald with two guarding diamonds on the third finger. Drew a long breath. "There! Now you're mine!" He raised her hand to his lips before he started the car.

Jean looked at the green stone as it caught the light. It was beautiful, even more beautiful than the ring her mother wore. But — she didn't care for emeralds — did the acceptance of it make her Harvey's? She shivered.

"Cold, Sweetness?" Brooke solicitously drew the rug higher about her throat. He did not speak again until he stopped the roadster in front of the door at Hill Top. Then he asked:

"Is your father at home?"

"He should be. Why?" She was conscious of the breathlessness of her voice.

As he inserted her key into the lock of the outer door he answered with exaggerated impressiveness:

"Because I wish to proceed according to the nineteenth century formula. No slapstick twentieth century methods about this engagement. Formally I shall ask your father for the honor of your hand."

Her spirit responded to the lightness of his voice. Harvey was a dear! She had been making a tragedy of her attraction to Christopher Wynne. Once engaged and married she would laugh at tonight's emotion if she remembered it at all. As they entered the broad hall, she demanded gaily:

" And if Hughie refuses? "

" Oh, we'll be married just the same." His eyes darkened, his mouth tensed, he took a quick step toward her. She retreated. He linked an arm in hers as he assured satirically:

" Cheerio! I won't kiss you again — at present. Come on! Let's find your father."

Hugh Randolph opened the library door in response to Brooke's knock. Two sides of the room behind him were lined from floor to ceiling with books. High steps on rollers provided a means by which to reach the top shelves. Most of the volumes looked as though they had been read and loved and read again. Against the time enriched oaken panels, above a fire, which sputtered, snapped, shot out licking red tongues of flame, hung the portrait of the first American Randolph, in the Cavalier dress he had discarded soon after he became a landowner in the new world. His brown hair, long and parted in the middle, fell in loose curls on the shoulders of his rich red doublet with its jabot of Vandyke lace. His beard was peaked. His eyes direct, compelling. The upturned ends of a small mustache, a broad brimmed hat with rich band and plume added their bit to his dashing ensemble. A strong hand gripped the rapier which hung from his sword belt. In spite of the suggestion of foppery in dress the face was that of a resolute man.

No more resolute than the face of his descendant, Jean thought as she looked from the portrait of her ancestor to her father who stood with one arm on the mantel. The lines between his nose and lips seemed to have deepened, his eyes were haggard. Was he horribly unhappy? Did life hurt everybody? For the first time it was beginning to hurt her. She tossed red fan and bag to a chair, held out both hands.

"Hughie, it's wonderful to have you back."

Color crept into his face, light into his eyes as he put an arm about her. His voice was gruff as he assured:

"It is just as wonderful to have you to come back to." He looked down at her, then at Brooke; "What have you two been doing this evening?"

Harvey cleared his throat. Jean answered before he could drag his voice up from the depths into which it apparently had plunged:

"We've come from — come is too tame for our experience — escaped from Sue Calvin's dance. Sit down here, Hughie. I'll play Scheherezade and tell you about that red and yellow horror."

She seated herself on the arm of a capacious chair as her father sank into it. She was uncomfortably conscious of Brooke, perched on the corner of the big table desk smoking cigarette after cigarette as with nervous volubility she related the events of the evening to the dramatic moment when a hand had appeared on the hangings. She stopped. As she hesitated Brooke carried on:

"It was the Reverend Christopher, vanguard of old Calvin. He handed your charming daughter out

the window to me and here we are. Coming home we
— we got definitely engaged. Hope you don't mind.
Came in to ask your consent. Old-fashioned stuff of
course but — but somehow it seems to belong to you
and Jean."

The girl looked at him through a sudden mist. Did
Harvey really feel like that about her? She had con-
sidered herself a typical product of her generation.
Hugh Randolph caught her hand resting on his
shoulder close in his, held it as he said lightly:

" Thank you, Brooke, for asking my consent. Even
if it is but a gesture, I like it. Let me get Sue Calvin's
party straightened out first. Who did you say rescued
you from the bay window, Jean? "

The girl's startled eyes met his intent ones? The
question had pounced. Why? Did he suspect that
she was not indifferent — indifferent — that was funny
— to Christopher Wynne? Her heart quickened, she
was conscious of heightened color. Brooke, who was
lighting a cigarette mumbled:

" Didn't I make it clear? 'Twas Christopher
Wynne."

Jean felt her father's eyes on her as he asked:

" Shall I give my consent to your marriage to
Harvey? He has intimated that you'll marry without
it, but, I'd like your o.k. Look at me, my dear, did
' good little Jean ' say ' Yes ' or was it her Terrible
Twin? "

Jean rose, faced him with one hand gripping the
mantel. With an effort she steadied her voice to
answer lightly:

"The Terrible Twin and I parted company weeks and weeks ago. Hadn't I told you that I dropped her into the river? It is 'good little Jean' who wants — who intends to marry Harvey."

Hugh Randolph busied himself with his pipe, avoided looking at her as he consented:

"Then as a nineteenth century father I'll say, 'Bless you my children!' As a modern parent I realize that you'll do as you like — but — I'll make one request, don't rush into matrimony."

Brooke slid from his desk perch as he protested:

"What's the use waiting? Jean and I have been pals three years. I don't at present spend half of my income — there's money enough now, there will be more later. I want to be married before Christmas — here in Garston — if Jean's willing I'd like to have Wynne perform the ceremony — I have a feeling that if he tied the knot it would be permanent."

"No! *No!*"

The girl's protest was breathless, poignant with terror. Her voice seemed to go echoing through the room, silent save for the purr of the fire. Then she laughed, a travesty of laughter. Stumbled into explanation:

"Imagine a twentieth century bridegroom taking such a precaution. If you want permanency we won't be married in that church. Hughie and mother were married there and they — " She met her father's eyes, tragic eyes. She had been cruel, thoughtless to use the wreck of his marriage as a barrier between herself and Christopher Wynne. Hugh Randolph rose, slipped his unsmoked pipe into his pocket.

" I understand, Jean. You are quite right. Harvey, you know, the whole world knows that my wife and I are muddling through life, neither of us happy, neither of us counting as we might in the scheme of things, because — she never loved me as a woman should love the man she marries. After Jean was born I discovered that always there had been someone else for whom she cared. God knows why she chose me. I want you two to wait for a while. Jean must be sure that she loves you enough to marry you — marriage fundamentally is a matter of sympathetic companionship shot through and through with gleams of passion, love. It should be productive of fidelity, loyalty, responsibility, of the stamina to see a difficult situation through if necessary. It is not just the business of two persons. A marriage which breaks down threatens the institution. She must not wreck her life, nor yours, Brooke, by mistaking her feeling for you. Be sure that the woman you love, loves you."

Jean's startled eyes met her father's. Did he suspect, did he know that for a mad moment she had been unbelievably swayed by Christopher Wynne? So swayed that Harvey's suggestion that he be the one to perform the marriage ceremony had torn that shocked protest from her lips? How could he? She hadn't herself analyzed her mingled attraction and aversion till she had stood on the window seat and met Christopher's challenging, burning eyes. She glanced surreptitiously at Brooke who was staring at her father. His face was older, graver than she ever had seen it as he admitted:

"I get you, Mr. Randolph. You think that Jean doesn't love me enough. You're right. I know that."

She slipped her hand within his arm.

"Harvey, I do love you, I do."

He looked down at her as though seeing her for the first time, smoothed a shining wave of her hair with an unsteady finger, caught her hand in his, bent suddenly and kissed her on the lips. Involuntarily she shrank away. He laughed, not a happy laugh, released her hands.

"I know just how much you love me, Sweetness, but —" he straightened his shoulders, added belligerently, "we're engaged, I'll tell the world tonight — and we'll be married before Christmas. I'll take a chance on anything — once."

He bowed with exaggerated formality and left the room. Followed the distant sound of a door closing. Hugh Randolph rapped his pipe against the mantel, observed:

"Fortunately an announced engagement isn't irrevocable."

"Oh, I must — I *must* marry him."

"What do you mean — *must?* "

"Hughie, you're ghastly. I didn't know that you'd care if I married — you see, I've played round long enough. I've really been out socially since I was fourteen. I am tired to death of theatre — teas — dances and round the circle again. Perhaps I'm not modern at all, perhaps I am old-fashioned. I would like to belong to someone. Someone who cared. Sometimes I have felt that I never really belonged. Mother loves me — in a way — but I am secondary to her work. I know that. You — "

"You have been first with me, Jean, since your mother left me to live her life in her own way."

The color was back in his face. He put his hand on his daughter's shoulder as he reminded:

"Marry Brooke if you are sure that he will make you — and what is quite as important — you are sure that you will make him happy — but, not until March. I will hold you to your promise to stay with me this winter."

Stay in the same town with Christopher Wynne until March! Impossible! Yet, she must keep her word to her father. She met his steady eyes, smiled gallantly:

"I will stay, Hughie, but, you'll give me an occasional leave of absence for a few days in New York, won't you?"

There was a trace of bitterness in his laugh.

"The Big Town! The clang and bustle lures you as it lured your mother. Perhaps I am doing wrong to make you wait, but — " he stared down into the fire for an instant, shrugged, filled his pipe and observed irrelevantly:

"So Christopher Wynne came to your rescue at the Calvins'. Sometimes I wonder if he made a mistake when he went into the ministry. His congregation is split into factions. The girl he loves — "

Jean had the sensation as of being held under water. After hours it seemed she rose to the surface, gasped:

"The girl he loves! How — what do you know about her?"

Her father's steady eyes met hers.

"Constance told me. It seems that Christopher has been mad about this girl for — she intimated for years. She won't have him because of his profession, she won't marry a minister."

Jean flamed.

"She won't. She must be dumb. Doesn't she know the good he's doing in this city? She won't marry a minister — "

"Would you?" crisply interrupted Hugh Randolph.

He answered a knock at the door. Christopher Wynne stood on the threshold. Jean's heart seemed to leap to her throat, coast to her red slippers.

"Come in!" Hugh Randolph invited cordially. There was a thread of determination in his voice as he reflected:

"Curious that you should appear at just this moment. Jean and I were discussing your profession — generally."

The girl managed a flippant little laugh.

"Generally! I should say, specifically. You asked me if I would marry a minister."

Christopher Wynne took a step forward as he demanded:

"And you answered?"

The girl's eyes met his defiantly.

"Not if he were the only man in the world."

"Not if he were the only man in the world — for you?" he asked steadily.

Chapter XVII

JEAN clenched slim hands behind her as she faced Christopher Wynne. His eyes were black with intensity. Why had her father forced her declaration of antipathy to the ministry? Did he know? Did he suspect how things were with her? Evidently he had no intention of pursuing the subject, as he observed:

"Heard that you were personally conducting Calvin over his house, Christopher. How come that you are here?"

Jean drew a little breath of relief. That thin ice had been safely skimmed over.

Wynne approached nearer the fire. Hands in his coat pockets, answered:

"After I had satisfied myself that the guests had escaped, that Sue and Flo were securely locked in their rooms, that Mr. Calvin was absorbed in taking account of the lavish outlay of refreshments on the dining room table, I slipped away to make sure that Jean got home safely."

"I'm always safe with Harvey. He's quite capable of taking care of the girl he is to marry," Jean interrupted passionately. She had the sense of living, breathing flesh hardening into steel as Wynne shook his head:

"You are not the girl he is to marry, Jean. You're mine."

The same bewildering sense of being swept helplessly along, that she had felt once when her canoe had shot through swift water! She caught her father's arm, held tight as though he were an anchor which would keep her from being snatched and swirled into the tide of love and longing which would fling her into Christopher Wynne's arms. The great emerald on her finger gave her strength to defy him. She managed a patronizing smile as she tormented:

"The Contessa was right, you have dramatic ability. No wonder that she and Signor Zambaldi covet you to the kidnapping point. You are so convincing. For an instant you made even me wonder — "

"If you love me?" supplied Wynne gravely as she hesitated under the disconcerting blaze in his eyes. "Why not be honest with yourself and — me? You do, don't you? You and I together — "

Impulsively, childishly, she pressed her palms over her ears to shut out the persuasive music of his voice. He caught her hands in his. Raised them to his lips before he demanded softly:

"Afraid to listen?"

She twisted herself free. Mocked angrily:

"We have with us this evening the most conceited man out of captivity! One would think you were Jupiter! That all you had to do was to nod, and presto, a girl would tumble into your arms. You've had a lot to say about my loving you — you've never committed yourself by saying that you loved me." Her voice broke in an excited sob. Her father patted the hand she had laid on his sleeve before he corroborated:

"She is right, Christopher. Not only that, but Constance told me that you had been in love with a girl for years."

Wynne's brows met in a sharp frown.

"Con told you that! She knows that the instant I saw Jean at the crossroads I loved her. For the last fifteen years I have been too hard at work to think of any girl seriously. As for telling her — I've felt that my state of mind — of heart — was too abundantly evident. My mistake." His voice deepened as he attested steadily:

"Jean, I love you. Will you marry me?"

The girl's fingers tightened on her father's arm. Defiant eyes on Christopher Wynne's she reiterated:

"Not if you were the only man in the world — now — please go!"

His colorless face flushed darkly. He took a step nearer, announced dominantly:

"I won't accept that refusal, I won't accept any refusal until — until with eyes on mine you swear that you do not love me."

Hours, years seemed to pass as she faced him, eyes defying his turbulent eyes. Once during the silence Hugh Randolph drew a long, hard breath; the fire sputtered; rain spattered against the diamond paned window. She dragged her voice up from the mysterious deep where it was chained:

"I swear that I don't —" Nervously she twisted the emerald on her third finger.

"Go on!" prompted Christopher Wynne implacably. "You needn't call my attention to that ring. Think I haven't seen it?" With a quick change of voice he implored:

"Forgive me if I'm cruel. I am fighting for your happiness and mine."

Jean flung out her hands in frenzied protest:

"Oh, go away! Go away! I'll never, never marry you! Isn't that enough?"

Wynne's low laugh set her heart pounding till it seemed to shake her body.

"Quite enough — for tonight." He caught her hands in his, pressed his lips to each pink palm before he added:

"Go to bed — darling — you've had a tremendous day — oh, I know about the bells — do you think that you could steal in and out of my church and I not know — feel that you were there?" Lingeringly he released her hands before he turned to her father:

"Forgive me for inflicting this scene upon you, Mr. Randolph, but, I couldn't permit Jean to believe even for another night that she was to marry Brooke — when her eyes have confessed that she loves me. Good-night, sir. Good-night — dear." He added the old-fashioned word softly before he closed the library door behind him.

Dear! Dear! Dear! It drifted like a tormented little wraith through the still room. Jean leaned her head on her bare arm flung along the mantel. Why didn't Hughie speak? How could she begin to say all she wanted to say? As though he sensed her appeal Hugh Randolph laid his pipe tenderly on the shelf, cleared his throat, observed with a tinge of gruffness in his kindly voice:

"I'll say that Christopher Wynne knows exactly where he's going and is on his way. Couldn't swear that you didn't love him, could you, Jean?"

The girl's voice shook as she admitted:

"I couldn't — honestly — but — don't speak yet, Hughie — I know that what I feel for him is merely a sort of — of — "

"Attraction?" supplied Hugh Randolph.

"That's just the word," his daughter approved eagerly. "It's so — so footless. Imagine me, Jean Randolph, as the wife of a clergyman. It just couldn't happen."

"I think it could or — or I wouldn't have asked you to come to me this winter — much as I always have wanted you here."

"Hughie!"

Her incredulous protest echoed through the silent room. With an effort she went on:

"You thought that — that — Christopher Wynne and I — " her voice failed. Hugh Randolph corrected:

"Hoped, is a better word. I wanted you to have your chance at the finest kind of married life — the road is rocky enough under the best conditions — and so, knowing what you are and knowing Christopher — I asked you to come here this winter."

"And you didn't really want me for yourself?" She felt her eyes brim with childish tears. Her father laid his arm about her shoulders.

"My dear, I wouldn't have taken you away from your mother for my own happiness — she needs you — but I felt that your greatest good came before anything else."

Jean stiffened.

"Sorry to disappoint you, but, you'd be more sorry if your wildly impossible plan materialized. As a clergyman's wife I'd be a hideous flop — I and the Terrible Twin."

"Thought you dropped your Twin into the river?"

Her laugh had an hysterical note:

"She can swim, that child. She's likely to confront me at any moment. Whether she comes back or not I will not marry Christopher Wynne if — if — I have to beg Harvey to run away with me. Good-night, Hughie."

Randolph caught her shoulder. His voice was stern as he reminded:

"You promised that you would wait until March, Jean."

"That was before I knew that you were on the side of Christopher Wynne. Some promises are better broken than kept. Good-night."

She heard the passing hours pealed by the silver chime of the crystal clock on her mantel, boomed by

the old timepiece on the stairs, intoned by the distant
church bell, as she fought each step of the way to freedom. She would go back to New York for a week or
two, she decided, stay till she had thought things
through. She would have her mother's apartment
quite to herself. Thinking things through didn't mean
that she would consider marrying Christopher Wynne,
it meant that she would consider the advisability of
marrying Harvey Brooke at once. In that marriage
lay safety, insurance against matrimonial shipwreck.

She dozed into sleep, sleep shot through and through
with troubled dreams. Into them gaily tripped a silver
chime. She raised heavy lids. Counted. Eight?
Impossible. She had barely closed her eyes. The old
clock on the stairs solemnly boomed the hour. The
steeple bell struck. As though to confirm these wit-
nesses Rosa appeared with a breakfast tray. Clear-
eyed, rosy-cheeked, pink linen frocked she apologized:

"Signorina tell me I call her prompt each morning
so she go to play the bells. I bring note from Signor
Randolph."

With an effort Jean flung off the spell of sleep.
Tucked her feet into satin mules, struggled into a flame-
color negligé, asked drowsily:

"What kind of a day is it, Rosa?"

"Wet, vera wet. Rain come splosh against windows."

All she had thought and felt and decided during the
long, wakeful hours surged through Jean's mind as
she felt the unaccustomed weight of the ring on her
finger. It was true then, she was engaged to Harvey

Brooke, she hadn't dreamed it. As she flitted from shower to dressing table, with Rosa an admiring super supplying her needs, she planned. She wouldn't take much in the way of wardrobe to New York. Her friends would not know that she was in town. She wasn't going for gaiety. She was going for a chance to sit down with herself face to face and talk things out. She answered the telephone. Fanchon Farrell's voice, punctuated by giggles, inquired:

"Make your get-away with boy friend all right last night, Jean?"

"Yes. It humiliates me to acknowledge that we jumped from a window. What evil genius whispered in Luther Calvin's ear that there *was* a party?"

"Some cat tipped him off. I hear that the darky band was scattered all over town, that they slept with their brass instruments for pillows. Did you ever hear so much noise? All that red and yellow was hideously unbecoming. Rumor saith that Christopher Wynne was in on the finish. Did you see him?"

Had she seen him! Jean waited to steady her voice before she answered:

"For a moment. Heard from Sue this morning?"

"Not a word. But, I hear she's eating out of her father's hand. What you doing this beastly day?"

"The usual schedule. Good-bye." Jean hung up the receiver with Fanchon's, Wait! I want — " echoing in her ears.

Later, as she pulled on the beige hat which matched her frock and rain-coat she remembered the note Rosa had brought which still lay amid the sparkling crystal and shining silver of the dressing table. What did Hughie want? She pulled the sheet from its envelope.

"Remember your promise!" That was all.

She tore the paper into tiny bits. She had told him last night — was it only last night — seemed ages ago — that there were times when a promise was better broken than kept. Should she tell him where she was going? Why not?

She wrote a note and gave it to Rosa to deliver. In it she explained that she was off to New York for a few days to try to get a perspective.

She went to the window. Beastly day. A spongy sky. Last night's mist had developed into a driving rain. Every bare branch and twig was beaded with crystal. Wet, bedraggled sparrows huddled under eaves. Lawns were sodden. The river, gun-metal gray, growled, muttered. Mists like furtive ghosts stole along its banks. White cottages gleamed like phantom houses behind the fog. Where was Christopher Wynne —

She forcibly switched that train of thought off the track. Glanced at the clock. Ten! Reckoning conservatively it would take her three hours to drive to New York in her roadster. She would unpack her bag at the apartment, go to a matinee.

She flew down the stairs, with her jewel box in one hand, bag-laden Rosa at her heels. Ezra Barker was beside her roadster at the front door. Little streams of water dripped from his soft hat to his slicker-covered shoulders, one more adventurous than the rest coasted down his long nose as he protested:

" You hadn't oughter go out in this rain, Jean."

" I'm neither sugar nor salt, Ezry. Put the bags in, please. Rosa, don't forget to tell Madama la Contessa that I will write." She stepped into the car.

" You come home soon, Signorina? " implored Rosa.

" I don't know how soon. Maybe never! " Jean flung back.

With his big, hairy hand glistening with moisture gripping the windshield, Barker protested:

" That was the Turrible Twin speakin', Jean. Course I know you're jest foolin', but I don't like your settin' out in that spirit. The roads is afloat. How far you goin'? "

" To New York — for a change of scene."

" By mighty, yer likely to git it. You'll be stopped by the police before you git fur. The bank was broken into last night. They're lookin' fer the burglars. Officer winged one of them but he made his get-away."

" How thrilling. It might not be for New York — but for Garston — Why should I be stopped? "

" They'll search every car fer the bonds that were stole. Don't you go today. No knowing what might happen."

" Don't worry, Ezry. Bye-bye! "

As the roadster shot forward she looked back and waved to the dripping, lugubrious figure. Poor man, she was a trial to him. She never seemed able to accept his suggestions.

How it rained! As she drove slowly across the

bridge she glanced up and down the river. Oily, sullen, it had an ugly look. Its color was a shade deeper, duller than the soaked clouds above. The usually white water of the dam which plunged and thundered had the yellowed tint of snowy hair which has been waved with an overheated iron.

A church clock struck the hour. Even with the slippery, muddy roads she would make New York as she had planned. Then what? The squeegee on the windshield swung back and forth, back and forth, whined monotonously. Would Christopher Wynne suspect that she had run away from him? Had she? Resolutely she thrust him from her mind and dragged Harvey Brooke into the spotlight of consideration. Gorgeous time he and she would have together. Harvey was a great playmate. No earnest-worker complex in him. Always she had wanted to go to Africa, South America. They could honeymoon through those countries, flying, sailing, motoring. Honeymoon with Harvey! The bottom seemed to drop out of her heart. She flouted herself. "You would feel lower in your mind if you were settling for life in Garston!" A minister's wife. She! Christopher Wynne — Back again! Couldn't she keep the bars up against him? Where was she when he had intruded? On a wedding trip with Harvey. Life held infinite possibilities of pleasure married to such a man. Of course she detested some of his ideas, hated his drinking — the Puritan Randolph in her was responsible for that — however, abstinence was becoming the fashion. It no longer was smart to drink. Absolute glowing health

was the present fetish, and the two were incompatible.
Harvey would fall into line. He prided himself upon
being an up-to-the-minute person.

The brakes of the roadster groaned as a policeman
in dripping rubber coat stepped forward with upraised
hand. She had been so immersed in thought that she
nearly had run him down. She smiled her traffic-cop
special as she explained unnecessarily:

" I almost didn't see you."

The charm worked. The officer touched his cap
from which water rilled merrily, grinned responsively.

" Sorry, Miss. We'll have to search your car."

" Search *my* car? "

" Bank robbed in Garston. We're giving every
motorist the once-over."

She laughed as she stepped to the soaked earth.

" Proceed. You won't find anything. I'm all out
of burglars and bonds today."

Embarrassed, obviously responsive to her friend-
liness, the beefy young policeman made a cursory ex-
amination of the roadster. Scribbled on a slip.

" Show this, Miss, if you're stopped again. Sorry to
have bothered you." He touched his cap. She smiled
acknowledgment and shot off into the rain.

It was after one o'clock when, hungry, damp, she
drew up at the ornate entrance to the apartment house
in which Madelaine Randolph lived. A glistening
coated doorman looked at her as though he were seeing
a ghost. Obviously he was disturbed. Why? A boy
seized her bags. Another stepped into the roadster to

take it to the garage. With top coat over her arm, the handle of her jewel case gripped tightly she stepped into the elevator. The gilt-braided operator grinned a welcome.

She might have left yesterday, so easily she had slipped back into place again, Jean thought as she put her key into the outer door of the apartment. She stood for an instant in the attractive foyer. How still. So still that almost she could detect the tones of her mother's voice like left-behind echoes floating about, even the scent of her cigarettes.

She sniffed. That scent was the real thing. The low rumble of a man's voice! In the living room? Had the apartment been surreptitiously sub-let during her mother's absence? It had been done. Was that why the doorman had stared at her in consternation? What a chance for a gentleman burglar — nonsense — the story of the bank robbery had unleashed her imagination.

She tiptoed forward. She would confront the intruders. Suppose they were to shoot? Silly! Her hectic imagination again. Persons sub-letting Park Avenue apartments weren't likely to carry firearms. The lessees doubtless thought they were taking title in straightforward fashion. She would enlighten them. She flung open the living room door — stood transfixed on the threshold. Stared for one speechless second!

Her breath caught in a sob. With a strangled cry, she flew through the foyer. Resolutely shut out the sound of a voice calling: " Jean! Jean! " Banged the outer door, ran down stairs, down, down, down!

Chapter XVIII

ON through the darkening afternoon. On and on
through the driving rain in the roadster . . .
how had she gotten it so quickly . . . Jean couldn't
remember . . . her mother's eyes . . . terrified eyes
. . . the great emerald on her finger . . . never again
would she see an emerald without remembering . . .
she would give the ring back to Harvey, she couldn't
wear that stone . . . had she clung to her jewel box
. . . yes, it was on the seat beside her . . . if only her
teeth would stop chattering . . . stairs . . . stairs
. . . stairs . . . nightmare . . . it had seemed years
before she had reached the street . . . had it really
been her mother in that room . . . she had written
that she had closed the apartment . . . a smoke screen
to keep her daughter away . . . the thought was unbearable . . . did Hughie suspect . . . poor . . . no,
one couldn't use that word in connection with him he
was too valiant . . . *her* mother . . . she had known
that such things happened, had heard girls callously
discuss the live and let live treaties of their parents
. . . that sort of sordidness wouldn't smudge her life,

she had told herself complacently . . . of course her father lived in one city and her mother in another . . . always she had felt called upon to explain that change, travel and metropolitan surroundings were the necessary atmosphere for a novelist, that her father was bound to his manufacturing interests . . . what a rush and roar that silly little brook was making . . . she was cold, horribly cold . . . too cold to shiver . . . would her heart ever stop aching . . . would her mind ever feel clean again . . . how could she have been so unsuspecting, she, Jean Randolph, so characteristically of her own age and generation . . . her mother . . . brilliant, beautiful . . . beloved by the public . . . letters, admiring letters in every mail . . . what river was she crossing . . . swollen, angry, snarling like a goaded beast . . . was she back in Garston . . . was that the roar of the dam above the bridge she heard . . . had she instinctively turned her face toward her father's home . . . home — what day was this . . . the concert — she had promised to usher at the concert this afternoon and she had forgotten it . . . she had driven on and on, hour after hour, an automaton at the wheel, thinking, thinking . . . if only one could switch one's mind into the reverse and unthink . . . if she had stayed with her mother this winter would this horrible thing have happened . . . it hurt unbearably . . . she couldn't endure the burn and smart . . . never, never had she been hurt terribly before . . . if only she could pour out her thoughts to someone . . . Hughie . . . no, *no* . . . the Contessa

. . . she would be caustic, she didn't get on with her daughter . . . she had said, " Little passions! Little passions content her! " . . . there was no one . . . unless Christopher Wynne . . . curious, how the mere thought of him warmed her . . . she couldn't go to him . . . troubled, desperately needing comfort . . . he might suspect that she cared . . . more than ever now she must keep the door between herself and him tightly closed . . . bolted . . . padlocked . . . that thought hurt too . . . if she were to marry him she would soon hate the narrow road a clergyman's wife would have to travel . . . she might prove as untrue as her mother . . . no, *no* . . . she never could endure herself if she were untrue to her standard of honor . . . she would marry Harvey . . . she really was fond of him . . . should she tell him what she had seen . . . no . . . whom could she tell . . . the knowledge was eating out her heart like caustic . . . she hated, hated, hated being hurt like this . . . across the bridge . . . she almost ran by that red light . . . she must watch the signals . . . where should she go . . . not to Hill Top, she might meet her father, her face would betray her . . . she shouldn't have come back to Garston . . . she was on the main street . . . how it rained . . . a cloudburst . . . the wheels of the roadster churned up fountains of water . . . where should she go . . . she couldn't drive round and round forever . . . she was almost in the heart of the city . . . the smell of wet asphalt . . . stark naked trees

. . . buildings, gray blots against pink mist reflecting the glow of the incandescents . . . glistening pavements . . . countless umbrellas with beige legs scuttling by . . . leaf-laden torrents cascading along gutters . . . jeweled street lights like cloudy opals rainbow-eyed . . . bells . . . wistful . . . mysterious . . . softly   blended — rhyming — chiming — swelling — calling — calling through the rain

Suddenly, inexplicably on the screen of Jean's mind flashed a picture. Velvet-smooth aisles like the spokes of a wheel sectoring mahogany pews brightened by the rich crimson of damask cushions, candles burning in massive silver sticks in the chancel, sumptuous red roses, soft tints filtering through a carved reredos behind an altar.

The church! Sanctuary! Even the memory of it steadied her mind. She could think connectedly. She would go there. She'd stay until she had thought things through. Her father believed her to be in New York. Her mother . . . she mustn't go back to that. Suppose the church were closed? Serve her right if it were. All her life she had driven indifferently, blithely by the open church doors . . . what need had she of church, she had asked herself . . . whenever she had questioned at all.

Would she ever get there? She was caught in a stream of traffic. Never had she known the city so crowded. The atmosphere seemed electric. Cars crawled on, in obedience to the wink of a great green eye sending up a shower of spray with every revolution of the wheel. Halted when the signal flamed red. Crawled on. Halted. Crawled. Whistles shrilled. Horns blared. She leaned forward. Impatiently cleared the windshield of moisture. She must get on. She couldn't live with this unbearable heart-ache.

The steeple clock ponderously struck the hour as she left her roadster at the curb in front of the church. Collar of her raincoat turned up, the handle of her jewel case gripped tightly, she raced up the three broad steps. The great outer doors were swung back in silent invitation. Across the vestibule . . . more doors. Inside she stopped for an instant. Breathed a little sigh of relief. Not a person visible. She slipped into a rear pew, shrank into its shadowy corner. Felt her taut muscles relax. The relief of it!

Softly lighted, faintly fragrant, hushed nave, glowing chancel, dusky transepts, as she had visualized them. The outside roar of traffic played like a soft lullaby against the walls of stone. Something reaching toward her out of the beauty and silence, something human, pulsing like an outstretched hand. Gleam of candlelight on silver, on red roses; flicker of flame picking out the gold and lapis and green letters above the altar:

Peace I leave with you, my peace I give unto you. Let not your heart be troubled, neither let it be afraid.

For an instant it seemed as though the heart in her breast swelled to bursting. A sharp sob floated upward like a little balloon broken loose from its keeper. An-

other followed, then another. Desperately she tried
to hold them back. This wasn't Jean Randolph, crying, she told herself, she would fight to the finish before she crumpled. She seemed helpless before this
crushing blow . . . if her mother . . . she must not,
would not think of her until she could control her
thoughts.

How still the church was. The silence enfolded her
like warm tranquillizing wings. Her spasmodic sobs
quieted. Head resting against the high back of the
pew through tear-drenched eyes she read and re-read
the illumined text above the altar. The flickering
candle-light quickened the gold of the last words to
living flame:

Let not your heart be troubled, neither let it be afraid.

"Neither let it be afraid," she repeated softly.
"Neither let it be afraid."

A hand touched her shoulder. A voice said:

"Jean dear, what has happened Let me help."

Startled, her heart beating in her throat, she looked
up into Christopher Wynne's face. In the soft light it
took on an unearthly whiteness, his eyes were dark
with emotion. His hand tightened on her shoulder as
he commanded:

"Come into my study."

Why not? Desperation in the question as she left
the pew. Why not fling her intolerable burden on his
broad shoulders, why not tell him what had happened?
That would break his hold on her. He would no longer

want her. How could he? How could he, she demanded of herself as she followed him to a door past which she had slipped daily for the last two weeks. He helped her remove her damp coat. Spread it over a chair to dry.

Her heart swelled to bursting again. A strangled sob tore up from its tumultuous depths. Christopher Wynne pushed forward a deep chair.

"Sit here." As she leaned her head wearily against its back and closed her eyes he asked practically:

"Had any luncheon?"

She shook her head.

"I thought not. What did you eat for breakfast?" He opened folding doors, revealed a compact kitchenette. Jean watched him listlessly as she answered:

"Oh, coffee and — and — coffee — and —"

"And that was all. Oh, you flesh-beaters," he mocked tenderly and set a kettle over an electric heater.

Her mind snapped back to normal with the rapidity of a ball at the end of a stretched elastic. Was that chocolate she smelled? She was faint with hunger. She hadn't realized it before. Back to her Christopher Wynne prepared a tray with china, silver, linen. The trace of laughter in his voice had the effect of righting her topsy-turvy world, of holding it steady as he observed:

"An empty stomach is an invincible foe, Jean. It undermines courage, spreads a smoke-screen which totally obscures the light of reason which keeps one's perspective true, keeps one seeing the big things of life big, the small ones small." He drew a table beside her chair. As she opened her lips to protest he commanded:

" Don't talk till you have eaten something. Mother used to say that she never made a suggestion to Father till after dinner. Hungry, he roared objection like a lion, well-fed he listened like a lamb. I never quite appreciated the truth of her statement until I entered the ministry. After a few months I installed that kitchenette. I consider it as valuable a part of the church equipment as the organ or the carillon. Many a man who has entered this room in despair, who had been too worried to eat, has gone out with head up and shield securely buckled on after receiving nothing more stimulating than a cup of hot chocolate and a biscuit. Here you are."

He set the tray on the small table. She watched the tiny spiral of steam which rose from the cup like a miniature Indian signal fire. Nothing more stimulating than chocolate, he had said. He neglected to mention the strength, the sustaining power of his personality.

" Drink every drop and eat every crumb of those crackers before I come back," he commanded before he left the room by a door opposite the one they had entered. As it swung open, Jean smelled the fragrance of roses, the odor of burning wax. That door must lead directly into the chancel.

She started from her chair. She would better get away before she capitulated to his tenderness. The aroma of hot chocolate assailed her nostrils, held her.

She was faint from hunger. With a hand which shook she raised the cup to her lips.

Literally she obeyed orders, drank every drop, ate every crumb. A sense of warmth, the surety that somehow the present tragic snarl would untangle, buoyed her spirit. She marvelled at the change in her outlook. How could it happen when . . . she winced. At least she now had the courage to go on alone, to keep her mother's secret.

For the first time since she entered the room she looked about. Two walls were book lined from polished floor to raftered ceiling. One was devoted to the culinary department, a cheery fire blazed and flamed up a chimney in the fourth. A broad table-desk occupied stage-center, laden with typewriter, writing paraphernalia, books, a slender crystal vase with three pink carnations. Floor lamps, softly lighted, invited to the occupancy of deep, cushioned chairs.

Hands clasped on her knees, eyes on the fire, Jean leaned forward, tried to analyze the sense of calm, which brooded in the silent room. It was not the calm of inertia, rather it inspired a determination to buckle on her armor that was the metaphor Christopher had used to meet life staunchly on her feet, to fight her way out to the light. Even if she couldn't change what had happened . . .

"Obeyed orders?" demanded Wynne from the threshold. He laid a crimson rose on her clasped hands. Had he taken it from the silver bowl on the altar, she wondered as she held its velvety petals against her lips before she fastened it at the V neck of her beige frock with the brooch she wore. He placed the tray in the kitchenette, closed the doors. Said lightly:

" My domesticity stops at washing dishes. Now . . ."

He drew a chair forward. Jean had the breathless sense she had at the dentist's when having adjusted the head-rest, the practitioner picked up an instrument with a preparatory. " Now " She proposed hurriedly:

" Mayn't I wash the dishes? "

" You may not. The caretaker does that. She keeps things in order here and Ezry Barker keeps her nose to the grindstone. I am well taken care of." His voice deepened to tenderness as he asked:

" Won't you tell me why you were out there, Jean? " he indicated the world which lay beyond the open door. Her hands tightened about her knee. She must not tell him. She answered as lightly as she could with the desire to fling herself into his arms, crush her face against his shoulder, battering at her resistance.

" You have diagnosed the trouble, perfectly. Hunger. I had driven home in the rain . . . thinking . . . thinking . . ."

" Of me, I hope." The darkening of his eyes belied the lightness of his voice.

" No. There was something else. I forgot that I hadn't eaten, my outlook got grayer and grayer. Not a gleam of color anywhere. I wouldn't inflict either family or friends with that mood. Happened to be passing the church . . ."

" Happened? I would say that you had been led. Go on! "

" There isn't any more. I saw the open doors, slipped in and then, the place did something to me. I cried as I've never cried before. And . . . and that's all."

" That explanation doesn't account for those heart-broken sobs, dear. Think of me only as one who longs to help you."

" Oh, if only I could! " she wailed desperately. Not until she saw the dark color surge to his hair did she realize the significance of the admission. She stumbled on:

" You're quite mad to even think of marrying me. Me! Jean Randolph! You — a — minister. Why . . . why . . . I never said a prayer in my life! "

His eyes, steady, tender, held hers.

" Perhaps you have in your inmost soul without knowing it when you have been terribly hurt."

" I never was terribly hurt . . . until . . . until . . ." the sentence dragged out in a shaken sob.

" Until today? Prayer becomes intensely real, intensely sustaining as a narrow conception of the things of the spirit broadens into faith, Jean."

Her broken laugh was the essence of skepticism.

" You don't believe that all one has to do to get what one wants is to — to pray for it? "

" Hardly. Faith without trying every possible way

oneself to make things come right, won't accomplish much. To me prayer is like an elixir of courage poured through my veins. It steadies, strengthens, clarifies, suggests. There is a new spirit abroad in the world, Jean. Any man who thinks deeply must move forward. Outward forms of faith change. But the vital truths strike their roots deeper and deeper as the years go on. As for prayer . . . remember those lines of Tennyson?

> " ' More things are wrought by prayer
> Than this world dreams of.' "

Jean's troubled eyes were on the fire as she demanded:

" How can one have faith in what one cannot see? "

" Have you never believed anything you could not prove? We wouldn't get far if we waited for certainty. Don't you realize that the whole world is run on faith? Think what an amount of faith the scoffing Contessa has in those Italian servants, they manage her establishment, run it honestly. Your father's business prospers largely because of his faith in the men whom he has selected as department heads. Your mother's faith in her literary agent — "

" Oh, Mother! "

For an instant books, fireplace, table-desk were inextricably mixed in Jean's vision. They dissolved into their component parts as Christopher bent over her, caught her hands.

" Jean! Jean! What is it? "

" Do I intrude? " inquired a dry voice from the threshold. It set waves of anger and hatred vibrating through the quiet room. It steadied the girl's shaken nerves as nothing else could have done. Luther Calvin! How hateful and forbidding he made religion seem by his sanctimonious attitude. Christopher Wynne made it real, as much a matter of course in one's life as sunlight, and as normal.

Wynne answered the man with agate eyes and patent-leather hair who stood in the doorway:

" No intrusion, Mr. Calvin. Come in."

" I will for fear that one of your parishioners, less understanding than I, might, and misconstrue this situation. Now I know why you wouldn't marry Sue. Doubtless you think she isn't quite the heiress Miss Randolph is. Well — you never can tell! You never can tell! "

Wynne's face was livid as he picked up Jean's coat and held it.

" Is your car outside, Miss Randolph? Sorry to seem to hurry you, but I have something to say to Mr. Calvin that I would rather you didn't hear."

Jean caught his sleeve:

" Oh, no, please! I — "

A thick-shouldered man in blue uniform with a plentitude of brass buttons unceremoniously elbowed Luther Calvin to one side as he entered the room. A police officer! What had happened? Had she parked

her car in the wrong place? The man was seething
with excitement. His rather childish eyes bulged, he
ran big, bony fingers through a mop of red hair
rampant, before he rejoiced:

"Cricks! I'm in luck to find you, Mr. Wynne.
We've caught the bank robber that was shot at. He's
Chick Sawyer, the man you had arrested the day you
were pinch-hitting for me. Got him in my house. He
was tryin' to launch a boat on the river. If he'd got
started, he'd cheated the law all right. A boat couldn't
live on that rough water tonight. The Chief says fer
me to keep him where he is. They can't come fer him
till morning, the storm's too fierce. The feller's about
all in. Can't last much longer. He's askin' for you."

"For me! Are you sure, Luke?"

"The guy insists he's got to see you. Got something to tell you. Sort of off his head. Terrible night
to drag you out. The streets are afloat. Floods north
of us but we're safe enough unless the dam should go.
It'll hold all right. Coming, Mr. Wynne?"

"At once. Jean —"

"Go! Go! Don't think of me. My roadster is
outside, why can't I drive you?"

"'Twon't do, Miss. My flivver'll get us through
traffic quicker. 'Twon't take us twenty minutes, the
other cops will send me through. Better hurry."

Luther Calvin rasped:

"I need your counsel, Mr. Wynne. Stay here and
let the law deal with that criminal."

"I'll come to your house, Mr. Calvin, when I get back from Carter's. I am needed there." Christopher slipped into his coat, picked up a worn, black bag, put a flash-light in his pocket. "What is it, Ezry?" he asked as Barker appeared at the doorway.

"Jest stopped to ask if we'd better not close the church early to-night. There won't be no one here." He stared at the girl. "By mighty! Thought you was in New York, Jean. Back ag'in! That's why yer mother 'phoned the Contessa thet she must see you, that unless she heard where you was before an hour, she was a-comin' to Garston as fast as a plane could bring her. The old lady sent fer me to know if I'd seen yer. She was all het up."

"Mother coming here!" Jean's voice broke in a sob. She sensed Christopher Wynne's quick glance at her before he directed:

"Wait an hour before you close the church, Ezry."

"All right, Mr. Wynne." Barker regarded Jean from under frowning, bushy brows: "How you goin' home?"

With an effort she smiled at him.

"My roadster is outside. When Mr. Carter came in I thought he had come to tell me that I had parked in the wrong place."

Barker slouched off grumbling audibly. Luther Calvin removed his overcoat, draped it with exceeding care for its contour over the back of a chair:

"I will wait here for your return."

"You may have a long wait."

Calvin walked to the shelves. Became absorbed in the selection of a book, persisted with condescending forbearance:

" I will wait here."

" Suit yourself. Come, Jean. Come, Carter."

Christopher Wynne did not speak again until he laid his hand on Jean's on the wheel of her roadster.

" Drive carefully. The pavements are treacherous. Don't barricade your heart against me — darling."

She closed her lids tight to shut out the ardor of his eyes, tried to close her ears against the caressing tenderness of his voice. She turned up the collar of her raincoat. How instinctive it was to be practical even when one's mind was a battleground of warring emotions. Turning up her collar and gripping the handle of her jewel-case! She thrust her hand to the seat? It wasn't there! Where had she had it last? Had she left it on the seat? Had it been stolen? Her diamond bracelets! Steady, she told herself. Think back. She had had it in her hand when she left the apartment, she remembered clutching it in the taxi on the way to retrieve her roadster. Remembered it beside her on the seat as she drove through the rain. She had touched it from time to time to make sure that it was safe. Then she had stopped at the church, had taken it with her.

She jumped from the car, ran up the three broad steps, past the great doors thrown wide in invitation. The world seemed to drop away as she entered the hushed silence. Unconsciously she tiptoed forward to the pew where she had sat. The jewel-case was there.

She dropped to the cushioned seat with a little sigh of relief. That was that. Stupid of her to leave it, but she had forgotten everything when she had followed Christopher Wynne to his study. What was there about him that made one cling tight to his hand in spirit? With him one wouldn't mind a stony road. Was it his daily companionship with — with — God? She had a curious sense of embarrassment in the thought, as though she had been unduly familiar with the Deity.

Oh, but she was tired of fighting. All night she had battled with the memory of Christopher's compelling eyes and voice . . . for hours since she had fought suspicion . . . that was too kind a word . . . of her mother. Why was she coming to Garston? Did she think that she could explain? Jean shivered. She must keep that memory locked up tight. She snuggled into the shadowy corner of the pew, tucked her feet up under her. This place was heavenly restful. Why should she hurry home? She had left the roadster unlocked! Safe enough. Automobile snitchers would be under cover this wet night. Ezry wouldn't close the church for an hour. Would he put Luther Calvin out of the study when he did? Devoutly she hoped so. Was the wounded man at the Carter cottage who had sent for Christopher the sporty individual with green eyes and mocking mouth who had been prowling about the cabin that Sunday? If he were she had done him an injustice. His anxiety to see Christopher now that he was perhaps dying proved that he really had been concerned as to his " salvation," as he called it. She bent her head to sniff the fragrance of the flower at her breast. Had it come from that bowl of sumptuous roses on the altar? Did a man as physically superb as Christopher Wynne, feel the need of prayer? He had said that prayer became intensely real, intensely sustaining as one's faith in it grew. She couldn't imagine herself praying. She just wouldn't know how to begin. She would remember the hushed quiet of this church all her life, would see the flickering light of the candles on that illuminated text above the altar. What did it all mean? How many prayers had been offered in the hundred years the building had stood? Did the echoes of those petitions still linger to give a sense of human warmth and understanding? Never, since she was a little girl and had parroted " Now I lay me " had she offered a prayer. What did one say when one prayed besides " Our Father who is in Heaven "? Irony that a man like Christopher Wynne, a clergyman, should think he loved a girl who never had said a prayer. He would forget her. She would marry Harvey. Was that a door banging? How far away it seemed. Ezry coming to lock up? Was it possible that she had been curled up in the pew thinking, thinking for an hour? If he saw her he would crab. She couldn't bear even his affection-prompted scolding tonight. She would escape before he appeared.

She looked back as she reached the door which

opened on the vestibule, looked back at velvet aisles, crimson damask, tiny flames sprouting from silver sticks, red roses, illuminated letters which seemed to flicker in the candlelight. A new world to her. Never would she forget her sense of security as she had entered it, never, she told herself as she splashed down the broad steps to her roadster.

Chapter XIX

COULD this be the defiant, insolent law-breaker whom he had had haled into court, this gray-faced, blood-stained man lying with closed eyes on the gayly flowered chintz couch in Luke Carter's house by the river? Could less than twenty-four fear-harried hours make such a change? He would be recognizable among an hundred by his twisted mouth. A man with abnormal features, of all others, should never stray from the path of honor, Christopher Wynne told himself as he bent and gently touched a dirty hand.

" You wanted me, Sawyer? "

Haggard eyes opened, rested on burly Luke Carter. With a masterly burst of profanity the man struggled to his feet. The officer laid a compelling hand on his shoulder.

" What's your hurry? You're spendin' the night here. We sure couldn't let you go out into this storm," the mockery left his voice as he added: " I've brought Mr. Wynne. You said you'd got to see him. Well, here he is. Now what you got to say? Goin' to tell him where those bonds are? "

His captive stared out of blood-shot eyes before he

caught Christopher's sleeve with skeleton-like fingers. By sheer force of will he dragged a voice coarsened by drink and roughened by exposure from somewhere deep within him:

"Gawd! I got to talk to, you, Parson!"

Rain beat and slashed against the windows. From below the house rose the roar of the river clawing and tearing at its banks. The strained silence within the room was broken by the monotonous tick-tock of an ornate clock on the mantel, Sawyer's labored breathing.

Christopher's throat tightened. The man was in a torment of pain. He was to be in Luke's custody until morning. Prisoner or not, he must be made comfortable. Of course he was a desperado, would unhesitatingly blow out his and Luke's brains if he saw a chance of escape, but, he couldn't escape. His hand closed strongly over the dirty, clinging fingers.

"I'm here for you to talk to, Sawyer, but first we'll make you comfortable. Luke, bring me a glass of water."

He turned his back, busied himself with his black bag until the officer returned. He added a portion of the contents of a bottle to the water, slipped his arm under Sawyer's head, held the glass to his lips.

"Drink every drop!"

The very words he had said to Jean an half hour, it seemed years, ago. Where was she? Safe at home by this time. The roads had been dangerously slippery when he and Carter had sloshed along in the flivver. Constance and Sally-May would be safely housed after the concert. The concert! Would the Contessa be furious with him because he had absented himself from the benefit which was to contribute to the fund to meet her gift? Tomorrow was the last day of grace allowed him. Either he knuckled or he would be asked to resign. Well, tomorrow was at least a night away. Many things could happen in a night.

Gently he lowered the tense shoulders to the pillow. Sympathized:

"Throbs like the dickens, doesn't it? I know. We'll try to ease it. Luke, come into the hall."

Outside the closed door he said quickly:

"Bring me a basin, a kettle of boiling water. Got extra pajamas?"

Carter scratched his mop of red hair, grinned apology:

"Cricks, Mr. Wynne! I don't wear nothing so classy. I ain't got anything but a night-shirt."

"All the better. Got a bath-robe? Bring that. Be sure Lucy's door is shut. Tell her I'll see her when I get through making Sawyer comfortable. He must be suffering intensely."

"Let him suffer. I guess he's got it coming to him. What d'you suppose he'd do to you an' me if he saw a chance to make his get-away? He's in my charge tonight. I don't know as the Chief would think I was doing my whole duty if I allow you to coddle him."

Christopher Wynne's laugh was short.

"Coddle him! Ever know the agony of a wound stuck to your clothing? I have. I'm no sentimentalist. Luke, the man deserves whatever punishment a fair-minded jury hands him. Meanwhile I'll take the responsibility of relieving his pain."

Under Carter's espionage, with his assistance, Christopher Wynne worked quickly, with practised skill. In an incredibly short time, bathed, bandaged, clothed in Luke's spotless contribution, a torrid bath-robe in place of muddy, blood-soaked clothing, Chick Sawyer, gray-faced, eyes closed in exhaustion, lay between Lucy Carter's wedding sheets. Christopher bent over him with a glass.

"Drink this. Then we won't touch you again. You can rest."

Eagerly the man gulped down the restorative. Head back on the snowy pillow he closed his eyes. As Christopher moved he caught his coat with his claw-like fingers. Protested weakly:

"Don't go! I — I — got to get something off my mind."

"I'm not going." Christopher sank into the chair Luke pushed forward, crossed his knees as though he were quite at home, as though spending an evening in the Carter cottage were part of the day's work. "I'm staying right here as long as you need me."

Two red spots burned hotly in Sawyer's gaunt cheeks, his eyes glittered feverishly as he indicated Carter with one shaking hand:

"Has the cop got to listen in?"

Luke stiffened.

"You bet your life I listen."

The weak voice roughened with contempt.

" Gawd! Do you think you're in fer a death-bed confession? No movie stuff in mine. If I goes . . . I goes . . . an' I takes what I knows with me. If I had a chance to snitch another couple of grands . . . but . . . I ain't had no luck since — since — " Christopher warned:

" Take it easy."

The man's closed eyes opened wide, too wide. Slowly, with his amazingly perfect teeth clenched he raised himself on one elbow.

" I'm feelin' fine. Like I was floatin'. That must have been powerful stuff you gave me out of your black bag. I was sayin' — I ain't afraid of snuffin' out — I — I — kinder thought that if you was standin' by — "

" I am standing by."

" Those words seem firm as a rock. You don't know why I wanted you, do you? Remember last night you had a call to come to this house, 'cause the Carter woman was dying? "

The question radioed pictures, impressions, sounds through Christopher's mind. The clearing on the hill — tree-tops silvered by moon-light — a fleecy cloud shrouding the spangled sky — sudden darkness — a stealthy human sound — the certainty that tragedy was biding its time — the maddening sense of futility that he could not drag it into the open — meet it — vanquished it — his prayer — his sense of close spiritual companionship as he went forward into the descending trail. He nodded thoughtfully.

"I remember. When I reached the house I found that no message had been sent from here."

Sawyer's eyes glittered with professional pride.

"Sure it hadn't. My partner — I had it sent. I meant to lay you by fer a time — teach you to keep your hands off honest, hard-working men; knew that as long as you was loose we wouldn't get nowhere with our business which had been goin' fine till you upset it. We had a deal on at the bank fer midnight. Had it doped out that if the town was all excited over you bein' missin' we'd pull things off easy." He choked, coughed, stubbornly resisted Christopher's attempt to ease him back on the pillow.

"No! *No!* I'm all right — feelin' fine. I got to tell you — maybe it'll change my luck. Haven't had any since I see it. 'Twas my bunglin' that queered the break last night. *It* was between me an' the thing I was doin'."

He passed a shaking hand across his glittering eyes. Hitched himself higher on his elbow, bent forward, brows knitted, stared at a distant corner of the room. The storm shook the house, tugged at the shutters, shrieked in uncanny glee. Luke Carter shifted his weight uneasily, looked surreptitiously over his thick shoulders. The walls seemed to echo Sawyer's weak, hoarse voice:

"Remember when you got to the top of the hill you stopped sudden as though you heard somethin'? 'Twas me! I stepped on a twig. How I cursed. You looked terrible tall in the moonlight . . . then it blinked out, but I could see you, even in the dark. I had you covered. Remember you stood still fer a minute, lookin' up? "

" I remember."

" Before I could fire . . . sudden . . . a figger shinin' like it was all lit inside, carryin' a drawn sword, stood beside you."

His eyes widened, stared into space.

" You stepped forward as if . . . as if . . . some-one'd told you you was safe . . . an' the shinin' figger walked close beside you as you come on, passed me hidin' there . . . holdin' my gun as though I was paralyzed. I — I've never had no luck since . . . always I'm seeing — seeing — that shinin' . . ." he covered his eyes with a shaking hand, dropped back on the pillow.

Christopher's eyes met Luke's childish with awe. The officer's voice was hoarse as he whispered:

" Sure I remember. You come to the door sayin' Lucy'd sent for you. Now what do you know about — "

The roar as of a Gargantuan bull loosed in the world's arena after years of heckled captivity rocked the house. Sawyer sprang to his feet as though forced erect by a galvanic battery. Christopher was already at the window. Luke Carter gasped:

" Cricks! What bust? " he ran to the hall, opened the door. Slammed it to shut out a stream of water. Christopher beside him whispered:

" The dam has gone. Get Lucy to the top floor.

Quick! Water's creeping in under the door! It's rising! It's reached the lower step."

As Luke took the stairs three at a time Christopher returned to the living room. Sawyer was swaying against the mantel.

" What was it, Parson."

" The dam. The country above here has been flooded. We must get to the top floor. Come."

He linked his arm within Sawyer's, half supported half dragged him to the hall. The sight of water lapping against the second stair braced the wounded man for a moment. Then he crumpled against the newel-post.

Christopher caught him before he fell. One arm about the man's waist, he half lifted half dragged him up the first flight of stairs. He could hear rain pelting against the skylight in the roof. As the water below rose it made a curious sucking sound like a sea-monster licking its lips. The rumble of Carter's voice came from the floor above. He looked over the banister. The water was half way up to the second floor and steadily rising. He must get Sawyer up one more flight. They would be safe there, there was always the roof. He caught the unconscious man round the waist. As he put his foot on the first step the lights went out. Christopher called:

" Got a lamp or candle up there, Luke? Help me with Sawyer! "

He could hear Carter grumble as flash-light in hand he came down. Not ungently the officer caught Chris-

topher's unconscious burden under the arms and lifted
him up the stairs to the accompaniment of indignant
protest:

"Cricks! Think of you luggin' this jail-bird up
them stairs. Why didn't you leave him? 'Twould have
saved the county a lot of time and good money."

"Leave a helpless man to drown? You know you
don't mean that, Luke."

Carter grunted a protest, struggled on and up. In
a bare room, with one dormer window, they laid Sawyer
on the floor. Christopher flexed strained muscles.

"So far, so good. Lucy all right?"

"Sure, she's a good soldier. She's in the other room.
Used her bean. Snatched up this electric lantern, told
me to get the candles, — we couldn't afford electricity
in this attic, lots of good 'twould have done us now,
if we had." He leaned over the balustrade, flashed
his light. His face was the curious color faces turn
when the blood seems to have been drained from beneath the skin. His eyes were big with anxiety as he
whispered:

"Water's up to the top stair of the first flight.
Where do we go from here?"

Christopher looked down at the hall below, at the
lapping tide, at the skylight above.

"We'll stay on this floor as long as we can. If we
take Lucy and Sawyer to the roof now they'll be soaked
by the rain, beaten by wind. We will keep them
under cover as long as possible. At any moment the
water is likely to subside. Go down to the bedrooms,

bring all the bedding, towels, anything you can find.
Take them in to Lucy. Tell her to tie and twist them
into ropes . . . it won't hurt her half so much as lying there listening to the rising water. While you are
doing that I'll investigate the roof in case we have to
use it. I hope we won't. Give me that flash-light.
You take the candle."

"You're crazy to put your head out, it will be blown
off, Mr. Wynne."

"It is fastened more securely than that I hope.
Get a hustle on." He lowered his voice, "Another
dam may break plunging its waters into our river.
We would have no time for preparation then."

"Cricks! That's so! "Carter agreed hoarsely before he picked up a candle and made his cautious way
down. Christopher, listening, heard a splash as he
stepped from the bottom stair. Already the water
had risen to the hall.

He fastened the electric lantern to his belt, mounted
the steps which led to the skylight. The bolt resisted
his first few attempts to slide it. Rusted? Every
moment counted. What a splash Luke was making
on the floor below. The water must be rising fast.
Would the skylight never open? The cords in his hands
and forehead knotted as he pulled again. It moved!
Another tug. The bolt shot back.

He stopped to draw a long breath before he raised
the window. As though the fury outside had been
cunningly lying in wait the wind banged it down upon
his head with a force which caused him to see whirling
suns and shooting stars innumerable.

The universe steadied. He pushed again. This time he thrust his shoulders through the opening. He freed one hand. Flashed the lantern.

The roof sloped gradually to the dormers. Between them and the ridgepole were fastened a row of cleats like a ladder, put there years ago to assist in fighting fire. Lucy and Sawyer could be tied to those dormers if worst came to worst and they had to flee to the roof.

He leaned far out. The wind caught at his breath. Darkness overhead. Not a light visible. Yes! The flying-field beacon! Slashing the blackness with its light-beam like an old-time pioneer blazing a way through the wilderness. That meant help. Help if it were needed. The roar of the river in front of the house was deafening. He pulled himself up. Looked over his shoulder. He could barely discern a white outline. The Randolph house at the top of the hill. Half way down a projection. The log-cabin chimney.

A hand gripped his ankle. Cautiously he withdrew his shoulders, gently lowered the window into place, backed down the steps. In the wavering light of the candle, Carter's grin flickered impishly:

" It's stopped rising."

Christopher leaned over the balustrade, watched for five interminable minutes by his wrist watch. The water in the hall below lapped gently against the lowest stair but made no gain. He drew a breath of relief:

" That's all right so far. Did you get those blankets and towels? "

" Yep, Lucy's tyin' them together. Think I'd better stop her as long as the water isn't making headway? "

" No. Work with her till you have four long ropes. Heard anything from Sawyer? "

" He called for water once. Cricks! Think of wanting to *see* any more water! I brought up Lucy's thermos, so I gave him a little, then he dozed off."

" He'll sleep. When the ropes are finished lie down yourself, Luke. You've been on duty all day, haven't you? I'll watch the water below. We won't signal for help yet, there are so many others in greater need of it. I hope that the flood will subside but, it's still raining. You and I must face facts. We have two helpless persons on our hands."

" Cricks! Helpless. I'll say they are. You take forty winks first, Mr. Wynne."

" No. I will call you at day-break. If there is no change I'll go off guard. Get those ropes ready first, remember."

Candle in hand, he bent over Sawyer. He lay where Carter had dropped him on the floor. The wind rattled the worn shades at the windows. A mouse scuttled in the walls. A murmur of voices drifted from the next room. He straightened the torrid bathrobe. The gray-faced man slept on, unconscious of pain, of danger, of defeat.

Christopher crept softly down the stairs. The water level remained as it had been when he had come in from the roof, even with the lower stair. He splashed into Lucy Carter's bedroom. Commandeered a jar of crackers, filled a small kettle with water, slipped vials from the medicine closet into his pockets. What an accumulation of bottles and boxes. Lucy must be the sort of woman who hated to throw anything away.

He deposited his loot in the room where Sawyer lay, dropped to the top stair from which he could watch the water in the hall below. If it rose two steps, he and Carter must get Lucy and Sawyer to the roof. He snapped off his light, he would conserve that.

Hands in his pockets, he leaned back against the wall. Now that he had stopped for a moment his muscles ached like the toothache from the strain of lifting Sawyer. Was he worth the effort? For the first time since he had heard it Christopher thought of the man's description of the " figger shinin' like it was all lit inside carryin' a drawn sword."

Curious. After his fervent prayer for help in the clearing on the hill he had been conscious of a sense of close spiritual companionship. Chick Sawyer in hiding to waylay him had seen a vision which had paralyzed his gun hand. Inexplicable . . . but . . . credible to one who believed in the close bond which links the soul that is man and the spirit which is God.

If only Jean could believe as he did. Whether she did or not he loved her independence, her defiance, her sense of honor, more than all else her beautiful self beating its wings against the wall her ignorance, prejudice, imagination, had piled stone upon stone against what she called religion. Foolish darling, as though religion were not as natural to man as breathing; as though it were not a vital force which gave significance and beauty to life.

One picture of her succeeded another as he sat there watching the oily gray tide that lapped like a drowsy tiger at the lower step. Pictures against vivid backgrounds. The main street with its darting taxis and lumbering busses; the drawing room of the Contessa with its lights, its elegance, its color; the log-cabin; dark eyes, aloof, passionately defiant; the fine, sweet line of her mouth tightening proudly when her glance met his; that dimple in her cheek made to be crushed under a man's lips; her lovely, slender body fashioned for the curve of a man's arm.

The last thought brought him up standing. How many hours had he sat there dreaming? Dreaming, with four persons trapped in this attic. He listened. Above the splash of the rain against the skylight he could hear Carter's staccato snores, Sawyer's stertorious breathing. A faint light spread through the darkness. Dawn! Thank God! Dawn, faint, wan, but still the harbinger of day. Day, which would bring release. He ran down the stairs, flashed his light. The water had not risen by so much as a hair!

A dull boom outside! The house shuddered. Christopher felt the color drain from his face. A landslide? A dam swept away? Would the water rise? Tense, breathless, motionless, flashlight trained on it, he waited. After what seemed an eternity he consulted the illuminated dial of his watch. Five minutes! Ten minutes! Was it his inflamed imagination or had the water risen? He bent forward. Rubbed his hands across his eyes again. He must be mistaken! It couldn't have covered the second stair in so short a time. He looked again. Raced to Carter's door. Thundered on the panels. Shouted:

" Luke! Luke! "

As the officer dazed with sleep stumbled against him he shook his arm:

" Wake up! We've got to get them to the roof. Water's rising a foot a minute! "

Chapter XX

IN the flickering candlelight Luke's eyes seemed like glass balls set in the whiteness of his face.

" T-trapped? " he stammered hoarsely.

Christopher countered with an assurance he was far from feeling:

" Not yet! Not with the roof over our heads, with the flying-field beacon on the job. Keep your grip, Luke. I'll open the skylight. When I click my heels give me a boost. Tie one end of a rope under Lucy's arms. Lift her up to me. Open the right hand dormer window. Wait for the rope end I'll fling you. Throw it to the other side. I'll catch it. We'll have Lucy safely moored. Understand? "

" Yep."

" Get Sawyer to the skylight. After I grab him repeat business with the left dormer. Bring the other two ropes and crawl out yourself! "

" Cricks, Mr. Wynne, it can't be done."

" Can't it? Look! "

Christopher pointed to the stairs. Water lapped against the fourth step from the top.

" It must be done." He nodded toward the skylight,

tried to laugh: " ' Came the dawn,' as they say in the movies."

Luke's spirit emerged from a cloud of apprehension.

" Sure we'll do it! Come on! "

Christopher pulled off coat and waistcoat. Rolled up his shirt sleeves. Mounted the steps.

" Ready, Luke! "

With all his strength he pushed up the window. With all its fury the storm beat it back. For an instant his courage faltered. What could individual effort accomplish in the face of chaos? Carter and he were puppets. Puppets! Not while he had an ounce of strength in his body! He pushed again. Thrust shoulders through the opening. Clicked his heels. Luke boosted. He catapulted to the roof. Rain hissed, glittered like sheets of theatrical gauze against the metallic eastern sky where dawn was wanly attempting to reclaim the inky blackness of the heavens. The steely light was reflected on the surface of the river now but a few feet below the dormers.

A shaft of gold swept the sky. The beacon! Christopher stood up. Waved his arms. Shouted. If only the light would rest for a moment on him. The wind lashed him to his knees. He thrust his head through the opening in the roof. The candle flame flickered eerily, burned low, but not too low for him to see the water almost at the top stair. He shouted:

" Hurry, Luke! "

He glanced over his shoulder at the light sweep-

ing the swollen river which seemed broad as an ocean
now that it covered what once had been meadows.

Would Luke never come! He looked down upon the
candlelight casting curious shadows on the walls and
ceiling, glinting on the gray water, creeping, creeping
up. He called again:

"Luke! Luke!"

"Coming!"

He came with an inert bundle in his arms, a rope of
twisted blankets trailing him. Laboriously he mounted
the steps to the skylight. His wife's head bobbed listlessly against his big shoulders. Had she fainted? So
much the better. She would be easier to manage unconscious of her peril. As he took the woman in his
arms he directed:

"Grab the end of the rope. When I twitch fling it
out! Rush for the right-hand dormer. Yell when you
get there!"

Carter's face framed in the opening was gastly.

"Hold her tight!"

"As though she were my own, Luke."

One arm about Lucy Carter, Christopher hitched
down the roof cleat by cleat. Gently he braced his
burden against the dormer. Twitched the rope Like
an over-stuffed serpent it writhed toward him. He
seized the end. Waited tensely for Luke's yell.
Terrifyingly near the river rushed, whirled, sucked.
The great door of a barn jiggled by wrigglingly alive
with — what were they? Black pin points of light!
Eyes! Rats! Grisly rats!

For an instant Christopher was as violently sick as when he had stumbled on the first dead man — an exceedingly dead man — he had seen in France sitting upright in a dug-out. Dizzily he clung to the dormer. With the back of his other hand he brushed away the sudden outbreak of sweat on his forehead. Luke's yell was as efficacious as a dash of iced water.

" Ready! "

Brain clear again, eyes steady, he flung the end of the blanket rope. Leaning far forward, watched. Dodging back caught it as it came round the dormer. Made it fast to the other end. Unconscious Lucy Carter was securely moored.

The beacon again! Balancing unsteadily in the storm Christopher raised his arms, shouted. His shirt sleeves flapped like tattered white flags. A great light silvered the roof. With a shout of exultation he waved again. The beam shifted. Moved on to a cliff of the river bank above. Disclosed a group of men and women. What were they doing? Taking pictures? Of course the newsreel men would be on the job. With a howl of derision the wind caught him, flung him on his face. He gripped a cleat. Struggled for breath which had been beaten out of him. Steel gray dawn had pushed back the sable pall above. Outlines were visible.

Cautiously, knee by bruised knee, he crawled to the skylight. Sawyer was already there. His eyes glittered in a face chalky, scarlet-cheeked like a clown's. He caught the limp man under the arms. Shouted above the din of the storm:

" I've got him! Boost, Luke. Help all you can, Sawyer! "

With the strength which only fever and terror of death can give, the wounded man crawled down the roof to the left dormer. A rope of sheets dragged after. Steadying, encouraging, digging his fingers into the cracks between shingles for a precarious hold, Christopher followed. Before he could twitch the signal for the release of the rope, Luke tumbled from the skylight opening. He sat with great legs sprawled while he shouted:

" Had to come! Water to my knees! "

Cautiously, puffing like a porpoise, he crawled and slid his way to the supine bundle which was his wife.

" No chance of mooring Sawyer to the dormer now," Christopher told himself. He turned and met the man's agonized eyes.

" I'd rather roll off than stand this damn pain, Parson."

" Keep your grip. Help's coming. Watch that beacon. Here it comes! They'll see us! " He waved his arms. Blinked in the blinding glare. " They've got planes out! Hear that whine! " He waved and shouted. Far up a sound like a pistol shot. " Hear that gun! They've seen us! "

Hands to his lips like a megaphone he shouted:

" Hear that, Luke! They've seen us! Help's just around the corner."

His voice cracked, rattled hoarsely in his throat. The light moved on. The roof went black. Sawyer's voice wavered through the darkness:

" Gawd, Parson, yer looked like a silver statue. I'll say yer white all — through. Yer might hev taken this chance to frighten a confession out of me — not that you'd got it — but yer never thought of it — did yer? "

Christopher bent to catch the last whispered words. He laid his hand on the thin shoulder.

" No. I never thought of it, Chick. I — "

With a demoniac shriek the wind caught him, carried him half way up to the ridgepole, flung him down. It shook the house as a terrier shakes a rat. Ripped off the roof. Swept it to the ravening maw of the river.

Stunned, dazed, Christopher pulled himself to his knees. Where was he? His mind steadied. The roof! Twisted off. Flung to the river. Moored against a jam of logs, the logs held by a clump of bushes. Bushes! Those were the tops of trees! Had the dormers come with it. Yes, Carter and his wife huddled against one. The other? Gone! He had been bending over Sawyer when the blast had seized him, flung him back, saved him! For what?

He crawled along the cleats to the ridgepole. For an instant the circling beacon illumined the remains of the Carter house. It sagged, tottered, a dormer waggled grotesquely like a lone, loose tooth in a senile lower jaw. Was that a hand clutching it? Sawyer's hand? Above it in a shoulder of the hillside lighted windows . . . the Randolph house . . . no . . . not high enough. The log-cabin . . . but the lights . . . no lights there unless — unless — the W. Vs. and their lamps! Trimmed and filled! The thought sent fresh courage through Christopher's veins. He turned at a sound behind him. Luke Carter was on his knees. Crazed by fright and anxiety he laughed loudly. Beckoned to his swaying house. Shouted:

"Come on in! The water's fine!"

It came. Wind and water lifted it. Twisted it. Flung it into the foaming river.

Christopher's strained eyes followed the mass of wreckage as it obsequiously bowed and bobbed its way down stream. Masses of pulp wood piled up against it. The dormer loomed like the periscope of a submarine. Slowly the current sucked it under. The water boiled and bubbled over it. Chick Sawyer had gone out of life as tempestuously as he had lived it. Eyes on the distant whirlpool Christopher petitioned fervently:

"Lord, now lettest thou that tortured, twisted soul depart in peace."

The rain dissolved into mist. The wind died down. A cold, steel light filled the exhausted world. It stole forward from all directions. Far off a timid shaft of smoke rose, spread like a woman's hair floating in the wind. Like a gray, leaping hound, the ravening torrent swept by, pitilessly exposing its loot. A tawny cat, crouched on the slats of a chicken coop, paws daintly tucked under its spotless shirt front, regarded Christopher through green slits as it sailed by; the floating corner of a man's blue coat; an old fashioned cradle, bucking, plunging, its pillow still holding the imprint of a little head; a radio loud speaker, its friendly voice silenced for all time; violently uptorn roots with earth still clinging; an aristocratic gold chair bobbing in company with a wooden bench of proletariat descent; a pony, whinnying frantically as it swam, its long mane floating like sea-weed. A dog, still, horribly still, caught in a jut of the roof, swaying with the current.

Christopher shut his teeth hard. Leaned far over. Tried to detach the stiff body. The roof tilted.

" Hi there! " Luke Carter shouted frantically. Christopher crept back and restored balance. Carter pointed to the hill which loomed above the raging water:

" They're trying to launch a boat," he yelled. He began feverishly to unwind the blanket rope about his wife.

A boat half way up the hill! How had it come there? The lights in the log-house windows! Jean's boat stored in the cabin! The W.Vs. and their lamps! Could the boat reach the floating roof?

As though in answer a detonation shook the world. A landslide? The river bank? Perhaps the cliff with the newsreel men! What a night! Had it been real or a fiendish nightmare? Above the moan and creak of timbers, the roar of water, rose a monotonous whine. A plane! Breathlessly he watched the winged thing approach, like a great darning-needle looking for a place to light. A seaplane! Flying toward them!

He shouted to Luke. Strained his eyes to follow the

plane as it coasted gently down, floated on the surface
of the water, taxied forward, forward toward the floating roof. Harvey Brooke, his face a colorless blotch
under his helmet, his eyes on fire, leaned far over the
side. Shouted:

" I'll bring one wing around. Swing yourselves up
to the cockpit! Room for both! "

For both. He hadn't seen Lucy. Luke must get her
aboard; he would get his chance some other way.
Christopher helped Carter lift his wife to the edge of
the teetering roof, jumped back quickly to restore
balance as the great wing maneuvered near. The plane
coquetted like a blooded horse impatient to be off.
Steadied.

" Now! " shouted Brooke.

With the elixir of hope flooding his veins Luke
Carter achieved the impossible. He climbed into the
cockpit with his wife in his arms.

Brooke yelled frantically:

" Where'd the woman come from? My God, I
can't take but two! "

" Go on! Go on! " Christopher shouted in reply.
Under his feet timbers creaked in the agony of dissolu-
tion. The current swept the plane on. The roof split
with a sound like the crack of doom. Sent him head-
first into the water. He came up gasping, caught a
projecting shingle. A glare of light. The beacon
again. He tried to pull himself up. He couldn't make
it. Above the tumult he heard a shrill call:

" Uncle Chris! Uncle Chris! "

As he clung in a desperate attempt to keep his head above water his mind juggled thoughts as a prestidigitator juggles colored balls. Sally-May's voice! Was that the bow of a boat creeping toward him? A wash of pale gold! The sun! Could he keep his head up till help reached him? He must. Bells? Ezra Barker's voice:

"Grab it! Grab it!"

Was this a boat bumping him? Was it worth the effort to lift himself? **His** breast seemed crushed in by the weight of water. The carillon! Was he back in France or were the bells really singing "O God, our help in ages past?"

With the words strength seemed to pour through his body. Muscles straining, heart pounding he pulled himself up to the accompaniment of Barker's agonized plea:

"Get to the other side, Sally-May, to balance. Careful you don't fall out! I'd never ought to have let you come, but 'twas your idea. By mighty! Hold on, boy! There you are! Almost up! Don't let go! *Don't* let go! There, a little more! The other foot over! There you are!"

Christopher rolled into the boat. Lay there in a daze. Through his consciousness pealed the bells:

"'Short as the watch that ends the night.'"

Sally-May implored close to his shoulder:

"Uncle Chris! Uncle Chris! You're safe! Pull yourself together. Say something — please."

His voice wouldn't come. Had it gone forever? As

though she divined the one thing which could rouse him the young girl sobbed on:

"You must pull yourself together, old lamb pie. The Contessa and Mr. Randolph are nearly crazy. Jean's missing! "

As a sudden change of wind will blow back the heaviest fog so Sally-May's words miraculously cleared Christopher's mind of confusion. He gripped her arm.

"Jean missing? "

Straining at the oars, skilfully steering the leaky boat between floating debris, Ezry Barker shouted above the turmoil:

"You hadn't ought to told him that yet, Sally-May! Ye see — " he cleared his voice desperately. "Ye see, Chris, they found Jean's roadster on a side street, only the wheels above water. 'Twas turned over. Empty! "

Chapter XXI

ON the curb of the sidewalk before the church
Jean had peered through rain and mist. Where
was her roadster? It had been a nightmarish day
from dawn to dark, but surely she had not dreamed
that she had parked it here? She looked up and down
the street starred with misty lights, each light reflected
on wet and glistening asphalt. Not so crowded as
when she had driven through. Had her car been
stolen? She had left it unlocked when she raced
back to retrieve her jewel-case. Why not, she had
expected to be inside a split minute, no more.

What should she do next? Rain rilled from her
soft hat, pelted her shoulders. Not a taxi in sight.
She couldn't stand on the curb forever. She would
better run back into the church. She could 'phone to
Hill Top from the study. Not so good! Luther Calvin
was waiting there. Serve him right if he waited all
night. After a trip to the Carter cottage on the river
bank in the storm would Christopher Wynne return to
the church? Not likely. Ezry was to close it in an
hour.

Ezry! He would take her home. Doubtless he
would monologue all the way, theme — her perversity,

The alternative to listening to his crabbing was to walk. She would be drenched. Better to wait for him. She need not listen to his tirade. She wouldn't sense much of it anyway. Now that the violence of shock and crying had passed she felt curiously light-headed, like a vacuum.

A vacuum perhaps, but she still could feel, she admitted, as she returned to the pew to await Barker's coming to put out the candles. Still could sense the peace, beauty, color of her surroundings. Her mind seemed like a huge ball of string, a mass of tangled thoughts. If she seized a loose end it led only to confusion. Why try to think? Why not rest in the security and comfort? Was her mother really on her way to Garston? Why? To explain the lie in her letter? Could she? Perhaps. Her imagination was her fortune. She must 'phone Harvey as soon as she reached Hill Top, tell him that she couldn't, just couldn't wear that emerald. Her breath caught in a ragged sob. Through her crept a dull ache as of a torn heart emerging from the soothing spell of an anæsthetic. She wouldn't let that agony get control again. She must do something. Jewel-case in hand she approached the chancel. Her troubled eyes wandered from altar to choir-stalls. The Organ! Why not test that while she waited?

Eager, interested, she examined the console. Nothing to daunt her there. Lightly she touched the ivory keys. Heavenly tone. Music stole through the silence, touched with sympathetic tenderness her raw heart.

Her fingers strayed from one lovely melody to another. Thought suspended, her spirit seemed to be floating in space, as though detached from her body it had gone adventuring into shadowy transepts, into rose-scented chancel, adown softly lighted nave.

A dull roar shook her back to actualities. An explosion? Swiftly she ran down the side aisle. Swung open the door. Dashed through the vestibule to the steps. Gazed incredulously. The main street was a river! Dotted with stalled cars! What was that dark cloud rolling toward her? A wave! A gigantic wave? Had the roar been the bursting of a dam? Carter had said:

" Floods north of us but we're safe enough unless the dam should go."

Safe enough! Where was he now? Where was Christopher Wynne? Where was her mother? Would she be warned of danger before she reached the flooded area?

A surge of water almost swept her from her feet. Precipitately she backed into the church her hypnotized gaze on the pursuing tide. Step by splashing step she retreated. Wave by oily wave the water lapped at her feet. She backed up the five stairs to the chancel. Fascinated eyes on the deepening water in the aisle, leaned against the altar. On either side the tall candles burned steadily, undisturbed, behind her the red roses breathed fragrance.

Safe! She drew an unsteady breath of relief. As though in derision a wave of angry water burst open the doors. A woman's blue hat fantastically crowned its peak. Swift, pitiless, it swept forward looting crimson cushions as it came. Through Jean's consciousness echoed her father's voice:

"Some day when you are caught in swift water, whirled, tossed, submerged —"

She dug her teeth into her lip to keep back a frightened sob. Coward! Knuckling at the first threat of danger. She wasn't tossed nor submerged yet.

"Pull yourself together!" she admonished. Sally-May would have said that. Sally-May! Where was she? Where was Hughie? Where — where was Christopher? At Carter's cottage on the river bank? If the main street were submerged what had happened there? She mustn't let her imagination loose. She must concentrate on getting above this flood. Then she might help others. The bell tower! Could she reach it without going through the church? There must be an exit from the chancel. That panel at the right was a door. The door which led to Christopher Wynne's study? Eagerly she pulled it open. Stumbled in sudden darkness. The lights were out! She clung to the handle of the door behind her dazed, uncertain. At one end of the room was a faint glow. The dying fire on the hearth. From out the blackness a metallic voice demanded:

"That you, Barker?"

Luther Calvin! She and old Stone Face alone in the church! She answered:

"It's not Barker. It is Jean Randolph."

"What do you mean by putting out the lights?"

Indignation proved a mighty gyroscope. It restored mental balance. There was a trace of mockery in Jean's voice as she demanded:

"*I* put out the lights? Don't you *know* that the town is flooded; don't you *know* that the church is filling with water; don't you *know* that you will be drowned if you stay where you are?"

His voice in the darkness took on a sepulchral tone:

"Drowned! *Drowned!* Do you think the Lord will let *me* drown? How would this church get on without me?"

All the contempt, all the fury he had inspired boiled up and over. Jean stormed:

"Get on without you! If you ask me I'll say a whole lot better. The congregation would have backed up Christopher Wynne in all he has tried to do if you hadn't interfered. If the Lord is on the job He will sweep you out with the tide along with that blue hat, clear His church of your narrow, bigoted —"

His harsh laugh sawed off the sentence.

"What have you done to this church and its minister? You're a malign influence. I felt it the first time I saw you at the Contessa's dinner with your naked back. Christopher Wynne couldn't keep his eyes off you that night. Your pagan grandmother is doing her best to ruin him. If he marries you his career will be finished. You, *you,* with your extravagant clothes, with a father who looks with covetous eyes upon a woman not his wife, with a mother —"

Jean hurled her jewel-case in the direction of the hateful voice. It struck something. Its contents

splashed into the water like a fusilade of bullets. Had
she silenced Luther Calvin for a time? Had she hit
him? She listened. Not a sound save the muffled
violence of the storm. Had she stunned him? Her
fury waned. The Terrible Twin again and she thought
that she had disposed of her forever. Suppose he were
unconscious on the floor? Suppose he were to drown?
She would be responsible. She must know. In the
inky blackness of the room her voice sounded weirdly
hollow as she called:

"Mr. Calvin. Mr. Calvin!"

No answer save the monotonous lap of water. What
could she do? There was no light. Feel her way
toward him? Go back? Go back for one of the
candles on the altar.

Swiftly she crossed the softly lighted chancel. With
a sense of desecration lifted a tall, wax taper from its
silver stick, shielded the wavering flame with one hand
as she returned to the door. She shivered. What
would she see? A man unconscious? Perhaps d-d-
dead? She set her teeth hard into her lip to stop their
chattering, lifted the light high.

She was at the top of three stairs in Christopher
Wynne's study. The flame of the candle was reflected
in numberless shimmers. The floor was covered with
water. Where was Luther Calvin?

Cautiously she splashed forward. The light cast
curious flickering shadows on the book-lined walls, on
deep chairs, on —

She laughed. Laughed till the dim corners flung

back the echo. Laughed till the candle in her hand wobbled treacherously. That sobered her. If that were to go out — she wouldn't let it. Cautiously she shielded the precious flame. She peered beyond it at the table-desk, met the fanatical glare of the man crouched in the middle of it. Unconscious! He? Nothing could be more alive than his agate eyes. She had thought for an instant, that a monkey on all fours had perched there. He looked like one she had seen in a Zoo. Sternly she repressed a spasmodic giggle. Never in her life before had she approached so near the borderland of hysterics. She wouldn't be a short-sport and let herself go now.

A fringe of glitter dangled from an edge of the desk. Her diamond bracelet. Hateful as the man was she must help him.

" I'll show you the way to the bell-tower, Mr. Calvin. You will be safe there."

No answer. Jean felt the water rising against her legs. Prodded indignantly:

" Hurry! "

As he still regarded her in stubborn silence she shrugged.

" Suit yourself. I'm going up."

She shielded the candle-light as she waded toward the hall door. She would rather lose her jewels forever, she decided, than go an inch nearer that hostile man to collect them. Her conscience pricked. Ought she to give him another chance? At the threshold she turned.

" Better come."

His reply echoed through the room like the clang of metal against metal:

" I told Mr. Wynne I would wait here. I *never* change my mind."

" Really! You and the Pyramids! Immovable! Do you mean that you won't let yourself grow? That always you will keep your mind in short trousers? Wait for him, then. I'm going up where it is dry."

She splashed her way into the hall. Wondered as she listened to the echo of her progress through the tomb-like silence if she should have dragged Luther Calvin to safety. Why worry? At present he was high and dry on the table-desk. She would much better watch her own step. The water clutched at her feet. One hand guarding the slender flame of light she struggled on. She reached the stairs. Gripped the rail. Pulled herself above the water level.

Slowly she mounted to the bell-tower. Water sloshed in her shoes at every step. With a feeling of security she sank upon the bench before the manual clavier. Drew a long breath. That was that! The flame of the candle flickered. Was it going out? Where was the flash-light Monsieur Bélique used about the keys?

With disturbed realization of the impermanence of the light she carried, she searched in a closet, on a shelf, pocketed a card of matches, she might need those. Having labored long and arduously to like smoking with no success, she didn't carry them. She returned to the clavier, found the flash-light in a nook apparently designed for no other purpose than to hold it. She pressed the switch. Light! A heavenly light.

Quickly she blew out the candle, laid it with the card of matches on a stand. She might need it again. Flash-lights were not immortal. Evidently the electric supply of the church had been cut off.

What next? Experimentally she curled her toes in her soaked shoes. Pulled off her rain-coat. As she sank into the capacious depths of the inviting leather chair she snapped off the current in the flash-light. Inky blackness! She wasn't mad about that. Even if she weren't she must conserve the light. How the wind shrieked! The tower fairly rocked. How the rain beat against it! Uncanny whispers among the rafters. Eerie rumbles in the bowels of the walls.

She shivered and curled deeper into the big chair. Wriggled her cold toes. The room was cooling off. The flood had put out the fires! That was the explanation. She would be chilled to the marrow before morning unless she could find some sort of covering. She could use the carilloneur's old coats!

She pressed the switch of the flash-light. Cautiously made her way to the bell-chamber. There they were! Top-coats. Short coats. Dark coats. Light coats. All shabby. Monsieur Bélique must have a coat complex. She piled three of the biggest, wooliest over one arm. Wrinkled a critical nose. Smelly things! Always she had hated the tobacco the bell-master used. She stopped an instant to listen to the fury of the storm.

Cautiously made her way back. Slipped her arms into one coat. Pulled off her wet shoes. Bundled feet and knees into another. Draped the third over her head and shoulders, settled deeply into the leather chair.

As warmth stole through her body her mind came wide awake. Was her father safe this horrible night? Had Christopher Wynne reached the Carter cottage? Could it stand against the rising water of the river? Oh, he must be safe! He must! Surely God wouldn't let anything happen to a man of such value to the world! God! Was she instinctively turning to Him? Calvin had said about Christopher:

"If he marries you his career will be finished."

Calvin! In the study! Alone! No fire! The man would be chilled into pneumonia. He had no extra coats for protection. There were several more in the bell-chamber. Could she get one to him?

She curled deeper into the warm nest she had made. Hadn't she urged and urged him to come to the tower? Let him chill! Insulting old hypocrite! The world, his daughters, the church would be infinitely better off without him. Just like him to be safely out of the turmoil when everyone else in the city who could would be breaking his neck to help, this fiendish night.

Everyone else! She wasn't helping. She was snuggling high above the flood while below her a man might be slowly getting his death from cold.

"Darn the Randolph conscience!" she sobbed as she threw off the coats. "I suppose I've got to try to help him." She tugged and stretched on her wet shoes.

"He couldn't see to follow me even if he tried."

Heavy coat over her arm, flash-light in hand she made her cautious way down the iron steps, down into the vault-like cold, the tomb-like silence of the lower floor. The last stair was covered with water. Not much higher than when she had gone up. She seemed to wade miles before she reached the study. The exertion took her breath. She leaned against the door as she flashed the light about the room. More nightmare? No one crouched on the table-desk like a monkey! No one in the room! The bracelet no longer glinted in the light.

Where was Luther Calvin? Had he waded to the street? Surely, if the water were ankle-high inside it would be feet deeper outside. Had he swum to safety? Had he been rescued? Not the last or he would have sent help to her. Whatever he had done, her responsibility was ended. She wouldn't carry the coat back. She looked about once more. Frowned at the pink carnations on the desk. Sue Calvin had put them there! With an inexplicable surge of fury Jean splashed forward, seized flowers and vase, flung them on the coals which once had been a fire. The tinkle of breaking glass gave infinite relief to the turmoil within her.

"You really are back again, aren't you, Terrible Twin," she said aloud and warily retraced her watery way to the stairs. At the top of the first flight, her light dimmed. Was it giving out? Horrible thought! Breathlessly she ran up to the next floor. If only she could reach the candle and matches in the bell-chamber while still there was a glimmer! Gone! She dropped to the stair. Leaned her head against the balustrade. It was frightfully cold. Looked as though she would have to sit there and freeze. She shook herself to her feet. Admonished contemptuously:

" Freeze! Short-sport! "

Resolutely she gripped the rail. In pitch blackness mounted the remaining stairs, wet skirts swishing about her knees. She stopped to visualize the location of the iron steps. Slowly, gropingly found them. Crawled up. Felt her way into the clavier room, stumbled against the leather chair and dropped into it. With shaking hands she piled the coats about her. Too tired to think, she leaned her head back and closed her eyes.

She dozed fitfully. Waking, flinched at the fury of wind and rain against the tower; sleeping, dreamed horrors. A lurid nightmare brought her up standing. Was she still dreaming or was the room lighter? She could distinguish outlines. The bench! Candle and matches. She didn't need them yet. She was stiff with cold. If she didn't move quickly she would freeze where she stood.

She groped her way to the bell-chamber. Was it light enough to see the havoc the night had wrought? She found the field glasses. Raised them to her eyes. Too dark for her to see. Was that the flying-field beacon silvering a great raft? Was it a raft? A roof! The searchlight was gone! There it was again! If only she could see! Feverishly she adjusted the

glasses. Better! Almost she could touch that thing
sticking up. It was a dormer! What dormer?
Carter's cottage? The floating roof! Two men on it!
One was waving his arms!

Christopher! Carter! *Christopher* in horrible danger! This hurt more than all the heart-ache of yesterday! A plane! Sweeping down upon the river!
Thank God! The men were lifting something into the
cockpit! The great winged thing swept forward! The
search-light remained steady. One man left on the
raft. One man waving his arms! He was gone!
Christopher in that furious river. Glasses at her eyes
Jean petitioned fervently:

"O God, save him! Please! I'll do the best I can
all the rest of my life if you will only save him! This
isn't a bribe! Really it isn't! I will try to be fine and
worth-while whether you save him or not. Please!
Please!"

Christopher was clinging to something! The steady
light shone on his shoulders. A boat! Where had it
come from? Could he keep up till it reached him? If
only she could help. Help?

The word struck a spark. She raced and stumbled
to the clavier. Steadied herself. With all her strength
set the bells to pealing:

"O God, our help in ages past,
  Our hope for years to come.
Our shelter from the stormy blast,
  And our eternal home."

Shivering with cold, dazed with fear and anguish, she played on and on. Struck the keys more and more feebly:

" I must keep on! I wonder — if I'm freezing — I'm so — so — " Her head fell forward in exhaustion.

A long, long blank. Her senses stirred. Was she really hearing voices? Men's voices? Another dream! She was too tired to raise her head.

" I knew when I heard those jangled bells — where we would find Jean! "

Was the voice really saying that or was she dreaming? Christopher's voice! It couldn't be. He was in the water! Perhaps she had died and — Arms caught her up and held her close. She was — somewhere where it was warm. From beyond an impenetrable fog came muffled voices:

" Jean! Jean! Listen, dear, your mother is in Garston hunting frantically for you."

Then one voice, hoarse, nearer, against her hair:

" Your bells gave me strength to hold on — darling. Open your eyes, Jean! "

Only Christopher called her — darling. If they wanted her to open her eyes she would, she supposed, though she was supremely warm — gloriously warm where she was. She lifted heavy lids. Looked up into burning dark eyes. Something within her numb brain clicked. Distinctly she heard a metallic voice warn:

" If he marries you his career will be finished."

Christopher's career! More important than for her to be happy. With all her strength she twisted free of tightening arms. The fog was lifting. Her mother — hunting frantically — why? She could distinguish faces, drawn, haggard. Christopher! Hughie! Harvey!

With strangled sob she held out her hands:

"Harvey! I knew you'd come. Your career won't be finished if you marry me. Will it? Hold me close. I'll never be warm again!"

She was slipping! Slipping! She clung to a wet sleeve, heard herself implore:

"Don't let me go, Harvey! Swift water! It's sweeping me to — him! Don't let me go!"

Chapter XXII

THROUGH a window, stripped of hangings and veiling net, Jean Randolph looked down upon an Avenue, upon the world's richest street, brimming with billions, representing three miles of millionaires. A Christmas crowd. Hurrying, jostling, good-natured, each individual steaming along at high on his own power as evidenced by frosty breath, gift laden, as evidenced by the red-ribbon tied packages under an arm. At the corner a portly Santa with an intriguing placard and a coin-box, prominently displayed, stamped leather booted feet. A stream of traffic, luxurious limousines and their less pretentious relatives — country cousins many of them — innumerable taxis, poured down one side of the roadway, poured up the other.

The girl gazed unseeingly at the distant wreath-bedecked windows. How the pattern of her life had changed in the weeks which had passed since last she had looked down upon the Avenue. Her mother was gone . . . forever. Jean shut her teeth hard into her lip to shut back an exclamation of pain. Her heart was twisted unbearably whenever she thought of that moment in the Contessa's great music room when she had been told. Madelaine Randolph had come to Garston to find her daughter. "To explain" she had kept repeating, "to explain!" When she learned that Jean was missing she had gone out into the storm alone, in a reckless search. She had not seen her husband, who was frantically hunting for his daughter. She had joined the newsreel men on the cliff — even in her turmoil of spirit it would be characteristic for her to store in her memory every tragic detail of that night — then the landslide and — swift water.

Swift water! That phrase of Hughie's seemed seared into her mind, Jean thought. She turned away from the window and glanced about the dismantled living room which once had been the rendezvous of the distinguished, the beautiful, the witty, the arrived and the arriving, but, never, never of the dull. Not much holiday spirit inside. The furniture stood in crates, pictures were boxed, china barreled. The logs sputtering and blazing in the fireplace seemed the one warmly human element. Only her mother's great desk and chair, a deep-seated couch, a little stand remained unpacked. She had kept those out for her own use while she remained in the apartment, which already had passed into other, eagerly awaiting hands.

She seated herself at the desk to resume the interminable task of sorting and destroying letters. Heart-wringing business this, dismantling a home out of which the occupant had stepped unknowing that she

never would return. Day had followed unreal day
— like dull beads on a string which Time relentlessly
counted off one by one — as she had sorted and disposed
of her mother's intimate belongings. Letters to be
read before destroying, others to be tossed unopened
into the fire as though they scorched her fingers;
stopping to re-live an occasion which the mere folding
of a gown had conjured from a care-free past; gaz-
ing down upon a box of intricately carved gold, seeing only the shimmer of the aquamarine sea before the
little shop where her mother had bought it; reading
through blinding tears, " Jean's first shoe " on the sole
of the bit of leather she had found in the strong box.
A short dark curl was there too, a marriage certificate.
The shawls had been the hardest to touch. Warm
colors, all of them. Gay, embroidered, dripping with
fringes, delicately fragrant with perfume. They
brought back the imperious lift of her mother's head,
the laughter of her flashing dark eyes, the ivory tint of
her lovely throat, the grace with which she had flung
one gorgeous corner over her shoulder, Spanish fashion.
They were alive with their owner's personality. Of
one fact these tragic weeks had convinced her, that in
spite of Madelaine Randolph's seeming absorption in
career and friends her daughter had been very dear to
her. That knowledge helped immeasurably.

A hand touched Jean's shoulder. Startled she
looked up. Letters scattered in a white drift on the
rug.

" H-Harvey! " she stammered. She glanced at the
door behind him.

Brooke's usually laughing eyes were steady with determination as they met hers. Hands on her shoulders he held her facing him as he commanded:

" Don't beat up Rosa for letting me in. She did her best as a watch-dog, but she couldn't resist my sunny smile. You and I have a little matter to settle. Why have you refused to see me? Why did you return this? "

He released her to show the gleaming green stone in his open palm. Jean only partially controlled a shudder.

" I — I — can't bear the sight of an emerald, Harvey."

Quickly he dropped the ring into his pocket.

"That goes for that. Perhaps you wouldn't let me come because you couldn't bear the sight of me? "

" Oh, no, not *that!* "

" What is it then? In love with Wynne? "

The sound as of many waters thundered in Jean's ears. She disclaimed passionately:

" Wynne! Christopher Wynne! You're mad, Harvey."

Brooke shrugged.

" Methinks the lady doth protest too fervently. I suspect that you are. Know why? " He hurried on before she could speak:

" I will go back to that fearful night of the flood to make you understand. After I landed the Carters at the flying field — having valiantly resisted an urge to chuck the woman overboard when I discovered that

Wynne had given up his chance at safety for her —
I sent the plane up again to try to help. Lost my
bearings. The face of the country had been changed
by the rush of water. I flubbed round for awhile,
finally crashed in the clearing in front of your log-
house, lighted as though for a party. No casualties,
except to the plane.

" If I live the one hundred and fifty years the scien-
tists are allowing us now, I'll never forget that cabin
room as I entered it."

He cleared his throat vigorously, leaned an arm on
the mantel, kept his eyes on the smoldering logs as
he went on gruffly:

" The Reverend Christopher was near the fire, coat-
less, wet trousers clinging to his legs, shoes oozing
puddles of water, ragged, soaked shirt clinging to his
shoulders, eyes like burning coals in his ghastly face.
Your father was staring at the man in dripping rain-
coat who had been sent by the Contessa to tell him
that his wife was out in flood and storm hunting for
her daughter. Constance Wynne was holding out a
steaming cup to her brother. She didn't care for anything but to get Christopher warm. Sally-May was
on the couch with a brown setter either side of her.
Those dogs knew what was happening as well as she
did, you should have seen their eyes. Good Lord, that
kid's a sport. It was she who thought of the lamps,
of the boat in the cabin, she, who with Barker and a
stranger whom they pressed into service, had dragged
that old leaky boat of yours down the trail.

" God! What a nightmare! Wynne was about crazy when he learned that you were missing. I can't live that scene over. When his mind snapped back to normal, he remembered the bells. Stuck to it that you had played them. That you were in the tower."

Jean pressed her hands over her eyes.

" This too much for you, Jean? "

" Go on! Go on, Harvey. I never have known really what happened. I couldn't bear to bring the memory of that awful night back to Hughie. Doubtless he had felt the same with me. What next? "

" We rushed Wynne home, stood over him till he got into dry clothing — he wanted to start on the hunt for you as he was — then paddled our way to the church. Found you huddled over the clavier. When Wynne caught you in his arms you looked up at him as though — as though suddenly you'd got everything in life you wanted. Then you pushed him away and called frantically for me."

Jean twisted cold fingers.

" I wasn't really responsible, Harvey. Talk about nightmare — " she shivered.

" I know, Jean, I know. But, you don't love me, do you? " His boyish voice broke. " Don't be afraid to tell old Harvey the truth."

" I do love you, I do, but — "

" Not enough to marry me. Your father is right. No man should start out as second choice when the first choice is lurking round the corner. That's all. There isn't any more."

Jean clasped her hands on his sleeve.

"Harvey! Have I ruined your life?"

He patted her fingers, grinned with stiff lips:

"No girl can ruin my life, Jean — unless she marries me while loving another man. I'd rather have you for my wife than any woman in the world but if I can't have you — "

"Happy Christmas, everybody!" Fanchon Farrell in green frock and turban, ocelot coat, a silver-papered, red-ribbon-tied, holly-garnished package under her arm, beamed at them from the threshold as she explained:

"Your father told me to ignore Rosa's protests, to fight my way in, if necessary. He thought you needed a girl friend all sweetness and light to play with. That's me."

Brooke's gravity dissipated like a light cloud before a touch of sun.

"I'll say it is. Now that you've come, I'll go."

Jean felt tongue-tied. What could she say to him that wouldn't rouse Fanchon's suspicions. He came to her rescue. Always one could depend upon Harvey in a social crisis.

"Sorry I can't take you out tonight as we planned, Jean, but I'm off on the midnight for Chicago."

Fanchon wailed:

"Chicago! Harvey Brooke! Aren't you to be in Garston for the Christmas eve celebration? Everybody's keeping open house!"

She was distractingly lovely as she looked up at him,

blue eyes pleading, a fluff of golden hair beneath the
brim of her green toque, teeth like pearls between
lovely lips, skin like rose-petals. As she looked at her
Jean felt colorless, lifeless. The loneliness and sorrow
of the last few weeks pressed down upon her like a
tangible burden. Brooke was staring at Fanchon as
at a revelation. He took a step nearer, promised gaily:

"After all, I won't go to Chicago. I will be at your
party." He flushed boyishly as he met Jean's eyes.

"Any objection?"

Suddenly life and the zest of living surged back
through Jean, like a returning tide.

"Objections, Harvey! I'm all for it. Good luck!"

As with a sheepish grin Brooke departed she invited
cordially:

"Don't stand as though you were about to fly away,
Fanchon. Sit by the fire? Have a cigarette?"

Miss Farrell withdrew her intent gaze from the
direction of the door. Observed as she sank upon the
couch:

"For the first time in our acquaintance Harvey
Brooke really looked at me." A green enameled lighter
waggled its red tongue of flame as she inquired with
exaggerated indifference:

"Turned him down, Jean?"

"Harvey and I are wonderful friends, nothing more,
Fanchon."

"I could see *that*. I couldn't bear the idea of your
being alone the day before Christmas. I know that
your father is coming tomorrow, he told me, but, what

a gosh-awful place in which to spend the holiday."
She glanced disdainfully about the dismantled room.
"You're the saving grace in that mauve frock, you
poor dear. Had you been in black I should have burst
into tears."

Sympathetic kindliness under the flippancy. Jean
understood. Perched on the table-desk she explained
soberly:

"Hughie asked me not to wear mourning. He
thinks we owe it to ourselves and our friends not to
carry an impression of gloom. We are not dining here
tomorrow, but at an hotel. I feel a little guilty about
deserting the Contessa but — "

My dear, don't worry about her. She has taken a
new lease of life since that — that — well, Garston
generally speaks of it as ' that awful night.' She has a
new scheme. She and Signor Zambaldi are to finance
young singers while they are working for the national
music scholarships which are being offered. I think at
last she has given up all hope of luring Christopher
Wynne into opera."

"Has he resigned? "

"Resigned! Haven't you heard? The congreation
of the Community Church has settled down once more.
Chris isn't the person who has resigned, it's Luther
Calvin. He was pushed out — practically."

"He pushed! I should as soon think of trying to
roll that granite boulder in front of my log-cabin down
hill. Who was the giant who performed the miracle? "

"A composite giant, the congregation. Haven't you

heard that it rose in its might and slew him — figuratively speaking — when it discovered that he had left you in the church the night of the flood? "

The dismantled living room faded into a hazy background against which Jean saw herself stealing down the stairs in an attempt to rescue Calvin. She could hear her feet splashing through water to the door of Christopher Wynne's study, felt again her surprise and consternation when she discovered that the late occupant of the table-desk had disappeared. She never had known what became of him, never had known how she had reached Hill Top. She had a dazed remembrance of being suddenly warm after being chilled to the bone, of men's voices, of the splash of water. As soon as possible after the service for her mother she had gone to the New York apartment. In her letters to her father she had not asked for news, he had refrained from giving any. She had lived as in a dream. Nothing had seemed real. Quite suddenly she felt that she must know all that was happening in Garston. She prodded eagerly:

" Go on, Fanchon. How did he get away? "

Fanchon crossed silken knees in the pose which hosiery advertisements have immortalized, blew an experimental smoke-ring into the air before she answered:

" His chauffeur had been told to return to the church for him at a certain time. He returned on a raft. Calvin said nothing to him about your being in the church, on the contrary hurried him away. When your father and the others reached the study, they found your jewels scattered on the wet floor, the case burst open. Then they found you."

She lighted a fresh cigarette before she went on:

"The horrible calamity is an Arabian Night's tale of wonders performed. I'll say one thing for it, it worked a miraculous cure. Lucy Carter's doing a day's work seven days a week not excepting Sundays and holidays. Specialists are now prescribing seaplane trips and flood as a cure for her special malady. As a g-grand and smashing climax, Luther Calvin demanded that the minister of the Community Church be indicted for having assisted in the escape of a felon."

"Assisted!"

"That's what he claimed. Just as though Chris had staged the gale which ripped off the roof of the Carter cottage, had prestidigitated the dormer, to which the bandit was clinging, into the flood."

"What did the authorities say?"

"Say! Having had the real story from Carter they laughed at him. That was the last straw for the long-suffering committee. It rose to a man — for once Dad saw red and saw it bloody — ousted Calvin and told Chris that he could do as he pleased in the church, that they didn't want his valuable time wasted raising money. And after all the hullabaloo there isn't any money to raise. Within twenty-four hours the parish had contributed the sum it had been haggling over for weeks, to aid the flood sufferers, and had politely but firmly informed the Contessa that it didn't care for her gift. Immediately Luther Calvin flung his real estate upon a lethargic market, took his two daughters and started around the world. Exit the Calvins from the city of Garston. Christopher Wynne must be grateful. One girl out of the way."

" Does he seem — grateful? "

Fanchon's blue eyes clouded.

" One never can tell what he feels. He has changed. He looks horribly thin. I suppose he hasn't yet forgotten his experiences on the Carter roof. His voice is still hoarse, has the most fascinating little croak, but, he doesn't laugh as he used." Jean sensed an implication in her voice as she added:

" Perhaps he is sorry that his sister is leaving him."

" Leaving! "

" Hadn't you heard? She is going abroad on a business trip. Sails New Year's day. I must go. I have a lot still to do at home. Chris is coming with the carol singers after the service, for hot coffee. The city will glow tonight. Lighted candles in windows, living Christmas trees blossoming with colored bulbs on every lawn, and a Community Church service. Chris Wynne is wonderful at any time, but his Christmas eve service is priceless. It might even touch you and you are the hardest-boiled female I know." She giggled. " I thought that long before this I would win your yellow roadster."

Eyes on the blinking, purring logs, Jean reminded:

" You were to get that only if I went to church because — of a man."

Fanchon fastened the collar of her fur coat. Laughed. Assured:

" I still have hopes. Too bad that you can't be with us tonight, but, I suppose you are not going out socially."

It rather sounded as though Fanchon were *afraid* that she might come, Jean decided. Aloud she said:

" Oh, I go out. Hughie believes that I need people and lights and music more than at any time in my life. I don't go to balls because I don't feel like balls, but I enjoy other things." An overwhelming desire seized her, she heard her own voice saying:

" I may drop in on you tonight. I shall go back to Garston this afternoon."

Chapter XXIII

HOURS later Jean stopped her yellow roadster on the bridge outside the city of Garston. Lights illumined the devastation the flood had wrought. An iron trestle twisted as though it had been part of a boy's toy railroad; a bush caught in the high branches of a tree, like a centipede trapped in a Gargantuan web; a shed leaning tipsily above the water; a crude fence to warn visitors away from the vicinity of the caved-in bank which was having its face lifted.

As a few experimental flakes of snow dotted the windshield Jean started her car. Resumed the train of thought which had been sidetracked. What driving force had sent her back to Hill Top? Not merely an impulse to combat Fanchon's self-satisfaction. The urge had persisted. She had called her father on long distance. His alarmed voice had responded:

" Anything wrong? "

And she had answered:

" No, Hughie. Would you be horribly disappointed if we had our Christmas at Hill Top? "

She could feel his surprise before he assured:

" Disappointed! Nothing I'd like better. The Contessa has been deeply hurt because you were staying away."

" Then I will come today. Rosa has a date with Italian relatives. I'll drive down. Don't wait dinner, I may be late. Things to finish here. Good-bye."

Mile after mile she had driven, time after time under her breath she had repeated Harvey Brooke's turbulent question:

" Are you in love with Wynne? "

Suppose she were, she asked herself. Suppose she were in love with Christopher Wynne? Did he really want her? She had had no word from him since she had left Garston. Luther Calvin had said that his career would be finished if she married him, but, Luther Calvin was discredited, he was out of the picture. Whenever during these last tragic weeks Rosa had brought in a tray of letters she had looked them over, heart pounding. Never anything from Christopher. If he really cared could he have kept from writing to her, coming to her? The Contessa had said that love was ecstasy, agony, suffering. She would say that it was slow torture, a monstrous nightmare of self doubt. But — even supposing that he still wanted her, could she make herself into the sort of woman who would help, not hinder him in his chosen work? She, who seldom had attended church. She, who never had said a prayer?

The last thought pressed a button in her memory. Promptly it released a series of pictures. She saw herself in the bell-tower watching the great light from the flying-field reveal tragedy and devastation; a swooping plane, a floating roof, a man signalling frantically for help, a man plunged into the rapacious river. As plainly as though it were being radioed she heard her own frantic petition:

" O God, save him! "

So that was prayer. In her terror instinctively she had turned for help to the Infinite, to a faith which had been bred into her, to a faith which had lain dormant, unsuspected. Christopher Wynne had said:

" Prayer becomes intensely real, intensely sustaining as a narrow conception of spiritual values broadens into faith."

The petition had steadied her. Had it inspired her to play the carillon? Muffled as though from beyond a thick fog Christopher Wynne's voice came back to her:

" Your bells gave me strength to hold on."

Never again could she be indifferent to spiritual values, deny their influence upon the conduct of her life. Never again be indifferent to spiritual values? Did that mean — ?

For the first time since the tragic night of the flood she laughed aloud. She patted the steering wheel with one gloved hand, confided with exaggerated sympathy:

" Hope you will like your new green coat, old dear. Fanchon doesn't care for you in yellow."

Snow fell with feathery daintiness as she entered the city, drove along the hillside road. It lay like diamond dust on men's shoulders. With fantastic convolutions it transformed wrought iron gates and balconies into marble carvings of amazing beauty. It capped chimneys. It lay like drifted, sparkling down on roofs and dormers. Everywhere trees had blossomed with crimson, green, gold and silver lights. An enchanted world. Candles flickered in wreathed windows which afforded tantalizing glimpses of package-laden, tinsel-fringed spruces. Through the snowy air drifted the music of bells, rhyming, chiming, joyously proclaiming:

" Noel! Noel! "

As the last lingering note drifted down the river to the sea Jean looked at her wrist watch. Fanchon had said there would be a church service. She was too late for the beginning — she might slip in in time for the final hymn.

As she stopped before the door at Hill Top whose every window was a-gleam with candles, a snowy figure stepped into the light of the car lamps. Ezry Barker to welcome her home! He caught the hands she eagerly extended:

" By mighty, here you be, Jean! A happy Christmas! Your Pa's gone to church with Miss Wynne. They waited for you till the last minute, then I told 'em as how I'd stay here till you come."

" Ezry, you're a dear! Want to do something for me? "

" If it's for the Turrible Twin, I don't."

Jean laughed. Put her lips close to his great hairy ear, warned theatrically:

" Hist! Speak low! I think I have given her the slip! "

Barker chuckled.

" By mighty, Jean, you're like the little girl I knew,

all twinkle, twinkle, like Christmas sparklets. What you want I should do?"

"Send my bags upstairs. I will drive to church. Have a man on hand to take this roadster to Miss Farrell's house when I get back. He must see her, tell her that Miss Randolph sent the car."

"Send the roadster to that Farrell girl! You jokin', Jean?"

"No, Ezry. I have lost it on a bet. I will run over to the Left Wing for a moment before I go."

Contessa di Fanfani in a thin black frock and pearls, was seated in an elaborately carved chair in her music room. Her head with its ruddy crown of beautifully waved hair rested against the high back. She flung off the suggestion of languor as Jean entered. Her greeting was tinged with emotion:

"*Dio mio!* My dear child! I did not know that you were coming."

Jean held tightly to the fragile hands in hers.

"I — I couldn't stay away. You and Hughie are all that I have."

She put one hand to her throat in an attempt to ease the contraction. The Contessa indicated a chair beside her.

"Sit there, Jean, while I talk to you." Her brilliant eyes were suddenly ringed by dark shadows as she ruthlessly broke down the wall of reserve which the girl had so painfully built up.

"I do not know what you stumbled upon that day you went to the apartment of your mother. I do not want to know. Whatever it was it sent her here that night as fast as a plane could bring her. She burst in upon me here demanding:

" ' Where is Jean, Mother? I must see her. I must talk with her. Jean misunderstood something. I swear that she misunderstood. I can't lose her. I can't. She is all I have, Mother, all I have. Help me to make her understand.' "

The Contessa cleared a real break from her musical voice, lightly brushed real tears from her dark eyes before she went on:

" After awhile she rushed out into the storm to find you. You know what happened. Christopher Wynne would say, ' She stepped into the next room.' I wonder —"

Her voice faded into a whisper, her head dropped forward, her brilliant eyes in their dark shadows stared ahead as though trying to pierce an invisible veil. The fire purred gently, diffused the pungent scent of burning wood. From far away came the faint music of a carol. Jean moved. The Contessa shook off the spell of absorption. Her voice held its customary ironic thread as she informed:

" The Community Church has refused my gift. *Dio mio!* Just as well now that Signor Calvin is not here to hold the purse-strings. Christopher Wynne must be thankful to have him and his daughter out of his way." She snickered. " Some day I will bribe that Sally-May girl to tell me what her uncle said when he refused the proposal of the granite Susie."

" She won't tell."

" Oh, yes she will. There is more than one way to get what one is after. I — " she left the sentence unfinished. Had she remembered that she had used those very words in regard to forcing a certain minister into opera? If she did she gave no sign as she added:

" Signor Zambaldi will arrive later to hear a remarkable voice. One of the carol singers. He has no religion-complex. I discovered him. The Wynnes are coming in after the service to help me entertain. I shall expect you, Jean."

After the service! Would she be too late to hear any of it? With an incoherent explanation Jean hurriedly departed. On the way to the church she mentally repeated over and over:

" Jean misunderstood something. I swear that she misunderstood."

Whenever, after this in the dark, the picture of her mother as she had last seen her alive blazed before her eyes she would force the Contessa's description of Madelaine Randolph's frenzied plea for understanding in its place.

The church was full to the doors when she reached it. Those taller than she pushed her forward till she stood at the front of the group. The aisle, like a broad, velvet path, stretched between her and the chancel. The surpliced choir sang with lusty fervor. The atmosphere was scented with the spicy fragrance of fir and balsam. Everywhere Christmas greens, the red of holly, myriad spear-heads of candle flame, fitfully illuminating the letters of gold and lapis and green above the altar, below them —

Jean's heart stood still. Raced on. Was that really Christopher Wynne? That impressive figure in the black gown? He was singing. His voice soared above the choristers. If only the Contessa could hear him, see him, could see the rapt, uplifted faces of the congregation, she must realize the power, the influence wielded by his voice in his church.

How far away, how terrifyingly remote he seemed. He love her, Jean Randolph! Not really. He had had a heart-storm, that was all. It would pass. Better for them both if she had not come back. If —

The song stopped on a triumphant note. The man in the chancel raised a commanding arm. As though moved by a master-mind the congregation sank to its knees, heads bowed. The power and the reverence in that upheld hand touched the group standing at the doors. With one accord men and women knelt and carried Jean down with them. For an instant she was achingly self-conscious, embarrassed. She forgot self as the rich voice petitioned:

" And now may the Grace of God
which passeth all understanding
be and abide with you all
through this joyous Christmas
season. May the candles on your
trees and in your windows
leave a lovely light which shall
linger in your hearts and homes
throughout the year."

"Amen! Amen!" softly chanted the choristers. The organ swelled into triumphant acclaim.

Jean wedged her way through a jostling crowd, a "Merry Christmas" crowd. Her face burned from embarrassment. Had she made herself horribly conspicuous kneeling at the entrance to that velvet aisle? She would have been more so, had she stood upright. Why shouldn't she have knelt? Before Christopher's upraised hand there seemed nothing else to do. If only she were not so afraid to show emotion. The Randolph reserve again.

She drove slowly in the wake of the swaying crowd which followed the carol singers. It formed a rhythmic pattern through which were woven barbaric strands of color, melodious harmonies of sound. A reverent crowd, as though to each and all the mystic function of the flickering candles in wreath-hung windows — to light the Christ Child on his way — was real, significant. The snow fell softly, whitening shoulders, rimming hats. As she sent her car up the drive to Hill Top the music of a carol rose from below:

> "O little town of Bethlehem
> How still we see thee lie!
> Above thy deep and dreamless sleep
> The silent stars go by."

A man appeared from the shadow to take the roadster. Ezry had not forgotten. Before she entered the house she looked up at the gleaming candles in the window, said softly:

" May they leave a lovely light."

" 'O little town of Bethlehem,' " she hummed as she entered the evergreen-hung library. Her father came forward eagerly, caught her hands.

" It's wonderful to have you back, Jean! "

She smiled up at him, her eyes brilliant with tears, her lips unsteady.

" It is wonderful to have you to come back to, Hughie." Her hands tightened on his. "You are looking simply gorgeous. What's happened? Discovered the Fountain of Youth? "

There was a note of emotion in his laugh.

" If not that, its first cousin. What changed your plans, dear," he asked as he took her otter coat.

She pulled off her soft turban which matched in color the amethyst velvet of her simple frock. Arm on the mantel, one slightly snow dampened shoe on the fender she looked up at the cavalier with his curled, brown hair, his rich red doublet, his plumed hat, at his strong hand on the rapier, at his compelling eyes. Her voice was unsteady as she repeated her father's question:

" What changed my plans? The spirit of my ancestors, Hughie." She hurried on before he could reply: "I hope that my return hasn't spoiled your tomorrow."

" Spoiled it! It has made it perfect. I feared that coming here might be hard for you, so planned for our holiday in the city. You know, you must know, Jean, that I love Constance Wynne. If it seems to you too

soon after your mother's passing for me to acknowledge it, remember that for years past she and I have
been as strangers, you the only bond between us."

Remember! Did Hughie know? She must not look
back. Her mother had said,

"Jean misunderstood! I swear that she misunderstood."

She slipped her arm within her father's.

"You can't be happy too soon to content me. I
would love to tell Constance that."

"Thank you. The Wynnes are helping the Glorious
Fanfani to keep open house for the carol singers. We
will see them there. Meanwhile, what is the situation
between you and Harvey Brooke?"

"A closed chapter. I found out the night of the
flood that I didn't care for him enough to marry him."

"Has she come?" demanded a breathless voice from
the threshold. As Hugh Randolph turned, Sally-May
Wynne exclaimed, "I see her." She dashed into the
room, preceded by the silky-haired setters. There was
snow on her brown beret, on the shoulders of her
goatskin coat, on the toes of her beige overshoes. The
Rover Boys shook off a shower of diamond drops before they squatted at either side of her like sentinels.
She held out a small, red ribboned package. The dogs
followed her every motion with their softly brilliant
eyes.

"For me?" Jean asked.

"Open it."

Quickly Jean slipped off the Christmasy wrapping.

Why should Sally-May bring her a gift? She lifted the cover of the small box. On a white satin bed lay a shining silver pin. A lamp. A tiny lamp. On its base the one word, Courage. On a card in a stiff, girlish hand was written:

> " The W.Vs. have the honor to
> inform you that you have
> been unanimously elected to
> fill the vacancy in the
> membership of the society."

Jean's troubled eyes met Sally-May's eager, expectant, behind their strong lenses, as she protested:

" But — but why honor me? "

" See what it says on that lamp? Courage. That was Flo's. She's gone. Forever, I guess," Sally-May swallowed an apparent obstacle in her throat. " The W.Vs. selected you in her place because you saved Uncle Chris the night of the flood."

" I saved him! "

" When you played the carillon. He said he was all in when the sound of the bells put fresh courage into him. Gee whiz! Why ask so many questions? Aren't you *glad* you're elected? "

Jean fastened the shining silver lamp to the old lace of her amethyst velvet frock.

" I am, Sally-May. I am! I will try my best to be an honor to the society."

" Then that's all right." The setters dashed before

her to the door, red tongues hanging, tails furiously wagging, waited for her as she stopped on the threshold to protest:

" I'm sick about your being engaged to that silly Harvey Brooke. I thought with W.V. training you'd be almost good enough for Uncle Chris. C'mon, Rover Boys! "

Followed the rush as of an able-bodied tornado through the hall, the distant bang of a door. Jean looked up at her father.

" Almost good enough for him? He must realize that I'm not even that. Hughie, I — I — haven't heard a word from him since I left here." She replaced wrapping and ribbon about the small box with meticulous care.

" You were engaged to Brooke when you left, weren't you? When we found you in the tower you thrust Christopher away for him."

" I know — I — is the Contessa really rid of her obsession to have him give up the ministry? "

" I hope so. Since the night of the flood she has not mentioned it. I think for the first time in her life she has realized what a man may accomplish in that profession. Christopher give up the ministery! God forbid! We need some native blood to take the place of the great New England clergy of the past. Are we to import all our influential preachers? " He lightened his voice: " Let's chuck problems. Let's be care-free tonight, Jean. You will help the Contessa entertain the carol singers and her guests, won't you? "

"If you think that my presence will not be misunderstood so soon after mother's going."

He put his hands on her shoulders, gravely met her questioning eyes.

"Don't let your sense of loss shadow the lives of others. Your grandmother, in spite of Carlotta's magic, is aging. She has missed you. It is Christmas, Jean. I hope that it may prove the happiest you and I have ever known." He released her. Suggested practically:

"We will enter the Left Wing from the front door. Want you to look down upon the lighted city. I will be back in a moment."

As he left the room Jean gently touched the shining silver pin in the lace of her frock. She a W.V.! Nothing wise about her. She had messed up her own life tragically. Would Christopher Wynne ever again tell her he loved her? Dear of Sally-May, though. If only she had a gift for her! Had she anything the child would like? Her eyes lingered on a shelf of books high up, her books, rare editions. She might give her one of those.

She rolled the steps before the shelf, mounted. Became absorbed in selection. Pilgrim's Progress! The very thing for Sally-May's present phase. Her father back again? She called over her shoulder as she pulled out a book:

"In a minute, Hughie! I am selecting a present for Sally-May."

"Don't I get one?" inquired a voice from the foot of the steps.

At the imminent danger of pitching headlong Jean turned. Christopher Wynne!

Was it really he? Really the same man whom she had seen in his black gown but a little while ago? Then he had seemed almost — almost divine. Now in his dark sack suit he seemed human, disturbingly human. The eyes looking up at her were alight with laughter, laughter which only partially veiled smoldering fire. She gripped her book tight as she dropped to a step out of reach of his extended hand. The room seemed uncannily still. The cavalier over the mantel tactlessly attentive, her mind alarmingly empty of ideas. She must say something. What?

" Coming down or — shall I come up? "

Hugging the book close Jean retreated a step. She had a sense of having run far and fast as she protested breathlessly:

" Don't come up! The — the steps aren't too strong."

" Afraid of me? Pull yourself together! " he imitated Sally-May's intonation to a note.

Jean's courage, which his sudden appearance had sent into a tail-spin, righted, soared:

" Nice way you have of saying, ' Welcome to our city, Lieutenant.' "

He took a purposeful step up.

" Coming down? "

Jean valiantly disciplined the tumult of her pulses, the aching longing to fling herself into his arms. Evaded:

" What's the hurry? " Desperately she tried to make her voice gaily indifferent, to keep all hint of hurt from it as she went on:

" I haven't been far away these last weeks and you haven't — cared to see me, you haven't even written."

For answer he lifted her from the steps as he might pick an apple from a tree, set her on her feet beside him, tossed the book under her arm to the table-desk, held her by the shoulders as he reminded:

" Play fair — darling. You were engaged to Harvey Brooke, weren't you? " As she remained mute he spread her slim rosy-tipped fingers on the palm of his hand.

" Ring gone? "

She nodded without lifting her eyes.

" I knew that you would not marry him once you had a chance to think things through. Alone in your mother's apartment I knew that you would get that chance. Perhaps if I hadn't had every moment filled trying to help here I wouldn't have been such a Spartan but," he crushed the slim fingers in his, " I have been tragically needed." He added softly:

" Miss me? Afraid to let me see your eyes? "

The telephone on the desk rang furiously. Jean feeling as though she were struggling free of a magician's spell, picked up the receiver:

" Hill Top! "

An excited giggle. Fanchon Farrell's voice:

" Jean! Do you mean it? "

With a furtive glance at Christopher Jean pressed transmitter close to her lips, said softly:

" I always pay my bets."

Was the squeal of exultation audible to the silent man behind her, she wondered. She suggested crisply:

" See you later, Fanchon."

As she hung up the receiver Christopher demanded

" So — you've lost your roadster? "

" Yes — I — made a silly bet with Fanchon when I first came that — that — "

" If ever you went to church — because of a man, you would give it to her. I heard of it soon, — very soon, — after you came here. She hasn't won the car. Why did you go tonight? Not because of me, did you? "

Her eyes wide with surprise met his:

" Did you know that I was there? "

" Did I know? " He steadied his voice. " You didn't go because of me, did you? "

" I — I — think not. The first time I went into your church it did something to me here." She laid her hand on her heart. Asked wistfully, " Sounds like sheer sentimentality, doesn't it? "

" Not to me. Some reach faith through a personality, some through nature, why not through the atmosphere of a church? All sorts and conditions of people can get comfort from the intangible spirit in any place of worship, where there might be nothing of universal appeal in the sermon."

Jean took a step nearer.

" You seemed like a different person in your black gown. Like a stranger. So remote — so — "

" Remote! I! Remote! Come here! "

He caught her in his arms. His turbulent eyes seemed to probe to the depths of her heart as he reminded:

" Remember saying that you wanted an honest-to-goodness lover? " He bent his head to hers. After a long moment demanded huskily:

" Well? "

The touch of his lips, the caressing richness of his voice swept Jean's mind and soul clear of doubt, of sorrow, of disillusionment. She felt outrageously gay, and young and carefree as she teased:

" I wouldn't have believed that a clergyman could be so human."

Christopher Wynne's arms tightened about her. His voice and eyes were grave as he repeated:

" Human! Who needs more to be human than the man who wants to minister to his people with sympathy and understanding? I — "

" Oh, Jean! " Hugh Randolph was half way into the room before the significance of the situation registered. " Sorry! But — but — oh well, come along to the Left Wing — when — when you are ready, children." His exit partook of the nature of a rout.

Cheeks burning Jean crushed on her soft hat. She refused to meet Wynne's disturbing eyes as he held her coat. Pilgrim's Progress under her arm she ran through the hall. On the porch she stopped to look down upon roofs sparkling as though frosted with diamond-dust, upon white carpeted streets, amber lights, the pyramid of red and green which was the

Community Tree. From below rose the music of a carol, from afar drifted the bay of a lonely dog, from the singing tower rang out the bells:

> "It came upon a midnight clear
>   That glorious song of old
> From angels bending near the earth
>   To touch their harps of gold."

Jean put hand to throat. The music had tightened it unbearably. What magic did the story of the birth of the Christ Child possess that it should come down through the years — almost two thousand of them — to be acclaimed again tonight by all peoples and all nations? Deep within her consciousness she felt a stirring as of a force awakening, preparing to buckle on its shield. Was the day coming when she would walk side by side with the man she loved, in his work, in his faith? Meanwhile —

Christopher's touch on her shoulder. She turned. He caught her close, pressed his lips lingeringly on hers. Unguarded eyes turbulent he demanded unsteadily:

"Hate it?"

The Randolph reserve hauled down its colors. With a gorgeous disregard of consequences Jean flung back recklessly:

"Love it!"